WRATH OF ABEL

AN ASSASSIN IS BORN

SIMON HARRAK

Second Edition

ISBN: 978-0-6480128-8-7

AN ASSASSIN IS BORN

Prologue

IT ALL ENDED AFTER THAT FINAL SHOT. IMME-
DIATELY HE HAD KNOWN.

Whose idea was it to take shots, anyway? he thought as he
woke up groggy with high-pitched ringing in his ears. *How
loud had the music been?* Wave after wave of humming vibra-
tions came from his left. His neck felt stiff. He gazed up at
the hazy ceiling and licked his dry lips. *Next time, no shots.*
He strained his eyes and looked over at the bedside table,
quick to realise it was his smartphone doing the vibrating.
Before he could reach out, it stopped. He rolled over and
checked the screen; seven missed calls from a number in Tartu. His head jerked back. He snatched the phone off the table and called the number.

"Oh, thank God," an old, husky voice on the other end
said. "It's Johannes."

A chill ran over his skin.

"Johannes? What's wrong?" he asked.

"You need to come home. It's Kraas. He had a stroke."

"What!?" he shrieked, sitting up suddenly. "No! Is he ok?"

"He…" Johannes said, trailing off. "I don't know. I went
next door to pick him up for hunting, and he was on the
floor. We are at Tartu Hospital. The doctors are with him
now."

He froze in place.

"Are you there?" asked Johannes.

"Uhh," he groaned, supporting himself on the bed with his free hand, his head spinning. "Yes, I'm here. I'm... I'm on my way, Johannes. Tell him to hold on. Please."

"Hurry, my boy," said Johannes wearily before closing the connection.

He stood up, struggling to hold his feet. His face and armpits turned damp with sweat. Water, he needed water, and a train ticket. No, he would take a taxi. The trip from Tallinn to Tartu was long enough. In minutes he was dressed. *Hold on, Kraas,* he thought as he rushed out of the door. *Please. Hold on.*

PART I

1

It was the worst flooding Berlin had seen in decades, a deluge of thirty-six relentless hours. Charlottenburg had somehow remained mostly unaffected, but according to the news, a large part of the city lay underwater. Underground train stations had become raging rivers. Transportation was crippled, and thousands of people were stranded. Meanwhile, Frederich Abel sat sheltered inside Novalis Café in Charlottenburg, cradling an espresso and staring out at the street. He was pondering how easy it would be to kill a man in those conditions.

It was the perfect setting, he figured. Especially at nighttime. The rain would shield the act, and the flood would hide the body long enough to make a clean getaway. The water would wash away any trace evidence. Looking into space, he squinted while chewing the edge of his thumb, immersed in his hypothetical plan. He grew breathless, picturing himself creeping up on his target in the rain with a clip-point knife in hand, the only sign of his presence being the sharp sting of a deep gash across the victim's throat.

Frederich, come back. His conscious voice shook him out of it. He blinked hard and gazed around to re-align himself with his surroundings. He caught the wide-eyed, earnest stare of a young girl with a blonde ponytail. The girl's mother spoke animatedly with the husband on the other side of their table, waving her arms as she expressed what was bothering her. With the parents distracted, the girl was on her own island, seated in open space with her tiny legs dangling. The ceiling light illuminated her hair from above, but Frederich could not help notice her grim frown. He returned her glare with equal intensity, causing her to lift her arm quickly and bury her face in it. She raised her head to check if he was still looking before he turned away and gazed out of the window again. Reality came sharply into focus, and the inescapable feeling returned. The dull ache in his chest reminded him that Kraas was gone.

The dissociative episodes were coming more often, he noticed. He knew the sinister thoughts were a symptom of something deeper. It was right there, tugging at him as he sat in his chair. It surfaced the day Kraas died, and had not let up since Frederich reached Berlin six weeks ago. If anything, the suffocating mood was growing stronger, allowing him no air to escape what felt like a cold void mercilessly sucking him in. The longer he spent alone with it, the more murderous and brutal his thoughts became, and the more difficult it was to get them under control.

He had few answers for this rising tide. At first, speaking to someone had crossed his mind. He decided against it. The urge to kill was not something you simply got off your chest. No, he was stuck with it. On unusually heavy days he would toy with the idea of driving his pistol into his mouth, feeling the cold steel pressing against his teeth, and pulling the trigger. Problem solved. There was something compelling, almost appealing about such a clean and straightforward solution. Picturing death in those moments gave him an eerie peace. He would spend hours curiously admiring the depth of this mysterious void, feeling himself being pulled in further, before a voice in his head intervened and ordered him out of the house. A few hours each day in Novalis Café among strangers' chatter on a backdrop of easy listening music kept him anchored, although it never completely freed him from the feeling. The morbid episodes kept coming, and the shadow remained his constant companion.

Novalis was usually the last place a misfit like Frederich would frequent. It was quaint and beautifully decorated. Its pastel-coloured walls, warm lighting and elegant decor drew in people who were looking for more than a quick bite or caffeine fix. Stylishly dressed women spent hours gossiping and giggling over lattes beside families lunching in their Sunday best. Within this vibrant, wholesome place was Frederich, dressed in all black, the whole time remaining withdrawn and distracted. His state of mind was not healthy, he acknowledged, but he had no other way to fight it. His daily routine of brooding and coffee in a family-friendly environment was all he could think of, and it had been somewhat effective. At least during opening hours.

He caught the waiter's eye and nodded, indicating he was ready for his glass of orange juice. The waiter nodded back, accustomed to Frederich's regimen. Minutes later the waiter brought the drink over with a smile then returned to the front. The staff at Novalis had learnt quickly not to bother with the chit-chat and to stick to the routine; each day two espressos followed by an orange juice, all now ordered with nods and gestures.

He sipped his juice and lost himself in his thoughts again while continuing to watch the deluge outside. When the staff began wiping down tables, he sensed his despair rising. It was time to face another restless night in the black, followed by another morning with only memories of Kraas to comfort him.

He stood up and looked around. He was the last one there. The earlier liveliness was gone, and Novalis felt still and unfamiliar. He put on his black leather jacket and made for the exit.

It was now dark outside, and the rain was coming down harder than ever, taking only seconds to soak him through. He pushed his mop of hair out of his face and walked faster. As he neared Savignyplatz, it became apparent that the worst of the rain had reached Charlottenburg. The street leading to his apartment was flooded. He sighed and began trudging his way through the water, which seeped immediately into his boots and jeans and weighed down his legs. He laboured forward, struggling to see ahead. The rain came down harder again and gave him vertigo, forcing him to a standstill. He lifted his chin to the clouds in frustration while water crashed onto his face and a sea of white noise filled his head. Could things get any worse?

From within the noise came a barely audible scream. He lowered his head and turned toward the source of the sound. He listened hard. It came again, this time from further down the street. Or had it been behind him? It was hard to tell with the rain. He waited a long time, directing his ears beyond the unceasing static. Finally, he shook his head dismissively. His mind was playing tricks. He lifted his leg and resumed pushing through the deluge. Then he stopped again. He noticed his heart was beating quicker and that his skin had grown more sensitive to the impact of the rain. His body never played tricks. He shielded his eyes with his hand and scanned the parked cars with their submerged wheels. There was no movement. He checked the entranceways of the apartment buildings. It was hard to know from his position if anyone was there. Then he turned back to one of the cars, a Mercedes SLK convertible. He moved a few steps closer until he saw it; the car's windows were foggy. Someone was inside. He plodded forwards without hesitation, his feet crashing against the water. He tried the front door. It was unlocked. When he pulled it open, his body shook. A brawny man in a light grey suit was in the driver's seat, bent over the passenger side and gripping a young woman in a chokehold.

The man spun around and looked at Frederich in surprise, his gaze fierce and unsettling and his chest heaving up and down. He had a crew cut and a long, bushy beard. The woman's hair was tangled, and her deep brown eyes were wide open and filled with terror.

"Help me!" she yelled.

Something primal electrified Frederich. He knew his training; maintain space while assessing the situation, and fight only if communication broke down. Despite that it blew past him, and he was too slow to catch it. Just like he had been the last time it came. *Oh, no.* The rage surged through and took him with it. His peripheral awareness sharpened, and all he could see was the man; all he could feel was an overwhelming need to destroy him, to reach inside and snatch the life out of him.

He stretched his arms out and yanked the man by his neck, using speed and surprise to drag him onto the flooded street face first. The man reacted quickly, jumping at Frederich's feet and knocking him off balance. Frederich now found himself in the water with the man's superior weight on top of him. Two hands pressed down on his face and submerged it. He tried pushing his torso up, then twisted left and right with his hips, but his opponent held fast. He grasped the man's arms. They were immovable. *Shit, he's a brawler.* It was all happening too fast. There was no space or time to think. The void was now his only comfort, seeping into him like morphine as he ran out of oxygen. The pressure in his throat and chest swelled, along with the tranquillity of the void. He let go and went with it, further than he had ever gone. The panic dissolved, and calmness reigned. His mouth opened, and water began pouring into his throat.

The woman's muffled scream sounded in the distance.

"Stop it! Let him go!"

Her words jolted him. He remembered that another life was in danger. He opened his eyes and turned his focus outward again, using the pressure of suffocation to propel him to act.

"Please!" came her muffled voice again.

He tried wriggling his body. When that failed, he instinctively lifted his knees and rammed them into the man's backside, forcing him to fall forward. He wrapped his left arm around the man's shoulder and with a mighty heave and twist of his body, dislodged himself and reversed their positions. He now had the high ground, and the man was the one underwater. He knew his advantage would not last long against his stronger opponent. He took the man by his shirt and pulled him up, then bent back and head-butted him with full force, smashing his forehead into the soft part of the face with a crunch. He sucked in a large gulp of air then brought his head down again on the man's nose before pushing him back underwater and choking him with both hands as tightly as he could muster. A gush of blood oozed out over the water's surface. The man struggled, but with only a fraction of the strength he had before. After some time, he stopped moving. Frederich continued to press down until he was sure the man was dead.

2

Her eyes stayed fixed on the dead body lying in the water while Frederich retched and coughed and struggled to regain his breath. Still faint, he turned his attention to the surroundings. He shielded his eyes from the rain with his hands and scanned the windows of the apartments and down the street for observers. There was nobody around — as far as he could tell.

That gave him a choice; he could call the police or flee. He looked over at the young woman. She had witnessed him start the fight, so self-defence was probably not an option. He *had* protected her from what looked like attempted murder. His lawyer could run with that. In any case, there would be consequences. Police interviews. A drawn-out trial. Media attention. He could imagine nothing worse. He would rather plead guilty. The best thing would be to clear his tracks and get the two of them inside, and decide later once the flood had died out. The police could do nothing in those conditions anyway.

He searched the body and found only a smartphone and a money clip stuffed with fifty euro notes. *Strange.* No ID. Was it in the car? Too risky to hang around and leave possible traces behind. The phone was useless. It had a lock code and could be tracked. He wiped it down and dropped it in the water, along with the money. He then hurried to clear the scene, first wiping the car's doors clean of prints with his jacket sleeve. He felt inside the water beneath the convertible and found it was too low, so he fought and struggled with the man's body until he could push it underneath an SUV parked in the next spot. The effort left him again breathless. He steadied himself on the side of the car for some seconds and waited for the lightheadedness to subside. Then it was time to go.

He went over and placed a hand on her shoulder. There was no reaction. She stayed in her place like a statue, still facing the dead body.

"We need to go!" he yelled over the noise.

No reaction. No movement. The sheer volume of rain was making communication difficult. Plus they had already lingered too long. He clenched his fists. *Stay calm, Frederich.* He took her by both hands and stepped in closer.

"We can't stay here! It's time to go!"

She turned to him with a stiff face.

"Please," he mouthed, pleading with his eyes.

She gave a slight nod. He nodded back then let one of her trembling hands go and led her with the other. As they moved forward, she turned around for one last look at the man's body.

They progressed slowly down the street without incident, trudging their way through the shin-deep water. Two blocks later they reached his building. The water level had now reached the front step. With steady hands he found his keys, and they made their way up the stairs to his first-floor apartment.

He switched on the light, revealing the hallway and series of four doors. The bathroom was on the right, followed by the kitchen and a modestly-sized bedroom. He led her

18

through his old-style apartment and into the living room at the back, leaving behind a trail of wet footsteps on the hardwood flooring. He encouraged her to sit on the three-seater sofa and switched on the lamp. She cooperated, still in a state of shock, and resumed staring at nothing. The curtains were open, he noticed. He went over to the window and checked the yard as well as the surrounding apartments before shutting the curtains. He went back over and kneeled in front of her. Her breathing was rapid and shallow.

"What's your name?" he asked, almost in a whisper.

After a long pause, she turned and faced him. Her mouth was partially open and her hands were still trembling. She swallowed hard.

"Ida," she said quietly with a hoarse voice.

He nodded, relieved that she was speaking.

"I'm Frederich," he said.

She blinked multiple times and took a deep breath, closed her eyes and leaned back on the sofa. He went inside, fetched a pillow and blanket from the bedroom and tossed them over his shoulder. When he returned, he found her peeling off her clothes. He turned around and faced the wall, and waited. He looked again and she was down to her underwear, while her sopping, brown skirt, black stockings, white t-shirt, brown platform boots and leather jacket were scattered at the base of the sofa. He covered her up immediately, refusing to allow his mind to wander. With the blanket over her body, she turned to lay down while he scrambled to position the pillow underneath her head. She closed her eyes and rolled into a foetal position. Soon after she was asleep, her breathing now slow and steady.

He went into his bedroom and opened the bottom drawer of his dresser. Beneath the clothing was a box, which he placed on his bed to unpack. Inside was his pistol, three boxes of ammunition and a suppressor. He loaded the pistol and silenced it. The gun had been in the drawer since he came to Berlin. Instinct told him that the man he had killed was no ordinary civilian. If so, he would likely have friends. Those friends would have the same violent tendencies. Frederich would need to stay vigilant. It was an impulse which came from years of training. Still, he was confident he had covered all the angles. Ida was the only loose end he could think of, and she was sleeping soundly on his sofa.

He carefully inspected the pistol. It had been a gift from Kraas for his seventeenth birthday which he maintained in immaculate condition. It was as much a weapon for him as it was a sentimental reminder of his father. When he was satisfied with its current state, he double-checked the safety then settled upright on his bed and placed the pistol beside him. His ears instantly began latching onto every sound, both inside and outside of the apartment. He heard the fridge humming inside and the movements of his upstairs neighbour. A dull pressure pushed against his skin. His temple twitched. He knew the telltale signs well. He was alert and ready to act, and he would remain that way for as long as he felt was necessary.

While Ida slept on, groaning and shifting at times, Frederich remained watchful, resting lightly only for short periods. The adrenaline from the fight eventually settled, and he began experiencing strange states of consciousness as the night wore on.

The first images came during a moment of light sleep. He saw the man's fierce gaze cutting into him, unflinching and uncompromising. He felt the man's fingers pressing into his face while it was underwater. He tossed and turned under the heavy weight and convulsed from the terror of being suffocated. Eventually, a moment of profound tranquillity broke through, where he looked down on the man's bloodied, lifeless face partially submerged in the water, his fierce gaze gone forever.

He jerked abruptly and was met by a howling sense of sadness and despair. It sucked him in and took his mind back to the day Kraas died. He saw himself in the back seat of the taxi as they raced down the number 2 from Tallinn to Tartu. His foot was tapping rapidly on the floor and he was urging the now annoyed driver to speed up. His phone rang when they were ten minutes away from the hospital. It was Johannes. He answered instantly.

"Johannes! Is he ok?"

There was only the sound of people rushing around in the background.

"Johannes?" he yelled again.

"Frederich," said Johannes with a weepy voice. Frederich's stomach knotted up. "He's gone. I'm sorry, my boy."

He left his body. The phone fell out of his hand. His eyes widened, and his lips began trembling. He was quick to realise how ill-prepared he was for this moment. He went numb, and the rest of that day and the next became a strange dream. He was now standing dumbfounded at the funeral, unable to cry. Random members of his village approached him, dressed in black, and offered their condolences with a soft touch on the shoulder. 'He was a great man,' they said. 'What a heartbreaking loss.'

It was now late at night, and he was sitting on the sofa in his childhood home staring at the moonlight coming through the window. He felt empty, desolate like nuclear aftermath, unable to grasp the emerging darkness. Without warning, the ground beneath him gave way and he found himself thrust headfirst into the infinite reaches of terror. The howling panic shook him like nothing before, and spurred an overwhelming urge to flee, to escape the place which had come to represent Kraas. That meant leaving Tartu and also Tallinn. The next day he met with Kraas' lawyer to discuss his inheritance, which turned out to be the house and 400,000 euros of savings. He looked on, stunned. Where did the money come from? The lawyer had no idea. His instructions were only to ensure a swift handover. Frederich reluctantly signed the papers. More condolences came. He returned to Tallinn, packed his bags and fled Estonia without alerting anyone. His only impulse was to escape and then stay in motion.

Green, transient landscapes passed by in the train window, including the farms, towns, forests and winding rivers of the countryside. The void was there, growing stronger as he travelled from place to place across eastern Europe, from Riga to Warsaw, Bratislava to Vienna. He had lived and slept beneath the shadow of Kraas' death, from hostel to city landmark, each day blending into the next until he reached Berlin, where something told him it was time to stop.

As he sat upright on his bed in the dark, it had all caught up with him. The unravelling process began with a thickness in his throat. *Shit.* The tears rose to the surface and he lifted the blanket quickly over his face. He clenched his jaw and stuck his head in but with no effect. After three months of tightly holding it in, grief came gushing out of him. He moaned and wailed while the image of Kraas' face grew vivid. Those sharp grey eyes would never watch over him again. He would never again see that bald head with the rough white stubble. Kraas would never pass by and rub the top of his hair again while he was reading, and he would never have the chance to complain about it while secretly liking when Kraas did that. *I miss you.* The words kept repeating in his mind, over and over, like a grief mantra, slowly cleansing him of his burden. The tears soaked his blanket until there were none left. Then, without meaning to, he fell asleep.

3

Michael Inselheim rolled up his shirt sleeves and wiped his forehead free of sweat. His associate handed him a cold bottle of water from the Jeep, which he used to cool the back of his neck. He rolled the bottle over his cheek and savoured a short reprieve from the desert heat. How did people live in such conditions, he wondered? He was hard-pressed to think of anything less interesting than the bland rocks, raw dirt and ugly shrubs which covered the Kazakh desert landscape.

"Ten minutes until launch," said Shirvan, having just spoken to the field team on the phone.

Inselheim nodded.

"Are they ready for post-launch?" he asked.

"Of course. The Neutralaser goes underground straight after discharge."

Inselheim looked out at the horizon where the dummy rocket would be launched, and his eye twitched again. After a short pause, it twitched again. He loathed waiting. That was why he refused to line up for anything, he thought, as he rubbed his thumb against the pale strip on his bare ring finger. It had been three months since he took his wedding band off, but having the finger naked still felt strange. He wondered how Mira would react once she found out that the project which ended their marriage was finally complete. She probably could not care less. She was happily wrapped up in her new life in London with Mr. Best-Selling Author, who judging by the photos was giving her all the attention she craved. Unlike Inselheim.

"*Eight minutes*," said Shirvan, staring at his watch.

Inselheim made a fist to stop himself rubbing his finger and began pacing back and forth.

"Stop fretting. It's going to be fine, Mr. Inselheim," said Shirvan from a distance.

Inselheim sniggered to himself. If Shirvan knew how bad their situation really was, he would be pacing right next to him. In reality, the very survival of the company was tied to the success of the Neutralaser project. They had nothing to fall back on. The test *had* to succeed — no exceptions.

Inselheim looked up at the crisp blue sky, beyond which over 1,000 operational satellites belonging to dozens of countries were in orbit. This would be the Inselheim Group's fifth rocket launch for the month. So far the cover story had held up, but they were pushing their luck. It had been over twenty-four months since Inselheim publicly commissioned the short-range ballistic missile project as a way to disguise the Neutralaser. No eyebrows had been raised yet, but it was a matter of time before the phone calls started pouring in from both East and West. Inselheim was proud of his cover project idea. It was a stroke of diplomatic genius. He had gifted his team something to test with as well as an excuse to fire rockets without raising suspicion. Far from adding yet another missile to the arms race, however, Inselheim was going to shock the world by revealing the device that would put an end to the threat of nuclear destruction. Most importantly, he was going to immortalise the Inselheim name. When all was done, the history books would extensively cover the life of Michael Inselheim; son of Thomas Inselheim and saviour of the world. He only wished his father would have been around for the moment.

His phone began vibrating in his pocket, disrupting his daydream. It was Brunswick.

"Hello, Kimberley," he said as he put the phone to his ear.

"Hello, Michael," said Brunswick. "How are you feeling?"

"Cool as a cucumber."

"Five minutes!" came Shirvan's voice from behind.

"Liar," said Brunswick.

"You?" said Inselheim.

"I'm nervous."

"Liar," said Inselheim with a slight smirk, which was the closest thing to a smile he had experienced in months.

"Well, nervous, but still confident," said Brunswick. "The team is in good spirits. That helps."

"Elias Khartoum called," said Inselheim flatly.

Brunswick sighed, then went quiet.

"What did he want?" she asked.

"He wants to do a cash pick-up this Monday. A fee of 250,000 euros as penalty for falling behind."

"They're tightening the screws on us. What are we going to do, Michael?"

"I've got the money. I'll fly back and meet him. Let's just get this right."

"We will. I've got to go. The team's ready for the launch."

"Four minutes!"

"Ok."

As Inselheim hung up, the gravity of the situation hit him. The lightheadedness came back and an ominous fear descended, causing his heartbeat to speed up. It had been a gruelling ride, which began when he slowly lost his grip on everyday company operations, becoming more and more engrossed with the Neutralaser project. As the Americans and Russians innovated beyond expectations, the Inselheim Group was uncharacteristically slow to respond. The worst blow was having to recall their newly released transport helicopter. Costly on-site repairs had resolved nothing. They had to redesign the fuel system from scratch, his engineers told him. After months of disruptions for his clients and the fatal crash in Ukraine, the lawsuits began. He had been warned early about the potential problems, but he had fooled himself into believing that his team would find a way to solve them. As the mistakes and costs piled up around him, he continued to roll the dice and grew more obsessed with finishing. Now he had no more rolls left.

Making matters worse was that bloodsucker, Kalakia. There was nothing more Inselheim could have done to keep him in the dark. The Neutralaser team did all of their work in the remote underground facility. Documentation and communication remained in-house and the facility had no internet connection. Inselheim had even refused to allow public road access. Paranoia was a must when it came to Kalakia. His people were everywhere, and Inselheim was sure he had been tailed earlier in the week on his way to the office. The Inselheim Group was by far the most profitable company in Germany and had been on track to overtake the mighty American weapons manufacturers in turnover. The more the company grew, the more demanding Kalakia had become. Half a million per week in extortion money became three million. Now Inselheim was coughing up over a million a day. The one time he tried to negotiate a reduction, he got a cracked rib courtesy of Kalakia's enforcer, Elias Khartoum. Inselheim had no choice. He would have to fly out early in the morning to make it back to meet him.

"Ready for launch, Mr. Inselheim."

Shirvan, Inselheim and the rest of the team put on their protective goggles and stared out into the flat, brown desert in anticipation. Inselheim tensed his jaw and held his breath.

"Ok," began Shirvan. "Launching in.. 10.. 9.. 8.. 7.. 6.. 5.."

"Come on," whispered Inselheim, curling his hands into fists.

"4.. 3.. 2.."

The nuclear-capable ballistic missile launched in the distance with a bright red-white trail of burning fuel behind it. It climbed steadily through the sky, shrinking gradually, continuing to rise until a bright blue beam shot out from the ground at an angle and caused a blinding flash of light to explode over the horizon. The rocket and its burning trail disappeared. Inselheim's jaw slowly fell open. Dumbfounded, he turned to Shirvan, who was on the phone with the field team. When Shirvan hung up, he removed his goggles and approached Inselheim with a grin.

"It's a success, Mr. Inselheim. The rocket has been destroyed."

Inselheim's throat felt thick and lumpy.

"Are you sure?" he whispered.

"One hundred percent. I just got word from Brunswick. The device is already in the underground tunnel and is being driven back to the facility. She says she'll be ready with the champagne," said Shirvan. "Congratulations," he added, tapping Inselheim lightly on the shoulder.

Inselheim blinked a few times. His hands began shaking, and he found himself chuckling involuntarily. His body tingled and lifted into the air.

"Woo!" he screamed in a cathartic fit of excitement.

He grew dizzy and bent down to support himself against his thighs as his eyes filled with tears. He surrendered with relief and thought of his late father, and how he might react had he been around to witness the moment. After decades of planning, years of risk, failure and constant stress, Inselheim had fulfilled his promise. His father's technological vision was a success.

"We did it," he whispered, picturing his father's plump red face. "We did it!" he screamed out into the open desert.

4

Frederich awoke abruptly with daylight coming through the crack between his curtain. His state from the night before seeped through immediately. He cursed himself for falling asleep for so long then jumped out of bed and marched to the living room to check on Ida.

She was still sleeping. He relaxed and leaned against the doorway. Her pale olive skin was glowing in the morning light, and her knotted light brown hair lay plastered over parts of her face. The rain had smeared eyeliner around her eyes and upper cheeks, and a red swelling had formed on her chin, presumably from a strike to the face.

He turned back toward the kitchen, then remembered his pistol was on the bedside table. He moved it into the drawer beneath then went to make coffee.

He had just prepared the Moka pot with water and roasted coffee when he heard a cough coming from the living room. He turned off the stove. Inside he found Ida slouched forward on the sofa with the blanket wrapped around her. He thought about what he should say to someone who formed their first impression of him as he killed a man. He cleared his throat.

"Hey," he said.

She turned to him with a sullen face and studied him. He swallowed and shifted his weight from one leg to the other.

"Hey," she replied.

"Are you ok?"

She pouted and shook her head.

"Anything I can do?"

"Can I have some water?" she asked with a hint of a Latino accent.

"Sure."

He went to the kitchen and came back. Ida gave him a brief look then accepted the glass and took a large gulp. He sat on the other end of the sofa and looked on. She stared into space for a long time and appeared preoccupied. Then she turned to him.

"I can't stop thinking that if you had not come, I might not be alive now. So thank you."

Frederich nodded. She looked away for a second then began shaking her head.

"Jesus, I can't believe Elias is dead!" she declared with a frown.

"You knew him?"

"Yes, we'd been seeing each other for a few weeks."

"Do you know his last name?" he asked. "I couldn't find an ID on him."

"No," she said, shaking her head.

"What happened? What exactly did I walk in on?" he asked.

She furrowed her brows and frowned while recollecting the events.

"First, I took the train to his apartment. When I got there someone was walking out of the building, so I didn't press the doorbell. It was so wet, and I just wanted to get inside. So I went straight up. When I got to the front door, I saw it had been left open. I was going to yell out when I came inside, but he was talking to someone on the phone called 'Inselheim'. I knew something was wrong because he sounded different — quiet and business-like. I'd never heard him speak like that before. So serious. He liked to joke around, at least with me. The last thing he said as I walked up behind him was…" She paused and leaned her head to the side. "It was something like 'Listen Inselheim, I'm either leaving your place with a money bag, or a body bag. The choice is yours.' Then he turned around and saw me."

"What did you do?"

"I froze. I didn't know what to do. He hung up the phone and then his eyes went cold. He didn't even try to play it off. He just stared at me. That was when I knew I was in trouble."

Frederich remembered the look the bearded-man Elias had given him in the car. It was ominous.

"Did you try to run?"

"No." Her eyes became glazed with tears. "I was too scared to move. He took my purse and phone and put them in the kitchen. Then he tied my hands and feet together and left me in the bedroom with the door open. I begged him to let me go, but he didn't reply. I was in there for hours, until it got dark. He didn't say anything. I was so scared I was shivering the whole time. Then he made a phone call, and someone came."

"Another person came?"

"Yes, he came inside the bedroom with Elias to check me out."

"What did he look like?"

"His hair was black, with a ponytail, and he was pale. He was tall, and he had a black trench coat on."

"Ok, what else?"

"He didn't say anything. He only nodded, and then they went to the other room. They talked about something. I couldn't hear. Through the door, I saw Elias give him my stuff and he left."

Shit.

"He took your phone and purse?" asked Frederich.

"Yes, my passport was in there too," she replied. "Then Elias came and untied me. He said we were going for a drive. That if I did anything stupid or tried to escape, his people knew who I was and they would murder my family, my best friends, everybody I loved."

She paused. Her lips were quivering. Frederich continued to watch on in silence. When she resumed, her voice became filled with rage.

"I mean, it was a fucking crazy thing to say! And the *way* he said it, and the way he was looking at me, and the way the other guy looked at me. I believed it. I still do. He's connected to something terrifying. I just know it." Ida had her face scrunched in disgust. Then it went stiff again with fear.

Frederich speculated about this Elias. If he were part of an organised outfit, then Ida would likely have been killed that same day. She was left with an impossible choice: try to flee and risk the lives of her loved ones or quietly go to her death. The swelling on her face gave a clue to her next move.

"You tried to escape when you got in the car?"

"Yes. I begged him again to let me go. But he just looked at me with his dead eyes and smiled. The Elias I knew was gone. Before we could leave, it started raining hard. You couldn't see outside. So we waited. I think he was expecting the rain to stop. The street flooded almost straight away. I wish I didn't, but I panicked and tried to escape. He was too quick. I didn't even reach the door handle before he pinned

34

me down. He punched me. When I screamed, he became angry and held me down by my throat. I couldn't breathe. Then you came."

Ida began trembling. Telling her story had been a point of focus which had held her together. Now it seemed the terrifying reality had caught up with her. Frederich watched the aftershocks of her trauma boil up to the surface. So far he had been analysing the information she was giving him for anything useful. It was time to put that aside.

He made his next move without hesitation, shifting closer to her and placing a hand on her shoulder. First a sob broke out, then she began weeping. He wrapped his arm around her and felt her despair, and with it, remembered her look of terror. He tensed his jaw and made a tight fist with his hand, furious again without knowing why. He had lost it, and not for the first time. He remembered when he snapped like that last, when that intruder broke into their house in the middle of the night and tried to kill Kraa... *Don't*, a voice warned him as the ominous shadow converged. *Don't think about that.* He blinked and shook his head, then took a deep breath to settle himself.

He looked down and focussed on Ida instead. After hearing her story, he was now convinced that his decision not to contact the police had been the right one. It was better to stay put for the time being, at least until some questions could be answered. Who was Elias, and what was he involved in? How much danger was Ida in? What would the police uncover once someone discovered the body? He could only speculate. For the moment he had to cast such questions aside. Ida continued to cry for a long time, and he continued to console her. There would be plenty of time to expose criminal connections and deal with the case of this so-called 'Elias'.

5

When Ida finally composed herself, sniffling and sitting up straight again, Frederich left her alone and went to his room to browse the news on his laptop. Nothing was breaking about a murder in Berlin. He gazed into space while tapping his fingers on the trackpad. The body must have still been under the car. He switched his focus to his sphere of control and went into the living room.

"Do you want to check up on your family?" he asked Ida, who was laying on the sofa underneath the blanket.

"Yes," she said, sitting up and looking alert. "But my family lives in Montevideo."

"You're from Uruguay?"

"Yes, but I've been living in New York."

"Ok. You should still get in touch with them. Any friends or anybody who needs to know where you are?"

"No, I don't think so. I was travelling with my friend Pia. She left a few weeks ago. We had a fight, and we haven't spoken since."

"So you're in Berlin alone?"

"Yes, I was on a world trip. Berlin was our latest stop," she said then looked down at the floor.

He watched her quietly but decided not to press further. His fridge only had a few slices of salami and a pair of eggs.

"Ok, I'm going to get groceries. My laptop is in the bedroom. I've set up a guest account for you to use."

He was about to reach for his phone to give to Ida but then stopped. What did he actually know about her? Was Elias really just a fling or was she in deeper than she led on? He could be coming back to an ambush.

"Are you ok?" asked Ida, having noticed his state of deep thought.

He made eye contact and tried to read her for answers. She was... simply there. Nothing in her words or behaviour had given him reason to doubt her.

"Here's my phone," he said, handing over his smartphone and his PIN code written on a piece of paper. "Call or message whoever you need to. If you hear or see anything suspicious, call 110 straight away, ok? I'll be quick."

Outside he scanned the street. Nobody was waiting. No police sirens. The parked cars within sight were empty. He relaxed slightly but remained alert for the entire walk. The flood had now subsided and the heavy rain from the previous night had reduced to a light drizzle. It was only a matter of time before the traffic got moving again and Elias' body was discovered.

At the supermarket Frederich was met with the Saturday evening rush. He picked up a collection of foods which satisfied his survivalist preferences; some ready-made sandwiches and protein bars, bananas and apples, a loaf of bread, peanut butter, oatmeal, milk, a large bag of mixed nuts and dried fruits and ingredients for pasta. He thought for a second about Ida and added a bottle of fresh orange juice to the basket. He then worked his way through the long queue and returned to the apartment.

After unloading the groceries into the kitchen, he went to the living room and found Ida fully clothed and seated upright with a hard stare on her face. She also had her leather jacket and shoes on. His pistol was resting on her lap. He knew where he had left it.

"After what happened I don't feel safe anymore," she said. "So I checked your room. Can you tell me what this is?"

Frederich narrowed his eyes.

"You went through my drawers?" he asked.

"What is this?"

"It's my pistol," he said bluntly, remaining standing in place. "Is there a problem?"

"Frederich," she said, frowning and rubbing her hand over her face. "I appreciate what you did. Really. And I feel like I should trust you. But I'm terrified right now. When I found the gun I had a panic attack. I was going to run away, but I'm scared to go back to my place. I don't know what's waiting for me there. I just... I don't know," she said, throwing up her hands. "I just need some reassurance."

"Ok. How can I reassure you?"

"Just... answer some questions. And please tell me the truth."

"Ok," he said, slowly approaching.

"No, stay there," she said, gripping the gun. The safety was still on.

"Ok," he replied, reaching his arms out with palms facing forward. "What would you like to know?"

"Did you know Elias? Are you part of some mafia group?"

"No. I didn't know him. And I'm not part of any criminal groups."

"So how did you get there in the middle of a storm? Nobody was walking outside in that weather. Only you happened to be there."

"I've been asking myself the same question," Frederich admitted. "One minute I was having a coffee, and the next I was walking home in the middle of a flood. Then I heard you scream. I've always had good senses."

"That doesn't explain the gun and how you could beat Elias. He was strong, and everyone was afraid of him. Do you work for the government? Are you with the military?"

"No, and no," he said, crossing his arms.

"Then what? You don't look like the kind of guy who would have a gun and be able to kill people."

Frederich took a deep breath. On the one hand, he understood her concern. She had been traumatised, and she had seen him kill a man. He would be just as untrusting in her position. Also, people always assumed he was a student or an artist. To understand him, a person would need to know his unusual history. He was still reluctant to tell her anything. He never spoke about his past to anybody. He considered his next step while she stared at him expectantly.

"I'm not part of any groups," he found himself saying. "I just had a strange upbringing."

"What does that mean?"

His palms grew sweaty. He rubbed them on his pants and sat down on the rug to get comfortable.

"I was adopted when I was seven. My father, Kraas Abel, was with the Soviet Army before he retired at the end of the Cold War. He was also with the Spetsnaz, which is kind of like a Russian Special Forces. I grew up in a village called Sassväku, near Tartu. It was just the two of us. When I got a bit older, he took me out with him hiking and hunting in the forest. Over time, I don't know, it just happened. He started training me. I noticed the guns he had around the house. I started asking him questions about his life. Imagine it for a second, an orphan and an elite soldier. How else were we supposed to bond? I learnt all kinds of things from him: hand-to-hand combat, firearms, survival tactics, espionage, military strategy, political theory. We spent hours in the forest rehearsing battle scenarios. I was an angry kid, and Kraas helped me channel my anger the only way he knew. I followed in his footsteps and he made me into a soldier."

The room fell silent and Ida remained perfectly still.

"You think I'm an idiot," she said.

"It's the truth."

She stood up.

"Look, I don't know what to believe, but I'm going crazy here. I'm going into the yard to get some fresh air."

She shoved the pistol into her jacket pocket and marched past Frederich.

"Wait.." said Frederich, reaching his hand out impotently.

Ida quickly stomped through the hallway. The door opened abruptly then slammed shut. Frederich frowned and scratched his head. His burning red face reminded him why he kept his past to himself. *The gun.* He was about to chase after her but was held back by his embarrassment. His face began burning again. He reassured himself that the safety was still on. He looked out of the window and followed her walk from the door to the bench at the back of the yard. He continued watching her, wondering how he could have told that story differently. Elias then popped into his mind and he took hold of his laptop. He looked out of the window once more at the brooding Ida then settled on the sofa and opened the Berliner Morgenpost website.

His eyes widened and he leaned forward. Under 'Breaking News' was a large headshot of the bearded man Elias. Frederich recognised the fierce stare. Laid over the picture were the words 'POSSIBLE MOB HIT IN CHARLOTTENBURG'. He clicked on the image immediately then began scanning the article. Elias' last name was 'Khartoum.' It rang no bells.

The article explained how the unsuspecting driver of an SUV had notified the police after running right over Khartoum's body while pulling out of his parking space. Frederich read further. Khartoum's criminal background was detailed. Five years prior, he was tried for the murder of a prominent French politician but acquitted due to 'missing evidence.' Six years before that, he was sentenced to fifteen years in prison for extortion but served only six months after new evidence emerged proving his innocence. He was twice charged with assault, but each time the charges were dropped. There were suspected links to organised crime. *Serious individual.* There was no mention of Frederich or Ida. That was a good sign. Frederich clicked out and checked the other news sites. Similar information was given, and each source claimed that there were no suspects at present.

He thought for a moment with his fist to his mouth then ran a search on 'Elias Khartoum.' An article came up from TZ Daily titled '21st century Illuminati under our noses.' It was written by a journalist named Jochen Weisman. Frederich read with curiosity as Weisman referred to Khartoum's remarkable acquittal rate in the German courts as the tip of a sinister iceberg. Weisman speculated that Khartoum had a guardian angel protecting him, then detailed an interview given by an unnamed source-in-hiding who claimed to have been tortured by Khartoum. According to Weisman's source,

Khartoum was a member of a worldwide criminal organisation, one equally as obscure as the Illuminati. The source claimed that Khartoum had stabbed his associate to death and had been extorting him for years before he refused to continue paying. The source had been tortured for hours in an abandoned warehouse in Zehlendorf until he was able to undo his bonds and escape. The dots could not be connected, admitted Weisman, and Khartoum had an uncanny ability to avoid prosecution. But the clues spoke volumes. Finally, Weisman quoted a name which gave Frederich a jolt and made the hair on his head stand up: *Kalakia.* The alleged mastermind of the organisation. Frederich could scarcely believe it. His lips parted and he put the computer down on the coffee table.

He recalled what he knew about Kalakia. There was the usual hearsay from the internet. Kalakia was a crime boss with deep ties to the Russian and Italian Mafia who tormented governments and murdered politicians to assert his power. To others, Kalakia was a modern-day urban legend spread using the power of the web, a symbol intended to distract from the real people behind the killings. Frederich paid no attention to the talk. He knew better. He turned his mind to the story Kraas had told him when he was 17.

It was in the middle of a harsh winter when he was still living in Tartu. He and Kraas were spending long periods by the fireplace after exhausting days of training in the snow. On one particular evening, they were discussing the corruption of lobbying in government and Kraas hinted that even lobbyists answered to somebody. When Frederich pressed him to explain further, Kraas topped up his glass with Vana Tallinn before settling in to tell Frederich about a group known in intelligence circles as *The League Of Reckoning.*

According to Kraas, the fall of The Berlin Wall had not only created space for a counterculture revolution, but also left behind a breeding ground where organised crime could thrive. An up-and-coming syndicate figure, known only as Kalakia, had emerged and established a base in Berlin for his unique brand of enterprise; extorting the world's politicians, bankers and billionaires. Kraas described Kalakia as a sociopath and brilliant tactician who commanded the loyalty of some of the most gifted killers in the world.

Kraas explained how The League originated in central Europe in response to rising wealth inequality and currency debasement in the capitalist world, eventually spreading to the United Kingdom and the United States before moving into Southeast Asia and then South America. The League's doctrine stated that concentration of wealth and power was inevitable in both the First and Third World, and that the State was unfit to resist it. A counterforce was needed to both police and tax the plutocracy. Using force, and murder when necessary, The League Of Reckoning would take excess money from the elite and funnel it back to the lower and middle class and the third world through proxy organisations. Word spread quickly. People were charmed by The League's principles, despite its brutal methods. Droves of criminals, military personnel and even civilians abandoned their lives and swarmed to join the organisation. The League's power grew exponentially and cast an ever-increasing shadow over governments and companies all over the world.

At first, the major powers resisted. An enormous bounty was offered for information leading to Kalakia's capture. Kalakia responded in ruthless fashion. In a day which became known as 'The Worldwide Horror,' various government figures and heads of companies were simultaneously assassinated on three continents, with the United States, the United Kingdom and newly-capitalist Russia hit the hardest. The death toll crossed 1,500 and shocked the world. A warning had been sent. The League would not be threatened. It was lethal, ubiquitous, highly organised and untraceable. The governments reluctantly fell into line. The major media companies were instructed to report on League activities as mafia rivalry gone global. The world economy was forced to adjust. Suddenly, no man or government could touch Kalakia, or even acknowledge him in public.

From then on, the name Kalakia was relegated to myth status while The League continued to hold the who's who of power hostage. Kalakia's loyal soldiers were everywhere, hidden among every population, ready to martyr themselves for The League. Kalakia had risen to become the most powerful man in the world. Any attempt on his life would lead to an apocalyptic upheaval involving the unhinged, wholesale slaughter of the world's elite.

How Kraas knew so much about The League, he did not reveal. At the time Frederich was deeply impressed by the story. He too felt compelled to become a soldier against corruption, to apply his training at the highest level. He hounded Kraas with questions. Who was Kalakia, and what did he do before he established The League Of Reckoning? How did The League manage to spread so quickly? How many members did it have? Why were the world's governments, with all of their resources and power, unable to stop Kalakia?

Kraas only chuckled and shut his eyes. He began snoring soon after, leaving his half-empty glass of Vana Tallinn on the table. Frederich had remained there that evening, deep in thought. He had noticed Kraas' reluctance to say more. It might have been the Vana Tallinn, but Frederich knew his crafty father well. He was hiding something. The next day Frederich asked again about The League Of Reckoning, but Kraas told him not to get hung up on conspiracy stories. Frederich continued to press the matter in the coming weeks but Kraas only grew more irritated. Frederich reluctantly let it go, assuming his father was playing games. He had no way of telling which part of the story was real and which was fiction. Nonetheless, he remained curious.

Years later when he moved to Tallinn he would research the events of 'The Worldwide Horror' with fervid fascination. It was an unprecedented event. The assassinations were brazen and skilfully executed. A sniper hit on a billionaire businessman in daylight in Manhattan. A member of parliament suffocated in his sleep. Knife attacks. Car bombings. Poisonings. Fatal beatings. The League Of Reckoning was a terror organisation of unimaginable scope and capable of unhinged brutality. Now Frederich found himself questioning whether he had killed one of its members.

He opened a new browser window and searched for 'Jochen Weisman.' He clicked on an article titled 'Award-Winning Journalist Jochen Weisman Dead.' It was dated three weeks after the exposé on Elias Khartoum. Weisman had died on his way home from work after his Audi TT collided with a tree. Drug and alcohol readings had returned nothing. TZ Daily ran a tribute article on Weisman's career, calling him a 'courageous, one-of-a-kind journalist' while praising his 'groundbreaking investigations into political corruption and organised crime.' When Frederich finished reading he raised his eyebrows. He knew not to believe in coincidence.

He felt a dull pressure in his head. The situation had taken a dangerous turn, above all for Ida, he suddenly realised. If no evidence came to light tying him to the killing, he could walk away. Ida did not share that luxury. He went to the window and looked out. She was still on the bench, staring into space, unaware that things were about to get far worse for her. He frowned. This was the last thing she needed. The second she left the building she risked being hunted by what could be the most vicious and dominant organisation in the world.

His mind began ticking rapidly, processing the situation from every angle. Tallinn. Kraas. Berlin. Ida. Khartoum. It dawned on him that he was just as involved as Ida. Before he could act, however, he first needed some questions answered. He took his phone out and made a long overdue phone call. It dialled for a long time before there was an answer.

"Hello?" said Johannes with his husky voice.

"Hi, Johannes. It's me. Frederich."

"Frederich?" said Johannes with a tone of disbelief. "Oh, my boy, thank goodness. We've all been so worried about you."

"I know. I'm sorry I didn't call."

"Are you in Tallinn?"

"No. I'm in.." He paused. It was probably safer not to tell Johannes where he was, considering what he had just learnt. "I can't say where I am. I just wanted you to know that I'm safe."

"Oh, Frederich. What's going on? We never had a chance to talk after Kraas died."

"There wasn't much to say, I guess. I just had to leave."

"I understand. It was a difficult day. Are you well?"

"Yes, I'm ok. How are you doing?"

"Huh," said Johannes, coughing and clearing his throat. "You know me. Carrying on."

Frederich's mouth softened into a smile.

"Good," he said.

"It's strange not having your father around. There's nobody to go hunting with anymore."

"Yeah, I know," said Frederich softly. "Hey, Johannes?"

"Yes, my boy?"

"I need to ask you a strange question."

"Yes?"

Frederich hesitated. Johannes and Kraas had been in Spetsnaz together for twenty-five years, had been on countless missions together, and had retired to the same town. If anyone had reliable information on Kalakia, it would be Johannes.

"Do you know anything about Kalakia and The League Of Reckoning?" asked Frederich.

Johannes fell silent. Frederich could hear him breathing.

"Why do you ask?" said Johannes finally.

"So you do?" asked Frederich.

"I need to know why you're asking." Johannes' tone had switched completely. It had lost its tenderness, and Frederich could sense the caution in the old man's voice.

"A friend of mine is in trouble," said Frederich.

"And you?" Johannes said. "Are you in danger?"

Frederich thought for a moment. As far as he knew, he was not. But that could change at any moment.

"Possibly," he said.

Johannes said nothing. Frederich waited. Johannes' reluctance to speak again was ominous. The longer the silence continued, the tighter Frederich's chest became. Johannes continued breathing on the other side. Frederich's grew shallow. A vein in his neck twitched. Still Johannes said nothing.

Then, without warning, the call ended.

6

Frederich pulled the phone from his face and checked the screen, confirming that the call had ended. He was sure Johannes had hung up on purpose.

His skin iced over as though someone had turned off the heating. What had he walked into? He turned the situation over in his head until his phone vibrated. It was a text from a number he did not recognise: "*Call me here from a pay-phone. J.*"

It was Johannes. Who was he worried would be hearing the call? That did not matter for the moment. Johannes was no paranoid fool, so he had a reason to be acting strange. But where was Frederich going to find a payphone? No point roaming around looking for something that was fast becoming obsolete. He decided he would take the S-Bahn directly to Hauptbahnhof main station. He could be there in fifteen minutes.

He stuffed his phone into his pocket and left the apartment. Ida looked up abruptly from the bench when he emerged outside and marched toward her. She stared at him with concern but said nothing.

"I need to go out for a couple of hours," he said.

Her eyes widened.

"Why? What happened?"

"I'll tell you everything when I'm back, ok?"

"What? No. You're scaring me."

"This is important. You have to trust me." He pointed toward the front. "Just stay here in the yard, and if you see anybody suspicious come through that door, you wait until it's clear and you bolt."

"Oh my God," she said, pushing a fist into her mouth.

"Look, as far as I know, you're safe here. You won't be in danger if you stay put. When I get back, I'll explain everything."

"Are you sure?"

"Yes, just stay put. Two hours and I'll be back. I promise."

She took a deep breath and nodded.

"Ok."

"Stay put," he repeated, afraid she might lose her nerve and run.

"I will."

That would have to do it, he thought. He handed her the apartment keys and left, scanning the street before jogging to the station. The train took two minutes to arrive as he paced back and forth on the platform. The ride was a blur, his mind turning thoughts over the entire way. At Hauptbahnhof he disembarked and forced his way through the crowd, pushing quickly down the stairs and frantically looking for a payphone among the many stores and restaurants. He found one minutes later at the bottom of the escalator leading outside. He dialled Johannes, and the call rang once before there was an answer. Nobody spoke.

"It's me," said Frederich, wondering if names were safe to use.

"Tell me what happened," came Johannes' voice.

"So you do know something?"

"Tell me."

Frederich took his mind back to Novalis Café, and went on to explain the subsequent twenty-four hours. Ida. His fight with Khartoum. The police discovering the body. He then explained what he had read in the Weisman exposé. When he finished, Johannes went quiet for a time.

"Where is the girl now?" came his voice.

"She's with me."

"Listen, you are not safe where you are, nor is the girl. Both of you get out of there and find a place to hide. No hotels. Do not use your bank card. No credit cards. Keep phone calls to a minimum. Do you have a friend in the city who can host you?"

Had Johannes lost his mind? thought Frederich.

"A friend? No, I'm not going anywhere. We got out clean. Nobody saw me."

"You do not know what you are dealing with, my boy. They will find out."

"Who? The League Of Reckoning?"

"Yes. Kalakia's people know everything."

"Joha—" Frederich tightened his jaw and balled his hand into a fist. "Is this line secure?"

"Yes," said Johannes. "But we cannot be certain."

Frederich huffed into the phone.

"I've never seen you like this. Why are you panicking?"

"My boy, The League Of Reckoning is not a fictitious entity; it is very much real."

"So everything Kraas told me is true?"

"Yes. The League goes far beyond your imagination. It has infiltrated every level of society across the globe. It only makes itself visible to those in power. The wealthy and the influential fear it. The common person only knows a tiny fraction of its terror. You killed one of its people. For that, you pay with your life. There are no exceptions. There is also every possibility that they will come for me."

"What!" yelled Frederich before searching around him. A man walking by in a suit and holding a takeaway coffee cup glanced at him then continued. "How do you know all that?"

"This is common knowledge, my boy — if you are in the right circles. I still have my intelligence contacts."

"So what do I do now? I run?"

"Yes, it is your only hope."

"What about you? And Ida?"

"I will be fine."

"No, from what you're telling me, you won't be." Frederich began biting his lip. His thoughts raced like freeway traffic as he searched for a solution. "What about going to the federal police?"

"My boy, you still do not understand. Every government entity has long fallen into line. They have no power. Anyone who defies The League suffers swift and terrible retribution. The League will mercilessly murder wives, children, siblings, parents, any person close to you. Nobody is safe. You must understand this."

"I don't believe that," said Frederich, shaking his head. "The CIA? Europol? Five Eyes? The military? They can't stop them?"

"The law has no power against these people. Nor does the military. This is asymmetrical warfare on home soil. Believe me, the West tried, but the cost was too high. They could not protect everybody. The politicians took comfort in their arrogance, ordering airstrikes on faceless terrorists thousands of miles away. This enemy is different. Now they pay the price with the lives of their loved ones."

"So nobody can stop them? How many people do they have?"

"No one knows precisely, but enough to control the globe. Kalakia's people are fanatical, and they are everywhere. His moles have infiltrated every major corporation and government agency. They feed The League a constant stream of intelligence about their superiors. When I tell you that nobody is safe, I damn well mean it. The world has long changed, my boy. The globalised system has led to mass disillusionment. We underestimated the disenfranchised — but not Kalakia. That clever bastard seized the moment. Now, it is too late. The balance of power has shifted, and every day more people cooperate with The League. Global control has all but consolidated, and it is in the grasp of one man."

"Jesus," said Frederich, drawing in a large breath. He leaned over and gripped the side of the payphone to support himself as Johannes' words sunk in. "Ok, I need to have a think," he said.

"There is no time for thinking," said Johannes. "Get out of there."

"I'll be careful," said Frederich. "I heard you."

"Do not be reckless. Call me anytime if you need help."

"I will."

Frederich was moving toward ending the call when he stopped.

"Wait, one more thing," he said.

"Yes, my boy?"

"Does the name Inselheim mean anything to you?"

"Of course," said Johannes. "Inselheim Group. The German arms manufacturer. Why?"

"I'm looking for someone with that name."

"Well, it's a family business," said Johannes. "The CEO is an Inselheim."

"Is he the only one?" asked Frederich.

"Yes, as far as I know. The father died a few years back."

"Your contacts, can they get me information on him? An address maybe?"

"What are you playing with here?"

"Look, I know this is asking a lot. And I know I've put you at risk. But I need your help if I'm going to find a way out of this."

"You still do not understand," said Johannes, raising his voice before breaking into a coughing fit.

"I do," said Frederich, waiting for Johannes to gather himself. "Please, just help me."

Johannes exhaled loudly.

"Call me back tomorrow, same time."

"Thanks. I appreciate it."

"Please. You are my son, too."

Tingles rushed over Frederich's skin, and his eyes welled up. *Keep it together.*

"Look after yourself, my boy," said Johannes.

"I will," said Frederich. "You too."

He put the phone down and wiped his eyes. He then stuffed his hands in his pockets and climbed the stairs to the platform two at a time. A plan had been forming in his mind throughout the conversation. Was he crazy enough to go through with it? Time would tell. For now, he had no other choice. Johannes did not get worked up for nothing. His message was clear: All three of them were in danger. Running was not an option. Doing nothing was not an option. Frederich had killed Khartoum, and for that he had to own his part.

But that was only half of it. Frederich had been drifting aimlessly since Kraas died. Now full of adrenaline and purpose, he grew ashamed as he realised how close he had been to giving up. If he had not heard Ida's scream, who knows what would have happened? In any case, he felt differently now. Khartoum had been the wake-up call he needed. He had died in the water under Khartoum's weight, and then returned — but not unchanged. The experience had stripped him bare and revealed his true nature. It was now clear; Kraas had trained him precisely for such a moment. He stood before a wide-open door, and only had to step forward. With the memory of Ida trembling and weeping in his arms, the plan finally emerged in its fullest form. To a reasonable person, it would seem insane. To Frederich, it made perfect sense. He took a deep breath, and finalised his decision. There was no going back. His time in the wind was coming to a close. He shut his eyes and gazed into the black unknown with full knowledge of what to do.

Step one: Find a way to make contact with The League Of Reckoning.

Step two: Admit to killing Elias Khartoum.

Step three: Ask for a job, and finally,

Step four: Negotiate Ida and Johannes' safety.

7

Ida stood glassy-eyed in the middle of the living room, her mouth wide open. Frederich had just shared with her what Johannes told him about The League Of Reckoning, as well as Weisman's exposé on Elias Khartoum.

"What is all this supposed to mean?" she asked.

"It means you were right. Whatever Elias is connected to, it's big."

Her hands began shaking. Her eyes darted rapidly from side to side, and her lips were quivering. When she looked like she was going to lose her footing, Frederich lunged forward to support her.

"No, no, I can..." she said, holding her arms out at full length. Before she could finish her sentence, she took a large inhale and stormed into the bedroom, closing the door behind her.

Frederich stood in place, unsure how to respond. For the second time, he felt powerless to help her. He walked over to the door and listened in but heard nothing. He went to open it then stopped himself and returned to the living room.

Hours passed. He thought again about going to her, but each time a voice stopped him. It told him that she should face it alone. That was how he would handle it. He spent the time sprawled on the rug, lost in thought. The void was there. Then he noticed that for a while he had forgotten about it. Did Ida have something to do with that? Who knew. It had been a complicated twenty-four hours.

He continued shuffling on the rug, unable to find a comfortable position. He was agitated, and she definitely had something to do with that. Why should he care? He barely knew the girl. She was in danger, and he had stepped in. Job done. End of story. What else was he expected to do? She had complicated his life, rudely walked out on him, and snooped around in his room. He owed her nothing. He thought about dropping her off at the police station and then leaving Berlin. That would be the easiest thing to do. She might have a chance in some witness protection program. He could take care of himself.

He sighed. Who was he fooling? Johannes could not have been more clear. Denial would do no good. He had to move forward with the plan. *They* had to move forward. Together. Something was holding Ida back, and it annoyed him most how blind she was to it. Finally, he had enough. He huffed and went to the bedroom door and knocked twice before going in.

The room was dim and still. Ida was hunched over beside the bed, her arms wrapped around her legs. She was frowning and gazing at the floor. He crouched down in front of her.

"I was out there thinking for a long time how I could help you with this," he said. "How to comfort you or something. Now I realise there's no point."

Ida suddenly shook to life and looked up, her eyes narrowed.

"First, I'm not good with that stuff," he said. "I was always expected to handle my fear alone. Comfort wasn't Kraas' thing. Plus, I'm afraid right now, and I don't have a clue how to make it go away. But that's not the reason."

"What then?" she asked.

"You don't need it. If you were going to break, you already would have. That didn't happen, and I have a feeling it won't."

"And how do you know that?" she said, scowling and raising her voice.

He looked sternly at her and shrugged.

"I know what I see. You don't need it," he repeated, then left the room and shut the door behind him.

For a long time the apartment remained quiet. It turned dark outside and he switched on a lamp, then returned to his position on the rug and fell into a meditative state. More time passed. When he heard the bedroom door open, he sat up and saw Ida standing upright in the doorway, her arms at her side. Her chin was raised and her eyes steely. He waited. She came up to him and sat down, reached into her pocket and took out his pistol. She placed it on her open palm and offered it to him.

"Ok," she said with a firm voice. "What are we going to do about this?"

"They have your passport. They know what you look like. You can't leave the apartment," said Frederich while grabbing a handful of mixed nuts out of the bowl and tossing them into his mouth.

He and Ida were leaning on opposite ends of the sofa, facing each other with their legs up.

"I don't care, I'll go crazy if I have to stay inside any longer," said Ida.

Frederich shook his head and glanced at his watch. It was almost 1 am.

"You can't leave," he said with a mouthful.

"Ugh, then what do I do, stay here for the rest of my life?"

"No."

"Then what?"

"We make contact."

"What? With who? The police?"

Frederich shook his head.

"With The League."

Ida went quiet, then pushed her eyebrows together.

"I don't understand."

"I can negotiate."

"You want to go to *them*?" she said. "That's crazy. We should go to the police."

"What do you think The League will do if they find out we went to the police? Even if I get off for Khartoum, do you think we'll be safe? They'll come after us, and nobody can stop them. Even if they can't get to us, they'll go after Johannes. He's too old to go on the run."

"If you go to them, they'll kill you."

"No, they won't. They don't know who I am. As long as you stay here, they can't reach you, which means they'll listen to what I have to say."

"That's too risky. I can't ask you to do that."

"You're not asking. I'm offering."

"Why?" she asked.

It was the moment for Frederich to come clean about his desire to join The League. If he could find a way to stir their interest, they could strike a deal: her and Johannes' safety for his services. It would be win-win. He had spent a long time rehearsing in his mind his conversation with Ida. He found

62

no real way to explain why him joining such a violent organisation made sense. Each imagined scenario ended with Ida in a state of outrage and disgust. Telling her about his upbringing with Kraas was one thing. This ran deeper, into a place nobody in their right mind would go. The only person to catch a glimpse of it was Kraas, and Frederich remembered how that had worked out.

"Do you have any other ideas?" he asked.

"Yes, I do. We can take Johannes with us and run away."

"No," he said, shaking his head. "I can do this."

"Frederich, no, I don't want you to be alone with them."

"There's no other way."

Ida picked a nut from the bowl and tossed it at Frederich.

"I should have shot you today, you know that?" she said.

"You left the safety on," he replied, smirking.

Ida frowned and gazed earnestly at Frederich.

"Why do you want to do this? You've risked your life once already for me."

"Honestly, I just want to get away from you for a few hours," said Frederich, lightly kicking Ida's foot and smiling. "You're too high maintenance. I figure chasing some bad guys would give me a break from the drama."

"Are you serious right now?" said Ida, her face turning red.

"Relax, I'm just playing," he said. "But seriously, it's my choice. I know how dangerous this is."

"Exactly," she said. "Even if they agree to meet you, how are you going to convince them to back off?"

One last chance to come clean.

A knot emerged in Frederich's chest and made it hard to breathe. A lie was a lie, no matter how well-intentioned. Yet there was no choice. He needed Ida on side.

"Johannes still knows people in the Russian government," he said. "He can call in a favour. All I have to do is make the initial communication. He takes care of the rest."

Ida stared at him for a long time while he maintained eye contact. The pressure spread to his throat, which grew lumpy. He swallowed hard. He knew he could not keep up the facade much longer. *Come on. Take the bait.*

"Fine," she finally said, throwing her hands up. "So how do we find them? I don't think they have an office which you can visit, or a public number you can call."

"I'm not sure yet," said Frederich, breathing easier but still not free of his chest ache. "Can you remember anything from your time with Khartoum? Any people you met, or places you went?"

"No, we spent most of our time at his place or in public. I met some of his friends, but I don't know who they are."

"Did you see anything in his apartment?"

"Uh uh," said Ida, shaking her head.

The room fell silent.

"Doesn't matter," said Frederich. "I'll track Inselheim down and get the information out of him myself."

"Wait," said Ida, sitting up. "Elias mentioned leaving Inselheim's house with a money bag. He's not going to make that pick up anymore, but that doesn't mean nobody else will."

Frederich smiled and began nodding. *Genius.* He saw where her mind was going.

"I have an idea," she said.

8

It was 9:11 pm when Frederich watched the billionaire entrepreneur Michael Inselheim drive his BMW 7 Series onto his fenced-off estate in Dahlem.

Late into the morning, Frederich and Ida had researched online for anything they could find on Inselheim. The wealthy businessman was a perfect target for The League. He headed the wildly successful Inselheim Group and had a family history of prestige and wealth, which began two generations before when his grandfather Heinz founded Inselheim Construction in the late 1940s, thriving on the rebuilding of post-war Germany. His father Thomas took the reins when Heinz Inselheim retired in the early 70s and was able to maintain the status quo until business wunderkind Michael was brought into the company in the late 80s. The father and son duo skilfully steered the business toward its reincarnation as Germany's major weapons manufacturer. Michael used his uncanny vision and charm to lure in the best talent and his father's political contacts to secure government support. With a green light from the top, The Inselheim Group innovated at a rapid pace, and by the late 2000s supplied military arms and equipment, guided missiles and helicopters to governments on three continents. It had defied the global hegemony and consolidated itself as an integral component of the German economy, employing over 70,000 people in the country alone.

Armed with this information, Frederich took the train back to Hauptbahnhof the next day and called Johannes, who had Inselheim's Berlin address ready. Frederich then walked to the city centre and visited a car rental agency. Meanwhile, Ida searched online for whatever she could find on The League Of Reckoning. That same day, Frederich drove his newly rented grey Renault sedan directly to Dahlem to stake out Inselheim's home.

Now upright and alert, he looked on from the street as the metallic gate to the property automatically slid shut. Inselheim got out of his car and marched inside, dragging his travel luggage behind him on wheels. The blond-haired Inselheim had on a fitted navy blue suit and a black tie. He was tall, fit and carried himself confidently. Frederich could not see his face, but he had no doubt that the man was Inselheim.

It was a cold, clear evening, which meant this time there was no torrential rain to give him cover. If things went as he expected, he would not need to leave his car. In any case, his target was not Inselheim, but the person Frederich and Ida hoped would be sent to make the pick-up in place of Khartoum, offering an opening into The League in the process.

Frederich waited and watched. Nothing happened. Inselheim's lights remained on until 11:34 pm, then the house fell dark. Save for a handful of passing cars, the neighbourhood remained perfectly still into the early morning. Frederich and Ida had admitted it was a long shot. The pick-up might have already happened, or it might have been carried out somewhere else. There was even the slim possibility that it was the wrong Inselheim, but that was doubtful. At 5 am,

Frederich watched Inselheim drive away to work before starting his Renault and making back to his apartment in Charlottenburg.

He took a three-hour nap, then went and purchased a pre-paid phone to communicate with Ida. After that, he walked to the KaDeWe department store on Kurfürstendamm and bought clothing for Ida including underwear, t-shirts and loose-fitting pants. She raised an eyebrow upon seeing his selection but said nothing. Frederich took another nap and then returned to Dahlem to continue the stakeout.

He arrived at 8:13 pm. Turning into Inselheim's street, he tightened his grip around the steering wheel. He approached the house and continued driving without slowing down. There was a black Mercedes E-Class with tinted windows parked by the side of the road in the same spot Frederich had been the previous night. He recognised the outline of two men in the front seats and noted the license plate. Fifty metres down the road he turned his car around so it faced Inselheim's house and parked. He took out his smartphone and studied the map of the area again before settling in.

At 9:47 pm, Inselheim's headlights approached in the distance then disappeared down the driveway. Frederich sat up and paid close attention. He was not surprised to see the doors of the black Mercedes open and the two men get out. They walked through the open gate and followed Inselheim inside. The pick up would take no longer than five minutes, Frederich figured. Four minutes later, the two men returned, one of them holding a duffle bag which he placed inside the trunk. Frederich switched on the engine, and leaving his lights off, made a U-turn and sped away from Inselheim's house. He took a hard left followed by another left then stopped at the turnoff to Clayallee. The map had shown that the men would either come from behind Frederich or pull out of Inselheim's street and turn left or right. Either way, Frederich could see them while appearing as a random car turning. Seconds later, he saw headlights coming out of Inselheim's street, and the black Mercedes turned right into Clayallee. They were going to drive right past him. Frederich put the Renault into gear and followed. He settled in twenty metres behind then let out a slow breath and allowed his shoulders to relax.

Traffic was light heading into the centre of Berlin. The black Mercedes led Frederich north through Wilmersdorf and Schöneberg. It then turned east into Kreuzberg and continued toward Neukölln. Near Hermannplatz the traffic increased, and Frederich took turns driving behind different cars to remain concealed. He was stuck in the left lane when the Mercedes made a sudden right. He braked hard, and the car behind him honked aggressively. He held up traffic for a few more seconds as cars rushed by in the right lane. More honks followed, accompanied by the fading sound of a man swearing as Frederich turned into the street.

He stayed focused, spotting the taillights of the black Mercedes a hundred metres ahead. He remained as far back as possible while the Mercedes took random turns through the backstreets. Then it tailed off and parked just off Karl-Marx-Strasse. He pulled over immediately and exited his car. The two men were finally in range. He studied them. They both wore black trench coats. One of them had a black ponytail and abnormally pale skin, which fit Ida's description of the man in Khartoum's apartment. *Bingo.*

Leaving the money inside the trunk, the two men went toward Karl-Marx-Strasse and turned the corner. Frederich followed, and noticed them entering a döner kebab shop.

Across the intersection was Neukölln Town Hall, and he sat on the stairs in the courtyard where he could see the front of the store. Minutes passed, until something caught his attention from the corner of his eye. He turned and spotted a young, well-dressed businessman with slicked-back blonde hair walking the way Frederich had come, looking busy with a cellphone to his ear. The man nonchalantly approached the car containing the money, unlocked it and got in. The headlights then came on and he drove away. *Smooth*, thought Frederich.

The car turned and went right by him, and he turned his attention back to the kebab shop. The two men eventually walked out, both of them lazily chewing on a kebab. The spot was perfect; crowded and exposed. Frederich marched over the intersection and approached them.

"Hello, gentlemen," he said unapologetically.

The men froze and looked sternly at Frederich, one of them having lowered his kebab mid-bite. They lifted their heads and pushed out their chests. Frederich knew he was not intimidating. He had on his black leather jacket and black jeans. He was dense but not overly broad. His unkempt, light brown hair, green eyes and soft features were disarming, and he preferred it that way. In critical situations, it bought him a split second while the other person weighed up the threat. But these men were professionals. They would never let their guard down, not even at dinner time. The man with the ponytail reached for the inside of his coat. Frederich swiftly revealed the pistol beneath his jacket.

"Ah, ah. No need for that. I'm only here to talk."

Karl-Marx-Strasse was a main street lined with Arabic restaurants, shisha lounges and waves of people wandering by. It was the worst possible spot for a shootout. The man hesitated but kept his hand in place.

"What do you want?" He had a typical enforcer's voice, husky and loud.

"You work for Kalakia, right?"

The men did not react.

"I'll take that as a yes. Tell him that the man who killed Khartoum wants to meet. A place of his choosing. I'll come alone, unarmed. If he doesn't like what I have to say, he can kill me then and there."

Frederich took out a folded piece of paper with his phone number and held it out. The men maintained their suspicious stance. Frederich took his hand away from his gun as a gesture of peace and gave a wry smile. The man with the ponytail motioned with his head to his associate, who bent forward and accepted the paper. Frederich then turned around and walked away as soon as it left his hand. He followed the road until a taxi approached. He hailed it and got in, leaving the two men and his Renault behind, along with any chance of being traced or followed.

9

The text arrived twenty minutes later as the taxi pulled up at Frederich's apartment: "*Tomorrow. 14:00. Linkstrasse 24. Level 6.*"

Frederich put his phone away and went upstairs. He found Ida seated upright on the sofa with her legs crossed and the computer perched on her lap. She had showered and was wearing the pants and t-shirt from KaDeWe with a towel wrapped around her wet hair. On the coffee table was a notepad covered in handwritten notes. Some colour had returned to her face, and the swelling on her chin had begun to settle.

Frederich paused and took notice. For the first time, he had a sense that he was staring at the real Ida. In the beginning, she had appeared stiff and lifeless. Her movements had been sluggish, and she was dissociated and gloomy. Her face and eyes were frozen from the shock. Then there was a shift when she emerged from the bedroom. She smiled occasionally and grew more assertive. She spoke up more, but with caution. Now Frederich looked over and saw something breathtaking. It was like night and day. She appeared graceful, collected and determined.

Ida put the computer down on the sofa and looked at Frederich expectantly as he approached and sat beside her.

"Looking good," he said with a smirk while signalling at her clothes with his eyes, to which she bent her head and raised her eyebrows.

"Well?" she asked.

"The meeting is tomorrow at two in Mitte."

"A meeting? Already?"

"I had some luck."

"Ok. Is it going to be safe for you to go?"

"It has to be. It's in the middle of the city. Nothing bad is going to happen there."

Ida nodded thoughtfully.

"Did you eat?" asked Frederich.

"Yes, I made pasta. I left you some on the stove."

"Thanks," he replied without moving. He turned his attention to the notepad on the coffee table. "What did you find out?"

"About Kalakia? A lot. And nothing. He's a phantom. His name is mentioned everywhere, and there are all sorts of profiles about him. His so-called lawyer was interviewed and described him as being tall and black. Someone claiming to be a Chinese businessman said that he and Kalakia did a construction project together in Hong Kong and that Kalakia's father was English and his mother was Chinese."

"Wow," Frederich said with raised eyebrows.

"Yeah, I know," she said, picking up her pen. "He's tall and white in one article," she continued, pointing to a spot on the notepad. "He's a politician, a media executive, a Russian oligarch. He's also muscly with a beard according to someone who claims to have worked directly with The League doing enforcement. I guess Kalakia hides behind this kind of misinformation. It's the same with The League. There are all kinds of conspiracy theories, and even if the truth was published somewhere, it's lost in all of this fake material. I really think that The League pays a team of people to spread as many false things on the internet as possible. Not that they need help. Everyone has an opinion. There are blog posts, news articles and all these comments on the discussion boards. People love gossiping almost as much as trolling. The craziest was an article claiming that Kalakia is actually Laurent Philippe, the movie star. I really hope it's not Laurent Philippe. He's one of my favourite actors. There's also a lot of talk about how the Illuminati became The League. That's what Jochen Weisman wrote, except he never connected The League directly to the Illuminati. Everyone knows The League exists, or at least that *something* exists. The Worldwide Horror more than proves this. The only problem is that nobody has a way to separate the truth from the lies. The mainstream media has been pushing this 'global mafia' storyline for years. I would say the only people who know the truth are those being blackmailed or threatened. It's clever. The League is everywhere, but nobody can define it. They're hiding in plain sight. I would be impressed if they weren't psychopathic monsters."

"They're definitely not stupid," said Frederich.

"No," said Ida. "So please be careful when you meet them."

Frederich nodded and gave a weak smile.

"Did you hear again from your family?" he asked.

"Yes. I called my mother. I also wrote to my friends in New York. They keep asking when I'm coming back. Everyone is ok."

"Good," he said. "Anyway, I doubt The League will do anything until they know the facts. Right now all they have is a passport and a dead soldier."

"I hope you're right," she said.

"It'll be fine," he replied, reassuring her with his eyes.

His words seemed to have an effect. Her face softened. Naturally, he could not guarantee anything. He was acting on instinct, and he had nothing to lose. He only hoped that his decisions did not hurt Ida.

"You know you don't need to go tomorrow," she said. "We can just leave and go somewhere safe. Anywhere. Pattaya? The Maldives? How about Narnia?"

His face melted into a grin.

"Narnia?"

"Hey, look. He smiles," she said.

His face filled up with a warm flush.

"And he blushes too! Where is my camera?"

The two of them began chuckling in unison, and Frederich felt himself slowly relax.

"So," she said, putting the notepad away. "By now you know about me. What's your story? I think I know more about The League than I know about you. And that's saying something!"

"I told you about me," he shot back.

"You told me about your secret ninja training with Kraas. What else?"

"Ninja training?" he said, laughing out loud.

"You know what I mean. Tell me about the *real* Frederich," she said, poking a finger into his belly.

"Ok. Well, yes, I grew up in Tartu, and I did *ninja training*. Then I moved to Tallinn when I was 19."

"Why did you move?"

"Kraas made me go. He said I needed to live in the real world."

"What did you do there?"

"I worked as a trainer at a mixed martial arts dojo and basically lived at the library in my spare time. I like history and philosophy. I also trained most days to stay in shape. I spent the rest of my time playing video games and at parties with friends. Nothing special, really."

"I can't imagine you partying," she said.

"With the right people, I enjoy it," he said.

"And you left Tallinn recently?"

"Yes," he replied, sensing the conversation heading into darker territory.

"How come?"

He went stiff. Ida noticed the sudden shift, after which she placed her hand over his. He flinched. The light conversation and her touch had melted his defences, leaving him feeling exposed and uncertain.

"You don't have to say if you don't want to."

He did want to. He was unsure how. Her eyes welcomed him to try.

"It's fine. Kraas died before I left."

Her mouth fell open.

"Oh, I'm so sorry, Frederich. Why didn't you say something before?"

"I don't know. I guess I wasn't ready to talk about it. It hit me kind of hard, and I haven't found a way to see past it yet."

"Is that why you were crying the other night?"

Frederich flinched again.

"You heard me?"

"Yes. I'm sorry, I should have come to you. I just couldn't."

"It's ok. I didn't really want company."

"How did he die?"

"He had a stroke, and I was in Tallinn partying when it happened."

"That's terrible," she said.

"Yeah. He was my family. We did everything together." Frederich thought of himself, scrawny and little, walking alongside the broad-shouldered Kraas in the forest, barely able to keep up. "He taught me a lot. How to think under pressure, how to fight, how to take control of any situation. He taught me to be a survivor. I was never afraid, even when I was in Tallinn alone. As long as Kraas was close by, I felt like everything would be fine. Then one day he was gone, just like that. And now — well, I don't know what to feel. Everything's dark."

Ida gave a sombre nod, her sad eyes holding Frederich's gaze. Silence fell over them. She had created the space, and Frederich had poured his sorrow into it. He felt intense relief. It was the first time he had spoken his feelings about Kraas' death out loud.

"So to answer your question, I ran away," he said, unable to tolerate the vulnerability any longer. "I left Tallinn because I didn't want to be there anymore."

"Do you think you'll go back?"

"I don't know," he admitted. It dawned on him that the recent events had sent him on a path which might keep him from ever returning to his old life.

"And you? What led you to a man like Khartoum?" he asked.

"Oh," she said, suddenly releasing Frederich's hand and straightening up. "I wish I knew. I still haven't made sense of everything. I've been too stressed to think about it. I keep picturing men with guns breaking through the front door."

"When did you get to Berlin?" Frederich asked helpfully.

"Only recently."

"You said you were travelling with a friend?"

"Yes. Pia. I was backpacking alone before that."

"Wow. What made you want to do that?"

"That's a long story," she said.

"We have time," he replied.

"Alright. Well, I had been living in New York doing marketing. It was ok, but I felt stuck. I was doing what I thought I should be doing, not what I loved. Like most people, I guess."

"What do you want to do?"

"My dream is to run a fashion company which promotes beauty and strength. My mother loves María Félix, the Mexican actress, and we used to watch her movies together when I was younger. Do you know her?"

Frederich shook his head.

"Well, she was the Marilyn Monroe of Latin America. So beautiful. She usually played a strong, femme fatale type character. All the famous artists loved her; even Diego Rivera was obsessed. There's this photo of them together, and he's gazing at her like a little boy, and she's just looking away like he doesn't exist. She had this presence and wonderful sense of style. She inspired me to want to get into fashion. So anyway, I figured it was now or never. If I wanted to have a chance, I needed to leave my comfort zone and start growing. But first, I wanted to see the world. So I quit my job and decided to go backpacking for a year. It was like a dream. I loved it. I spent the first few months in Southeast Asia, then I met Pia when I was in Jerusalem. She was travelling alone too, so we teamed up. We went to Istanbul together, then we came to Europe.

"We loved Berlin. The parties, the vibe, everything. So we stayed. We rented a room in Neukölln. But Berlin can be so dirty and dark. We felt like dressing up for once and getting away from the grungy part of the city, so we went to Club Marie in Charlottenburg. Elias came to us when we were drinking cocktails at the bar. Something drew me to him. He looked handsome in his black suit, and he made me feel safe and excited. We talked, and I gave him my number. Then we began to see each other. It moved quickly. I'm not even sure how or why. I didn't care. I was infatuated. One day Pia became angry at how much time I was spending with Elias, and she wanted us to leave Berlin, but I said no. I was having too much fun. He took me to the ballet, we had nice dinners, he bought me gifts. I didn't want to backpack anymore or hike in forests and be bitten by mosquitos. Things were perfect, and I wanted to keep it that way. I was acting like a teenage brat. We had a big fight, and Pia left without me. That was two weeks ago. I can't believe how stupid I was."

"How much did you share with Elias about your life?"

"Now that I think about it, not much. He wasn't interested in personal things. It was all superficial. He planned and controlled everything, and I followed."

Frederich remained quiet.

"You probably think I'm naive and stupid," Ida said, her face turning red.

"I don't think you're stupid. But I do think you're allowed to be naive some of the time. Following your impulses and taking responsibility for what happens is how you learn, right?"

Ida pushed back a smile.

"All I see from this is that you're human," he added.

She let out a slow breath. Then she collected herself and turned toward him.

"Does that apply to you as well?"

"What do you mean?"

"I have a feeling that you're angry you couldn't be with Kraas at the end. You mentioned the party like it was something to be ashamed of."

Frederich remained silent, unsure how to respond.

"Do you feel like you abandoned him?"

Silence.

"All I saw from your story was that you're human too. You were living your life, and you lost someone you loved."

The mirror had unexpectedly flipped, and Frederich recoiled at what it was showing him. He felt an intense urge to storm out, or at the very least, to snap back and tell Ida she had no idea what she was saying. There was more to it than she could know. Mostly, he was overcome by the longing to see Kraas again, to be in his company and to tell him that he loved him for all that he had done and all that he was. There was never the chance. Ida was right; Frederich did feel like he had let Kraas down. Kraas had been his father and his best friend. While Kraas fought for his life, Frederich was drunk. He *should* have been at that hospital. With Ida's eyes on him, he refused to break down. One time was enough, and she had heard him. He pushed it all away and instead allowed himself a smile of admission. She had read him well.

"See?" he said. "Naive, but definitely not stupid."

10

Frederich took the U2 to Mendelssohn-Bartholdy-Park and arrived at Linkstrasse 24 at ten minutes before 2 pm.

He entered the lobby, which had dozens of business people moving in all directions, either rushing out to meetings or casually returning from lunch at the Arkaden Centre. The building had three elevators. Frederich followed a man and woman into the middle one, which had just opened its doors. The woman pressed the button for level eight, then turned and asked Frederich which one he wanted. He replied six then noticed at the same time as the woman that the gap between the buttons for five and seven was covered by a metallic square. There is no access to level six, she declared. She assumed he had to take the stairs. Frederich thanked her then swiftly kicked his leg out between the closing doors and stepped off.

He scanned the area. Before he could find the stairway entrance, he was approached by a short, bald man in his fifties wearing a black suit and a light grey tie. He had a scarred, wrinkled face, a thin, white moustache with a long, stringy goatee and he carried a permanent smirk. Frederich noticed that his left earlobe was missing. The man appeared measured and professional but might easily have been a soldier in his younger years.

"Please come with me," the man said before making back for the entrance.

Frederich followed him outside and around the side of the building. They approached a plain, unmarked door and the man took out an access card and scanned it on the reader. The door opened with a click. Inside, the man asked Frederich to place his hands against the wall while he thoroughly frisked him. Frederich's pockets were empty. He had come without possessions as a precaution. The man led Frederich up twelve narrow flights of stairs. The entire way up Frederich found no doors for any of the other levels, only security cameras at the top of each flight. When they reached the sixth floor, the man's access card allowed entry through another unmarked entrance which led to a tiny room with a large, steel door. This time the man held his face in front of the scanner. After a loud beep, the metal door began sliding sideways. They crossed through, and it slid shut behind them.

Frederich flinched. Inside was not what he had expected. There were no office partitions or carpet, no printers or fax machines, and no sterile meeting rooms with large oval tables and bottles of sparkling water. Instead, the entire level was gutted like an industrial warehouse. There was no sign of the outside floor-to-ceiling windows. The floors and walls were bare concrete, and the room was ablaze from a series of fluorescent lights. In one corner sat stacks of barrels with stickers that read 'corrosive', and beside them, hanging by hooks, were three chemical suits. Along the right side, metal chains with wrist cuffs came down from the ceiling above. A hydrant protruded from the floor nearby and had a pressure hose attached. What appeared like dried blood stains were splattered in random spots on the floor. In the back corner were shelves with various metallic cases. There was also a door which Frederich assumed offered a secret route into the basement. A harrowing sense of doom descended on him. He had walked directly into a death chamber, cunningly built into an inner-city office building.

He turned his eyes to the middle, where six men stood beside two facing chairs. He separated them immediately into three hierarchical categories. There were four large men dressed in varying combinations of black street clothes. They were the enforcers. He recognised two of them from the kebab place the previous night, including the pale man with the ponytail. Among them was a tall, slim man with slick, jet black hair who wore camouflage cargo pants and a light grey fleece jacket. He had small, beady brown eyes, a long, thin, hawkish nose and a stony stare. He was the number two.

Frederich paid extra attention to the last man standing at the side. *Hello, number one.* He was medium height, had a large, muscular build, a thick neck, a long, bushy, greying black beard and bald head. His face was weathered, and his eyelids curved downwards, giving him a predatory expression like a tiger. He had on a buttonless black shirt and baggy black pants and combat boots. Judging by his attire, he was just another crew member. As a matter of fact, there was no visible indicator of status or affiliation anywhere. No coherence in clothing or tattoo markings in sight. Still, Frederich was sure the man with the beard was the leader. He radiated something the others lacked. He stood firmer and looked calmer and more confident.

Frederich had all eyes on him when he approached with his chaperone. He ignored the other five men and looked directly at the man with the beard, who stared him down silently for ten long seconds. Frederich waited. Then the bearded man gave a dark, wry smile and stepped forward and spoke.

"At first, when news came to me that Elias had been killed, I was angry," he said, his voice resonant and deep. "I had my suspicions about who it could be. I ordered the people responsible to be found and dealt with immediately. When the police discovered no traces at the scene, I sent my people to take over. They are far more capable and thorough. When *they* found nothing, I grew concerned. It seemed that a ghost had killed Elias. Then, I receive word that a young boy has fessed up, and he wants to meet me personally. That, I must say, was quite unexpected."

Frederich maintained eye contact with the man throughout his monologue. He was fierce, measured and eloquent in his speech. He spoke with a hybrid English accent which gave away traces of British, German and possibly Russian, and he could have come from any of those nations. The only thing Frederich could confirm about him was that he was a figure of absolute power. Then it hit home. *Meet me personally*. Frederich lifted his head slightly and narrowed his eyes.

"You're Kalakia," he said, to which appeared the tiniest of twinkles in the man's eyes.

Frederich was surprised. He had not imagined a man of Kalakia's stature would emerge so easily.

"Have a seat," said Kalakia, motioning toward a chair with his eyes before sitting opposite. "So. Tell me why you killed Elias, and what it is you want. But be concise. If I feel you're wasting my time, well... even a young man like yourself is wise enough to know the situation he is in."

The room grew quiet, and Frederich weighed his words. Adrenaline was blasting through him, and his hands were on the verge of trembling, but he knew the importance of maintaining calm and control.

"Killing Khartoum was pure coincidence. But this is not: I want to join your organisation. Concise enough?"

Nobody reacted initially, until the slim man in the camouflage pants broke rank and marched quickly toward Frederich. He pulled a large hunting knife out of his pocket, slid it out of its pouch and put the sharp end against Frederich's neck. He leaned forward.

"You little vermin," he said with a shrill, angry voice. "I'm going to enjoy killing you. Every. Single. Second."

Frederich did not acknowledge the man. His gaze remained fixed on Kalakia.

"This here is Felipe Vivar," said Kalakia. "He was a close friend of Elias. So you will have to explain yourself to him. His will be the last face you see in this life."

Frederich leaned into the knife. The sharp sting of the blade entered his neck, and he felt a tiny stream of blood rush down. The shadow drew nearer as he began to accept his fate. He continued staring at Kalakia, whose eyes did not wane from what he was witnessing. His mind turned to Kraas, and his longing for the void to take him grew. The life in him faded like a lamp running out of gas as he pressed his neck harder against the knife. Vivar obliged, pushing the blade harder in turn, the pace of his breathing increasing and his excitement building.

"Felipe, stop," said Kalakia calmly before standing up and walking over.

"No. Let me finish him!" Vivar's exhilaration was boiling over. "He wants to die! I can see it in his eyes. Can't you see it?"

"Yes, I can see it. Take the knife away."

"Aaah!" shrieked Vivar like a madman, raising his head toward the ceiling before removing the knife from Frederich's neck.

Kalakia placed a calming hand on Vivar's shoulder then approached Frederich and crouched down in front of him. Frederich could hear Vivar gathering himself with long, deep breaths.

"Now, I must say, I am intrigued," said Kalakia, narrowing his eyes.

With the threat having eased, Frederich's heart began pounding hard again. Inside, the pressure was about to burst, yet he remained still. He now had Kalakia's attention, but it came with an ominous undercurrent. He still could not understand why Kalakia was there talking to him. Kalakia was also showing an unsettling curiosity in him. He had not stopped studying Frederich since the meeting began.

"So, you are not resigned to death," said Kalakia. "You have only already surrendered to it. And you come here and ask to join our organisation. Why?"

"I'm not asking for anything," replied Frederich. "My path crossed with Elias Khartoum's, for whatever reason. Things turned violent. I proved to be the better man. Again, for whatever reason, he happened to be tied to you. I sensed an opportunity, and I took it."

"You are saying that fate has brought you and me together?"

"That's exactly what I'm saying."

Kalakia looked deeper into Frederich's eyes. Neither of them flinched.

"So?" asked Frederich.

Kalakia gave Frederich a cold, contemptuous grin then stood and walked back to his seat. "I am not convinced. You can kill, and you do not fear death. How do I know you can be loyal? How do I know you have the discipline to work for me? And there is still the matter of you killing one of my soldiers. I cannot overlook that. Do you assume Felipe here will forget it?"

"No fucking way," Vivar blurted.

Frederich knew if he wanted to turn Kalakia, he would have to raise the stakes. He was also aware of the weak link in the room. He came up with a plan to kill two birds with one stone.

"Firstly, I don't believe a man like you has gotten where he is without his instincts," said Frederich. "If I did have potential, you would have already seen it. You've been watching me closely enough. Secondly, I have a way to settle Khartoum's death." Frederich turned and looked at Vivar for the first time. "You're a hunting man, right? Besides the obvious, the clothes and the knife, I see you have the killing… spirit. So here's my proposal." He turned back to Kalakia. "We set a time, a place and an even playing field. Felipe can have his chance to hunt me down and kill me. If he succeeds, then it's decided. Problem solved. *But*, if I get the best of him, then the girl goes free, and we assume that fate decided that I join your organisation."

Vivar began laughing loudly and hysterically, his shrill voice filling the room.

"Yes!" he yelled. "An old-fashioned hunt. It's perfect!"

Kalakia finally abandoned his poker face and chuckled lightly.

"Let me have this," said Vivar, turning toward Kalakia. "For *Elias*."

Kalakia's face turned serious again. He clasped his hands together behind his back and began walking to the other side of the room while Vivar followed, pleading to him with a low voice. Kalakia stopped thirty feet away and stood listening to Vivar, who was leaning forward and speaking directly into his ear while signalling toward the shelves. Kalakia appeared to be thinking for a long time until he finally gave Vivar the nod he had been waiting for. The two men then walked back toward the middle.

"Weapons?" asked Frederich as they approached, not wasting time.

"Knives, guns, booby traps, your mother's rolling pin if that's all you can get, I don't care," said Vivar.

"Location?"

"Let's do it at Tiergarten," said Vivar, referring to the inner-city park not far from where they were. "And don't worry, the police won't stick their nose in."

Frederich nodded. *These guys love to flaunt their power in public spaces.* He had explored Tiergarten during his first week in Berlin. It was a park with low-density trees and various walking paths and open spaces throughout. They would be fighting to the death in a place frequented by tourists, locals and the homeless. A logistical challenge, but workable without police interference.

Frederich still could not shake the feeling that something sinister was at play. He had been allowed to dictate terms almost without resistance. It was not what he had expected from what was supposedly the world's most powerful organisation. Most unsettling was Kalakia's stare. What was he looking for?

Frederich turned and noticed that Vivar had retrieved a metallic bracelet from a case on the shelf. Vivar crouched down in front of Frederich, lifted his pant leg and locked the bracelet around his ankle.

"For you, my little rabbit," said Vivar, his beady eyes now almost a pinprick in size. "A little invention of mine."

Vivar stood up and stepped away, and someone else came from the side and stuck a swab in Frederich's mouth and began rolling it around inside his cheek. Caught off guard, Frederich leaned back and tried slapping the man's arm away. The man was unfazed by Frederich's reaction, taking a plastic cylinder filled with liquid and placing the swab with Frederich's saliva inside.

"Be there at midnight," said Vivar. "That's when we will activate the device. If you stand still for longer than a few seconds, it will make a noise and tell me where you are. I don't want you hiding out."

"The game should be done before daylight," said Kalakia. "Stay within the park boundaries. The ankle bracelet has a tracking device. I will be watching. And do not worry, nobody will give Felipe your location. That would spoil the fun."

"Enter from the east side of the park by the Brandenburg Gate," said Vivar. "I'll come from the west."

Kalakia turned to Frederich's chaperone.

"Francois. Show young Frederich the way out."

Frederich turned his head quickly and looked at Kalakia with wide eyes. *He knows my name?*

"Do not overestimate your power, boy. You are a long way from Tartu," said Kalakia.

The words hit Frederich like a gut punch. *He knows where I'm from.*

"Look at his face!" said Vivar with another chuckle. "He has no idea what he's gotten himself into!"

"Oh, and one last thing," said Kalakia. "Did you expect you could keep Ms Garcia safe inside your apartment in Charlottenburg?"

Frederich's body went cold. *Ida.* Francois placed a hand on his shoulder. Frederich cleared his throat and stood up mechanically. Kalakia was now openly grinning, and his gaze was burning into Frederich's most vulnerable inner spaces. As Francois led Frederich back toward the steel door, Frederich's legs grew suddenly weak. It seemed he had made a fatal mistake.

11

Ida Garcia gazed out of the window into the yard, mindlessly stroking her hair. A stampede of anxious thoughts had been gnawing at her since Frederich left for the meeting two hours earlier. Was he being tortured? Was he even still alive? She pictured herself alone in his apartment in dead silence, the day turning to night with no trace of him and no word of his fate. It was harrowing to imagine.

A dark cloud of fear had set over her the second Frederich left to meet The League. Fear of what was to come. Fear for Frederich's safety. Fear, she realised, had been her constant tormentor since she had stepped into Elias' apartment that day. Luckily, Frederich had appeared out of the darkness, a knight without shining armour. His armour was dark and obscure. Behind his boyish demeanour, he was cold and calculating. At times he showed glimpses of something more, someone warm and vulnerable, but it never lasted. His other side was morbid and brutal. He had killed Elias with no sign of regret. Ida was curious about the warmer Frederich, the one who had invited her in with his sad eyes, but she also had to acknowledge that without the callous killer, she might be dead - gone from this world, with no chance to say goodbye to those she loved. She thought about what Frederich had shared about the day Kraas died. She picked up the phone from the table and dialled her mother.

"Hello?"

"Hey mamá, it's me."

"Ah, hello mijita, how are you?"

"I'm fine. I just wanted to hear your voice."

"I was having a coffee with tía Magdalena before, and I was telling her how nice it was to hear from you two days in a row. Now it's three."

Ida teared up, and a laugh broke out.

"Of course. I hope you made enough coffee for three," said Ida with a sniffle. "I'll be home before you know it."

"I hope so. Is everything ok? You sound sad."

"Yes, I'm fine. Don't worry. I just felt like checking in."

"Ok."

"Hey mamá," said Ida. "I love you."

"Oh, mijita. I love you too. Are you sure you're ok?"

"Yes, more than ok. I have to go now. I'll call you soon."

"O… Ok."

Ida closed the connection and exhaled slowly while wiping the tears that had collected around her eyes. She resumed watching the yard for a time before resting on the sofa. Eventually, her homesickness gave way to the paranoid thoughts which circled her mind like vultures, ready to devour her sanity. Two hours became three, and her hope of seeing Frederich began to wane. *Where is he?*

A scratching noise at the front door shook her out of her thoughts and sent a jolt through her. *He's back!* She stood up excitedly, unsure if she should greet him at the door. She decided to wait. Her breathing grew shallow. The scratching continued. Finally, something clicked into place, and the door squeaked open.

"Cover the door. I'll get her," said a man's voice.

Her body turned cold. They had come for her. She remained petrified in place, the life sucked out of her as it had been at Elias' apartment. There were slow footsteps in the hallway. She was in the back room with no path of escape. She began trembling and broke out into a sweat. She listened carefully. Her eardrums twitched with each footstep. She held back the urge to scream. More shuffling. More footsteps. A long pause. Then he was in the doorway, dressed in all black. His face was sweaty and pale. He had an unkempt, receding hairline, a thick neck, large belly and fat hands.

He stopped when he saw her and observed her coolly from his position. He snickered. His eyes looked cold like Elias', but also predatory. They revealed to her the horrors which he had in mind for her. She had nowhere to go. There was nothing she could do now — except fight. There would be no saviour this time. No police. Frederich was not going to magically appear. She began breathing rapidly. Her nostrils flared. Her eyes widened. Hatred possessed her. Her senses flared up like a bright lamp. Her rage was all she had now.

The man walked calmly toward her with a cocky grin. When he approached, she lifted her leg and stomped her heel into his knee as hard as she could. He screamed out in pain and stumbled forward, and she met him with a knee to the groin while also belting out an angry roar. The man collapsed to the floor, wailing from the pain. Ida felt a surge of excitement at the sight of him paralysed before her. Now there were fast, approaching footsteps in the hallway. Her thinking was sharp and resolute. She knew she would not have surprise on her side this time. The second man would be ready for a fight which she could not win.

He appeared in the doorway and paused, scowling when he found Ida backed up at the window and his partner collapsed on the floor in agony, grasping at his groin. He hesitated. Ida, propelled by the adrenaline, sensed the opportunity for escape. She turned toward the window and twisted the handle. Directly beneath her was the concrete path, and further out was the open yard covered in grass. She turned back and saw that the man was still near the doorway, but had begun marching toward her with vengeance in his eyes. He drew his gun. She climbed up onto the windowsill, and without hesitating, she jumped.

12

Frederich sprinted from Linkstrasse 24 back toward Mendelssohn-Bartholdy-Park, his thighs burning as he pushed up the grass hill separating the station from the office buildings. He hurriedly dug his phone out of his pocket and called Ida. The dialling persisted as he climbed the stairs to the platform. No answer. He tried again while pacing from side to side. Another long wait. Still no response. He clenched his fist and let out a groan. *Calm down, Frederich. Focus on what you can control.* He took one long, deep breath and dialled again.

"Frederich!" came Ida's voice through the speaker along with the sound of street traffic.

"Ida! Are you ok?"

"I am now. I don't know where I'm going. I think I lost them."

Her heavy breathing made it difficult to understand her, and he could barely hear her voice over the background noise.

"Lost who? What happened?"

"They came for me, Frederich. They broke in. I fought one of them, and I jumped out of the window. How did they know where you live!?"

"I have no idea," he said. "I underestimated them. Ida, I'm sorry."

"Don't be sorry, Frederich. Just stay safe. Please."

"I will. Listen, meet me at th—" He stopped and looked down at his ankle. Tracking device. Kalakia would have been furious to find out that Ida had slipped through his fingers.

"Frederich? Hello?"

"Ida, I can't come out to meet you yet."

"What! Why not?" she yelled.

"They're tracking me. They're probably listening to this conversation. Do you have somewhere you can hide for the time being?"

"No. I don't even know where I am. Frederich, please come."

"If I come now, you'll be in danger again. Stop running for a second, take a deep breath and think."

For a time he could hear only the sound of traffic.

"Ok, I have someone," she said.

"Good. Don't make any phone calls or use the internet. Just go straight there and stay put."

"Ok. I'll go now."

"You're sure you're not being followed?"

"Yes, I'm sure. I'll keep my eyes open."

"I'll call you when it's safe."

"Ok."

Frederich let his head fall back as he looked up at the sky in relief, causing the cut on his neck to throb with pain. When he winced and straightened up, he caught sight of a woman staring at his bloody neck before she turned away. He would have to take care of the wound first, he thought.

He studied the train platform. There was a group of teenagers assembled in a circle, as well as a couple in their 60s waiting at the edge of the painted safety line. It seemed like nobody was trailing him, but he could not be sure. He could not be certain of anything. He turned and looked out over the hill and saw nothing out of the ordinary. He allowed himself to grin openly with pride. Ida had fought back, and she had escaped.

He steeled himself again. His relief would need to be short-lived. Kalakia might have eyes where he least expected, and in less than nine hours, he would be locked in a game of cat and mouse with that psychopath, Vivar. He had told Ida they would see each other soon. That would not happen unless he was focused and prepared.

He considered the facts and variables. The battle would be in an inner-city park littered with low-density forest, making it challenging to maintain cover. It would be dark but well lit in the open spaces, and he had to expect there would still be people there in the middle of the night. Because of his ankle bracelet, he had to stay on the move, which would make him more vulnerable than Vivar, who could stalk him from a distance. He would also be tracked, but he hoped that Kalakia would keep his word and not relay his location. One option was to stand in an open, exposed area and challenge Vivar to a fight — man to man. But that would leave him vulnerable to a gun, and it would attract unwanted attention. It would also cost him his only real advantage; as long as Vivar was in hunting mode, he would be on a string, and Frederich had a chance to influence the outcome. No, an open fight would not work. Frederich had to lure in his hunter while remaining on the move — without being recognised. For that, he would need a damn good camouflage. He went about making his preparations.

It was 11:32 pm. Frederich sat in the S1 headed north toward the Brandenburg Gate. A lady approached and offered him a 1 euro coin. Her concerned eyes and warm smile assured him that everything would be fine. At first, he waved it off, but she insisted.

"Bitte," she said. *Please.*

He accepted her offering and thanked her with a humble nod. If anything, he felt validated that his disguise would work.

The journey to finding his camouflage began when he had taken the underground to Neukölln and went straight to a pharmacy to buy a bandage and tape for his neck. He then visited some used clothing and vintage stores and picked out the most ragged pieces he could find. To widen his body, he had on three pairs of pants with old, dark brown corduroys on the outside. He was also wearing a black hooded jumper and a thick, soiled, dark grey trench coat. He covered his head with a light grey beanie and wore an old, tattered pair of hiking boots which he packed when he left Tallinn. His nails, hands and face had dirt carelessly rubbed into them. In his left hand he carried a bottle of beer containing tap water, and between his legs was an Ikea bag filled with random bits of the cheapest clothing he could find. He also had a small torch in his pocket. Beneath his jacket seam sat his fully loaded pistol.

The train stopped at Brandenburg Gate station, where he disembarked and made for the escalator. He stumbled forward with slow, purposeful steps, appearing oblivious to the commuters who overtook him one by one. He progressed slowly and ascended the stairs at Pariser Platz at 11:46 pm. At 11:52 pm he passed under the Brandenburg Gate, taking a swig of his 'beer' and receiving glares from a pair of tourists whose photo he had interrupted. At 11:55 pm he entered Tiergarten through one of the eastern gates.

The air was cold and fresh, and the leaves were showing their autumn colours. Most importantly, the trees had barely begun shedding, which meant they would provide Frederich with plenty of coverage and with it, darkness in which to hide. The recent deluge would have softened the ground, making treading in the dark quieter. The summer crowds had long thinned out. Enough so, Frederich hoped, to avoid any innocent bystanders being struck by a stray bullet.

He followed the bare path until 12:00 am, when the bracelet made a tiny beep. He estimated it would take Vivar fifteen minutes to reach the middle of the park, where the chance of them meeting would increase considerably. A third of the way in, Vivar would cross the road at Hofjäger-allee. Tiergarten had a spider web of pathways, so Frederich would need to draw Vivar into his sector of the park.

He moved west for a while, then turned left and continued until he reached a tiny creek which began at the southeast end and ran up to the north side of the park. He stood still. The anklet let out a harsh squeal which surprised him with its intensity. His pulse rate stepped up, and a burst of urgency shot through him. Now Vivar would be on the move. Frederich forced himself to remain calm using slow, stomach breaths. He then stumbled forward again and relaxed his body, but kept careful watch of his surroundings.

There was chatter in the distance, and he saw the outline of a couple holding hands and looking around in confusion. Not far from them were three others perched on a bench, appearing equally concerned. They were talking amongst each other, puzzling over the source of the high-pitched sound. As Frederich walked by, taking another swig of his bottle, they paid him no attention.

He pushed forward, following the path along the creek in a northwestern direction. At one point he came across a gang of five teenagers occupying a bench. Their loud chatter and laughter gradually stopped. They went silent, suspiciously watching on as Frederich slowly laboured past them while taking another swig of his bottle. One of them giggled, and they whispered something he could not make out. He continued forward another hundred metres to another dimly lit opening with a pond in the middle. The surrounding area looked abandoned.

His stomach tensed up. From the corner of his eyes, he noticed the outline of a tall, skinny figure in the trees to his left. *Vivar.* The figure remained in place for some seconds, then disappeared into the forest, apparently satisfied that the drunken man fumbling his way through Tiergarten posed no threat.

Frederich continued down the winding path while maintaining a careful eye. There was no further sign of Vivar. He listened for any voices or movement in the vicinity but was met with only the sound of cars in the distance. Ahead of him was a pitch-black patch of grass leading into the trees. It was time to reel Vivar in. He discarded the bag and bottle and took out his pistol. He stood still until the ankle bracelet sounded and then immediately sprinted forward, away from the overhead lights and into the darkness where he slowed to a crawl. He crouched down and paced slowly with knees bent while taking deep, calming breaths. He aimed his pistol with both hands into the black.

He held his breath and listened hard. Almost a minute passed without a sound as he slowly slithered across the grass. He inched forward to the edge of the forest. The outlines of the trees were vaguely visible in the almost pitch-black darkness. He felt the ground for some seconds without looking down and located a large twig. He picked it up and tossed it across to his left into the forest then travelled right. Seconds passed in silence before he heard a faint footstep. He studied the woods carefully, hoping to spot an outline at which to fire. He focused too hard and forgot to take a step. The ankle bracelet began squealing. *Shit.* He leapt forward in panic, and a bullet smashed into the tree above him. Another two cracks of a suppressed pistol sounded, and two more rounds flew past. His immediate impulse was to fire back blindly, but instead he moved behind a thick tree for shelter and began slowly circling it with tiny steps. His heart was now beating loud enough that he could hear it. Him trying to control his breathing against the torrent of adrenaline was sending shockwaves through his body. He sensed the urgency of the situation. Suppressed or not, the bullet cracks would be heard throughout the park. He had to end it before it spiralled toward a shootout.

He took out his pocket torch. With his pistol in one hand, he held the torch in the other and extended his arm back while taking micro steps. He maintained his thumb on the button, inhaled deeply and then swiftly pressed down while tossing the torch forward like a grenade. It deflected off one tree, then another, then fell to the ground, illuminating the area and revealing Vivar standing in the far distance holding his pistol with both hands. Vivar's head had momentarily turned toward where the torch had landed. *Move!* Frederich came out from behind the tree, took aim and fired two bullets in quick succession at Vivar's chest, sending him to the ground. He ran forward and picked up the torch and shone it down. Vivar had landed face first and was not moving. Frederich checked for a pulse. Vivar was still alive. Five bullets had already been fired, figured Frederich. One more to finish the job. He pointed the pistol against the back of Vivar's head, ignoring the high-pitched squeal now coming from the ankle bracelet.

He hesitated. His body was pulsating, urging him to finish the job and then leave the scene quickly. There was something else. Like a firestorm it had engulfed him. He closed his eyes. *Pull the trigger!* said a voice in his head. He tightened his grip on the pistol until his body trembled and he began sweating even more profusely than before. The squeal grew deafening, and the ferocity continued to build behind his trigger finger, begging to be unleashed. *Do it!* He opened his eyes, unwilling to give in but unable to tolerate it any longer. Then he looked down and noticed his gun, and instantly sensed a shift. The feeling was still there, but it was being channelled through his pistol. He now had the choice; he could walk away and let his foe fight for life, or he could engage the feeling and put an end to Felipe Vivar's time in the world. He decided. He pulled the trigger and blew a hole in the back of Vivar's head, sending blood and brain splattering toward the dirt. His fingers tingled. Especially his trigger finger. He straightened up and looked down on Vivar's bloodied, dead body, and enjoyed what he saw. With a smile on his face, he allowed a deep sense of relief to wash over him.

13

Kalakia stared at the map of Tiergarten on his tablet screen with raised eyebrows, unsure what to make of what he had just seen. First, he had watched Frederich's blue dot travel steadily westwards through Tiergarten then follow the river northwards. Just before 1 am, the blue dot and Felipe's red dot had converged on a spot and had barely moved. Kalakia anticipated the decisive moment when Felipe would put an end to the farce. Now the blue dot was on the move again, this time southwards down Ebertstrasse toward Potsdamer Platz, and Vivar's had not moved. Kalakia disabled the alarm system on Frederich's ankle bracelet and shook his head. Frederich had indeed won. He had beaten yet another high-ranking League soldier, this time a twelve-year veteran.

Kalakia stroked his beard and thought back on the entire fiasco. Upon landing in Moscow, he immediately got word that Khartoum had been assassinated on the street. When it emerged that a young man had made contact and admitted to the crime, he grew curious. Nonetheless, he was happy to have Felipe deal with the matter in his twisted fashion. Kalakia had more important business to attend. Then League Intel got a hold of the Karl-Marx-Strasse surveillance footage and identified the boy as Frederich Abel, adopted son of Kraas Abel. Suddenly Kalakia was paying close attention. Soon after he was back in the air, returning to Berlin.

He felt compelled to meet Kraas' son. During the meeting at the facility, he had studied Frederich carefully, and he was confident that Frederich did not recognise him. Kraas, always the man of principle, had managed to keep his mouth shut. Still, Kalakia was not fooled. There had to be more to it. He knew Kraas too well. There was *always* some hidden motive with him.

As the meeting at the facility progressed, something else became clear to Kalakia; Frederich was Kraas' protégé. He moved, acted and spoke like his father, and was equally bright. Now Kalakia had seen enough to know that Frederich's recent successes were no fluke, which meant the boy could no longer be taken lightly.

The safest, most logical step would be to eliminate Frederich, find the girl and have her also disappear. She was a loose end, and Frederich was a reckless upstart with a death wish. Kalakia thought for some time, remembering Frederich's amusing explanation on how they came to meet. Then he made a decision which surprised him. Maybe it was time to let 'fate' have a say in the matter.

The threat was gone. The adrenaline had subsided. Now Frederich was wandering with no particular destination in mind. He only wanted to stay on the move for a while, to come back to himself. He passed a long row of bars and restaurants and stole the occasional glance at the patrons inside, who were laughing amongst each other and exchanging stories. He stopped at the large intersection at Potsdamer Platz and waited at the crossing in his ragged clothing, surrounded by dozens of people, bright lights, and shiny billboards.

Momentum kept his mind turning, and the scene from Tiergarten replayed like a vivid dream. He recalled his rapid heartbeat, the sweat on his body, his heightened sense of awareness. Standing among a crowd of people at the crossing, he closed his eyes and saw Felipe Vivar's stiff body like it was right in front of him. He bathed again in a feeling of satisfaction before being interrupted by a knock to his shoulder. When he opened his eyes, he saw that the crossing light had turned green and the crowd was migrating across. A teenager walking ahead with his posse of friends looked back and with a wave indicated his apology for crashing into Frederich.

Frederich pushed forward on autopilot. The traffic gradually died down, and the number of people outside thinned out before he reached the waterside at Hallesches Ufer. It was deserted. He stopped at the bridge and looked over the canal. With his senses still peaking, he became mesmerised by the water shimmering in the streetlight. He found an unexpected vibrancy in the stillness, noticing himself immeasurably aware of every detail. He smirked. *Nothing like a whiff of death to make you feel alive.*

He closed his eyes again, and the momentum took him back to Tiergarten. His smirk died away. He heard the sound of bullets hitting the trees and flinched like he was there. His tense, alert body urged him forward to kill an enemy who no longer existed. He tried to counter the unrelenting visions by picturing Ida, but Vivar's lifeless body appeared instead and stayed there until he opened his eyes again.

He had been lucky to miss those bullets, he admitted, but his opportunity to triumph had not come by coincidence. *Study your enemy.* Kraas had repeated the phrase so often that Frederich habitually practiced it with everyone he met. It had taken him seconds to read Vivar, whose guise was simple to see and even easier to exploit; he lived for the hunt. *Pride comes before the fall.* Vivar was so obnoxious Frederich could almost smell it on him. Maybe it was just his breath. In any case, the way he dressed spoke volumes. All that remained was to give him a taste of the kill and then invite him to play a game. It felt effortless. Vivar was blinded by his thirst for revenge and egged on by Frederich's supposed inexperience.

In the case of Kalakia, Frederich had nothing to go with. The head of The League Of Reckoning held his cards close and gave nothing away. Frederich had expected nothing less from the man. Despite this, he still felt he had the situation under control. His anonymity protected him. Ida was the missing link, and she was tucked safely away in his apartment. Then Kalakia showed his hand, and with it, shifted the balance of power. *Lesson learnt.*

Frederich relaxed his shoulders and focussed again on the shimmering lights. The only movement around him came from the occasional passing taxi. He wondered what was next. The answer arrived minutes later in the form of a black Mercedes sedan. It pulled up behind him on the bridge, and the ponytailed man and his associate got out. The ponytailed man marched straight up to Frederich, took a key out of his pocket and bent down and unlocked the ankle bracelet. He passed it to his associate.

"Unzip your jacket," he said. "Hands out."

Frederich complied, and the ponytailed man frisked him, pushing extra hard on the areas where Frederich wore multiple layers. The man found the torch in Frederich's pocket and twisted it open, removing the batteries and studying the inside briefly before reassembling the torch and returning it to where he found it. He searched further and discovered the pistol. He stashed it in his pocket.

"That's mine, you son of a bitch!" said Frederich, taking a step forward with clenched fists, furious at seeing a stranger holding the gun Kraas gave him.

"You can have it back after the meeting. Get in."

With those words, Frederich relaxed somewhat. They drove back to Linkstrasse 24, where he and the ponytailed man entered through the same door Francois had led him earlier in the day.

When they got inside the secret sixth level, Kalakia was waiting for him with Francois. Frederich sat in the chair in front of Kalakia, who looked over his shabby attire and muddied skin for some seconds then began chuckling. He was measured even when he was amused.

"This is how you misled Felipe? *Mein Gott.*"

"Camouflage isn't just for the hunter," Frederich shot back.

"Kraas trained you well," Kalakia said. "I guess it was inevitable. The retired life must have been incredibly boring. What a sad end to an excellent career."

"Tell me how you know so much about my father," Frederich said.

"Adoptive father," replied Kalakia. "Knowledge is everything, young Frederich. I have eyes everywhere, and access to any information I need. Do you think I would be speaking to you without knowing your background, your movements or your affiliations? You will learn not to underestimate me, the same way I have learnt not to underestimate you again."

"Too bad Felipe won't have a chance to learn that lesson," said Frederich with a sly grin.

Kalakia gave Frederich a long, stern look but said nothing.

"So what's next?" asked Frederich.

"You have proven your talents beyond a doubt, but first, you need to pass our background check. Our team is taking a more thorough look as we speak."

"What are they hoping to find?"

"We cannot have a mole in our organisation. We need to be certain you are who you appear to be."

"Do you think I'm a mole?"

"It does not matter what I *think*. Only the facts matter."

"And if I come up clean?"

"Then you join us, as agreed."

"And what will I be doing?"

"What do you think? Covert liquidation. Knowledge is nothing if we cannot enforce it. Anyone who defies The League must be put down. Anyone who threatens the existence of The League must be put down. Without exception. Finding men capable of violence is easy. Invisibility, resolve and adaptability are rare commodities. I need people who can carry out complex tasks skilfully under pressure. That is where you come in."

"And the men I kill, who decides their guilt?"

"It is not a matter of guilt. Think of it as containment."

"Containing what? Power?"

"Correct. The unquenchable thirst for wealth and power must be opposed. Without The League, the world would again plunge into chaos."

"Again?"

"Oh, come. Have you not studied your history? The rise and fall of empires? Think of it as a heated room. The warmest air rises to the top and remains there, meanwhile those at the bottom are deprived. In such cases, revolt is inevitable. Your task will be to help us fight corruption anywhere it occurs, to draw out the stale hot air, so to speak, allowing the process to begin anew. This does not just apply to the political sphere. Business and cultural figures must also be kept in check."

"So you're saying that The League is the judge and jury presiding over every government, organisation and individual on this Earth?"

"Yes. The League is the government of governments and the world police."

"And what about the drug cartels and organised crime?"

"Drugs and crime are not our concern. That fight I leave to the authorities. Crime is already shunned in a civilised society. Not even the great Pablo Escobar could penetrate the Colombian government and rise to national power. The horrors of his deeds were too much for the populace, and foreign political power helped finish him off."

"Who keeps The League's power in check? Aren't you just another authoritarian?"

"Ah, the age-old question," said Kalakia, lifting his index finger. "Who has the right to absolute power? We shall have that discussion after your training."

"What training?" asked Frederich, furrowing his eyebrows.

"You are being sent to our facility near Zürich. The training course is a compulsory requirement for all recruits. Call it a test of your commitment and loyalty. After you are done, you will be stationed back here in Berlin. Then you begin your work."

Kalakia handed Frederich an envelope.

"Your plane ticket is inside. The flight leaves in two days. Somebody will be at Zürich Airport to pick you up."

Frederich paused and considered this latest twist. He knew what he was signing up for when he made his decision. Besides, high-level training was no problem for him. He was raised with it.

"I have one last question," said Frederich.

"Of course you do. You want to know what happens to the girl."

"Yes."

"What do you want to happen to her?"

"I want you to leave her alone. She's no risk to you."

"I disagree."

"She won't speak. I'll make sure of it. And who would believe her, anyway? It'll be just another thread in your insane web of misinformation."

Kalakia thought for a moment in silence.

"If she opens her mouth, I will hold you responsible. My retribution will be swift and absolute, and those she loves will be the first to feel it. Do you believe that?"

"Yes."

"Good. Then you have my word. She will not be touched."

Frederich nodded. He could barely mask his relief.

"I will also spare the old man," continued Kalakia. "But if he pokes his nose again where it does not belong, he will die like his contact at Russian Foreign Intelligence. He is retired. Tell him to act like it."

Frederich shook his head in disbelief.

"There really is nothing you don't know, is there?"

"One more thing," said Kalakia, not skipping a beat. "You are responsible for disposing of Felipe's body."

Frederich turned and looked at Kalakia.

"You're joking, right?" he said.

"Afraid not. No matter how vile a man is in life, you must show respect for the dead. Let this be your punishment for that earlier remark."

Frederich fell silent and snapped his jaw shut. *You conceited bastard.* He began grinding his teeth. He wanted to resist Kalakia's order with every part of his being. Kalakia had ample resources to deal with Vivar's body. Both of them knew that. By giving Frederich the dirty work, Kalakia looked to assert his dominance and remind Frederich who was in charge. First Kalakia was sending Frederich to Zürich with almost no notice, then this. It was humiliating. It was also a test of his loyalty. *Choose your battles, Frederich.*

"Have me dropped off in Neukölln," he ordered, now refusing to look at Kalakia. "I'll need my car."

Kalakia nodded at the ponytailed man.

"Be quick," said Kalakia. "Daylight is near. We do not want any innocent children coming across our dear, fallen Felipe. My people in Zürich will keep me informed on the progress of your training. If all goes well, then we will see each other again in six months. Good luck."

Kalakia had barely finished speaking when Frederich stood up and marched swiftly toward the exit, the ponytailed man in tow.

14

It was inching closer to daylight when Frederich drove his Renault sedan into Tiergarten, entering via Hofjägerallee near the Victory Column. He travelled along the footpath with headlights off, paying little attention to the man sleeping on a bench who sat up and looked on curiously. He approached the edge of the forest closest to Vivar's body and went forward to prepare to back in. He put the car in reverse and slammed his foot on the accelerator. The wheels spun in place and sent chunks of dirt flying into the air before finding traction. The car lunged backwards, and Frederich slammed the brakes just as he reached the trees. The car slid briefly then stopped with a loud thud. A middle-aged man taking his dog for an early morning walk approached as Frederich slammed his door shut.

"What the hell are you doing?" the man yelled from a distance.

Frederich had by now lost all patience. Kalakia had pushed him too far. He took out his pistol and pointed it at the man.

"Your wallet. Give it here," he said.

The man gasped and took a step back before putting his hands up.

"Your *wallet*," repeated Frederich when it seemed like the man had not heard him.

After a short delay, Frederich's message registered, and the man complied. He reached into his pocket with shaky hands and produced a black leather wallet. Frederich snatched it from his hand and pulled out his identification card, inspected it, then flicked the wallet back in the direction of the man.

"Now piss off, Viktor," he said, placing the identification card in his pocket. "And if you speak to the police, I'll be visiting your place on Turmstrasse while you sleep."

The man fumbled on the ground with trembling hands, making numerous attempts before clutching his wallet.

"Gerold, come!" screamed the man as he stormed off, where his dog emerged from a bush and followed him down the footpath.

When Frederich returned to Vivar's corpse, he saw that blood covered most of the torso and head, and a large pool had collected beneath the body. He put on his leather gloves. He cursed under his breath as he dragged the body, straining from the weight, but with Vivar's thin build he managed to make it to the car without stopping. The area was now clear of people, and he could only hear the sound of birds chirping in anticipation of daylight. With one heave he lifted the corpse and pushed it into the trunk, where he had laid out layers of cardboard collected from his apartment block's recycling bin. While he was there, he had gone into the cellar and sifted through his neighbours' storage spaces until he found a shovel. He was only going to borrow it, he had insisted.

He traced the blood left behind from Vivar's body with his torch and kicked dirt and leaves over the trail. He used the shovel to dig a small hole and buried the bulk of the remaining pool of blood. With Vivar's body secure in the

114

back, he snaked his way along the footpath out of Tiergarten and left Berlin, taking the A13 south toward Cottbus almost two hours away.

He turned off before Lübbenau and drove toward a dense forest area. He found a secluded opening by the side of the road and rolled in as far as the forest would allow. By the time he decided on a suitable place to bury Vivar, it was early in the afternoon, and he knew he would not be done before the morning. He rang Ida's phone.

"Hello?"

"Ida, I can't make it back today," he said with a flat, dull tone. "We need to meet tomorrow."

"Tomorrow?" said Ida. There was a long pause. "Is everything ok? Where are you?" she asked.

"I'm fine. Look, I really can't talk right now. There's just something I have to deal with today."

"Ok," she replied.

"You're ok? No sign of Kalakia's men?"

"No, not since I left your apartment. I'm fine."

"Good. Then I'll see you tomorrow. 1 pm at the Lustgarten in Mitte."

"Ok. 1 pm at Lustgarten."

He ended the call and put his phone away. He was not himself. He knew that. In his current state of mind, he had use only for anger. Kalakia was enforcing his authority. Frederich understood that. But the only authority he could ever tolerate was Kraas, and Kraas' commands came with good intention. Like Frederich's non-negotiable 5 am wake-up time, for example, or Kraas' insistence that Sunday be a day of rest. It was about structure, discipline, and what was best for Frederich. Kalakia was toying with him because he could. That made him viscerally upset.

115

To avoid getting too worked up, he turned his focus to digging. The soil came apart easier than he had hoped. He would never have imagined during the last week's storm that he would later find himself in the middle of nowhere, with a shovel, digging a grave and feeling thankful for the deluge. It was a nice concession considering the situation.

He toiled throughout the day and into the night, channelling his rage toward completing an eight-foot-deep hole in the ground, adding an extra couple of feet to keep the wolves away. By 2 am the following morning, Vivar's corpse was tucked deep in the Spreewald forest. By 4 am Frederich was back at his apartment and shortly after that he was showered and in a deep sleep.

Frederich took the S-Bahn to Hackescher Markt and crossed the Friedrichs Bridge into Lustgarten. To his left stood the Berlin Cathedral. To the right was the monolithic Old Museum, under which sat Ida, patiently waiting on the front steps, dwarfed by a series of neo-classical columns. When Ida noticed Frederich approaching, she got up and marched forward, wrapping her arms around him and holding his body tight against hers. Her warmth seeped in and filled him with something obscure and gentle, an energy he rarely felt. He lifted his arms and wrapped them around her in turn, and they remained locked together for a long time.

"I don't think I can explain how glad I am to see you," she said, taking his hand and leading him to sit beside her on the steps, which overlooked the open grass area. "Are you ok?" she asked.

It was a good question. He felt... different. The emptiness was still there, but it was now more than an inconvenient presence; it was a *part* of him. He first noticed the shift while standing over Vivar's bloodied body. It had given him intense gratification, much like killing Elias Khartoum, only now it felt permanent, more rooted. It seemed each kill had allowed the void to become integrated, like a body part.

"Frederich, tell me what happened."

"I'll tell you," he replied. "But tell me first, did they hurt you?"

"No, I'm fine," she said. "There were two of them. They broke into the apartment. It was crazy. I became another person. I was so focused." She smiled, and her face brightened as she recalled the events. "I used self-defence moves I learnt when I was younger without thinking. I mean, I jumped out of the freaking window!"

Frederich looked at Ida with a warm expression and nodded.

"What happened to you, other people would have broken down. You have amazing strength, Ida. I don't think I've met anybody like you."

"Thanks, Frederich," she said, her eyes softening.

"And you should know, you're safe now. Nobody is going to lay a finger on you. I promise."

"That's great," she said halfheartedly. "How do you know that?"

"I spoke to Kalakia. We made a deal."

"What kind of deal? Did Johannes convince them to back off?"

"No," said Frederich with a head shake while biting his lower lip.

Ida tilted her head and inspected Frederich's face. Her expression darkened.

"Frederich, I want to ask you something, but I'm afraid."

"Then don't ask," he replied.

"No. I have to know. Where were you the whole time?"

Frederich remained silent. She was reading him again.

"Something happened. I can see it on your face. You're different," she said.

"I need to leave Berlin tomorrow," he said.

Her eyes widened.

"Why?"

"I'm joining The League. I'm working for Kalakia now."

Her mouth fell open. She had been sitting side by side with Frederich, but now she shifted back and created a distance between them.

"You're what?"

"There's a lot you don't know about me, Ida."

"What's that supposed to mean?"

"It means there's something in me that's not normal."

"And? We're all weird in some way," she shot back.

"This is different. I belong there."

"What are you talking about? Bullshit! I've *seen* you, Frederich. You killed Elias because you had to. You were protecting me, and he was going to kill you first. They kill because they want to."

"There's more, Ida. And that's the part you don't want to see."

"No," she said, shaking her head vigorously. "No!"

"Ida, plea—"

"Frederich, they tried to kill me! And now you want to work for them? How? *Why?*"

"I never wanted them to hurt you. I was trying to protect you. I made a mistake the other day, and I'm sorry."

"So when you said Johannes had contacts who could help, you were lying, weren't you? You were planning this the whole time."

"I had no choice. You have to understand…"

Frederich felt cornered. His face was burning red now. He was not prepared for this conversation. Ida went quiet for a time.

"Fuck!" she blurted as a sob broke out. "Are… are you going to kill people for them?"

He paused. The moment he had feared was coming.

"Yes."

Ida stood up and took a step back, her face distorted and horrified, her eyes filled with tears. She opened her mouth to speak but then stopped. Instead, she turned and walked away. Frederich watched her march down the grass and past the fountain in the middle, and as she did, his shoulders and stomach grew tense. There was no point going after her. She was too close now, and it was only a matter of time before she was irreparably hurt.

His body began burning up. A feeling of frustration rose up to the surface. What did she expect from him anyway? What did she want to hear? The truth? The *real* truth? That Khartoum was not his first kill? That in the middle of the night, a man with an old vendetta had broken into their house and tried to kill Kraas without calculating on Frederich's presence? That Frederich had foiled his attempt and chased him into the forest and caught him? That he had beaten him with a frenzy of fists and snapped his arm from the elbow? That he had picked up a rock and in a psychotic rage had pounded it over and over into the man's skull until only a bloody, mushy, crater remained? That he had blacked out, and when he came to, was met with Kraas' terror-strick-

119

en face? That what he had done was so horrific, not even a seasoned soldier like Kraas could face it or even speak about it? That he had a demon inside him. That at his core, he was a savage. Was that what she had wanted to see? No, it was better this way. It was his burden, not hers. She had been through enough.

When she reached the sidewalk, she turned and looked back wistfully in his direction. He kept his eyes on her. She lingered briefly among the passing pedestrians then turned suddenly and disappeared down the street, leaving Frederich with nothing but his anger and a cold, empty feeling in his chest.

15

Without an alarm, Kalakia rose out of bed at 5 am, like every other morning. By 5:30 he had showered, groomed and dressed himself before stepping into the outer section of his top floor penthouse apartment, where his breakfast was waiting for him.

He stretched his neck left and right then walked past his dining table and approached the window. Beneath his feet was the Grand Luxus Hotel at Zoologischer Garten. Ahead of him was the Berlin city landscape, which he could see from any position since the apartment was lined all around with tinted, bulletproof glass from floor to ceiling. This was the first of many of Kalakia's security requirements. The original, multi-room penthouse suite had undergone extensive renovations. The only access to the apartment now was through a reinforced metal door, and even after the facial scanner had granted permission, Kalakia would need to approve access from the inside before the door opened.

He had dwellings in almost all the major cities, including Moscow, New York, Tokyo, Budapest, London and Dubai. He preferred Berlin, but he understood the importance of mobility. Creating the illusion of omnipresence was a cornerstone of his power. That was why he was going to be in London next week, and Tokyo after that. When he switched cities, he did so without warning. He could be both nowhere and everywhere, depending on if you were his enemy or ally.

Behind him was his walled-off, fireproof private area containing his bedroom, bathroom and study room. His study was the size of a small house. It included his work desk, volumes of history and philosophy books, and anthologies of military strategy which filled up dozens of bookshelves and dated back to Ancient Greece. When he was not coordinating The League's business, he locked himself inside and absorbed every ounce of knowledge he deemed worthwhile. The outside section of the apartment contained an open plan kitchen and dining area. A 360-degree tour revealed a museum of rare artefacts, early twentieth-century art nouveau paintings and various curated furniture pieces. Kalakia imagined a look inside his apartment to be like diving into his mind; it was fortified, uncluttered, well-endowed and all-seeing.

He checked his watch then sat down to have breakfast. Francois would soon be coming up for the morning briefing, a daily routine which they broke only when there was an emergency that required action. For example, a spiteful delegate from the British government had lied to a member of Mossad and a League soldier was needlessly killed. Or a billionaire Silicon Valley 'disruptor' who refused to pay his tribute had hired muscle for protection and had encouraged other entrepreneurs to join his pitiful rebellion. Then there were those who threatened to expose The League by speaking to a journalist. Kalakia did not expect the ship to sail smoothly all the time, but he did insist that problems be solved immediately, and he made sure to oversee most operations. Complacency was never an option.

There was no such crisis that morning, but Kalakia was still bothered by something. He let the feeling sit for a while over breakfast before fetching Frederich's file from a cabinet in his study to read over again. He poured himself a black coffee then took out a copy of a report written by a Kaspar Tulmus of the Tartu police:

10.03.1996

A call was made to the police hotline at 10:03 alerting to the discovery of a lost boy, age so far unknown. At 10:41 I arrived at the home of Kraas Abel (Loom-Turinga 18, 51071, Sassväku, Tartu), who found the boy roaming alone in the Järvselja forest while hunting for boar. Mr. Abel is a retired soldier and lives alone. The boy appears to have been abandoned and is showing signs of malnutrition and shock. There are light scratches on his face and arms, and four deep gashes on his back, which Mr. Abel has bandaged up. The boy's attire at the time, according to Mr. Abel, was black shorts, a tattered, bloodied plain grey t-shirt and no shoes. It is not clear how long the child had been in the forest. My estimate is two days. Mr. Abel states that he obtained new clothes for the child from a neighbour with a young son. My initial enquiries with locals have revealed no knowledge of a missing boy. The boy currently remains in the care of Mr. Abel and is resting in the spare bedroom of Mr. Abel's home. So far, the missing person's database shows no child fitting the boy's de-

scription. I have alerted the authorities in Tallinn, and
they are currently in transit.

Kalakia turned to a follow-up report by the Tallinn Police
the following day, signed by a Frani Fullda:

11.03.1996

*A boy, aged seven years (estimate) and identity un-
known, was today taken into the custody of Tallinn Police and moved from the home of Mr. Kraas Abel to
East Tallinn Central Hospital. According to a report by
Kaspar Tulmus from the Tartu Police, the boy was discovered alone in the forest. The boy has so far refused or
been unable to speak. The boy's clothing at the time of
his discovery has been inspected, and the name 'Frederich' was found marked on the inside tag of his t-shirt.
An initial evaluation by doctors and psychiatrists at the
East Tallinn Central Hospital has been carried out and
the child has been diagnosed with post-traumatic stress
and shock. He is exhibiting a dissociated, unresponsive
state of mind and a suspicion toward members of the
police, welfare officials and doctors who have tried
speaking with him. I am now handing the case over to
the child welfare agency, but will continue to investi-
gate and make routine checks in the missing person's
database in case something shows up. In the meantime,
the child welfare agency will decide where the boy will
be housed after he is discharged from hospital. The
child has so far refused to allow Mr. Abel to leave his*

side, and Mr. Abel has agreed to remain with the boy
for the time being.

Two days wounded in the forest, thought Kalakia. At that age. It should have killed him. He was an exceptional specimen with a talent for adaptability. That was one of the reasons why Kalakia had spared him. Another was because of his indispensable qualities; he had no next of kin, showed no fear of death, and had so far managed to avoid the lure of power. Not even 250,000 euros of Inselheim's cash was enough to entice his desires. There was a deeper motive behind his actions that went beyond greed. He was pure potential ready to be forged. He was also Kraas' boy. That was, Kalakia hated to admit, the most compelling reason.

Kalakia was not forgetting that Frederich had killed two of The League's high-ranking men. It was more than enough to warrant a death sentence. The League did not tolerate weeds in its garden. In response to Frederich's actions, the men had made their outrage known, and demanded he be made an example of. Matthias Vidrik had been especially vocal, even with the good fortune of being promoted to Felipe's position. While Kalakia was aware of the doctrine, as a leader he could not ignore the bigger picture, which meant he sometimes had to break the rules. His men were unaware that The Council was insisting on a succession plan, and that Kalakia doubted the worthiness of the front-runners. The Council had secretly drawn up a list of 24 potentials from all over the world and had been pushing to debate the selection process. There were days when Kalakia wished he had never established that panel of eight, cynical old men, and that was precisely why he had done it. Critical voices were necessary to help sharpen his leadership abilities, even if most of the time The Council simply nagged him.

If he had had a son, the succession process would be greatly simplified. A brief look into history, however, explained why he had not taken this route. The French Revolution was compelling proof why being a blood heir did not guarantee the strength, wisdom or nerve to rule well. Louis XVI had learnt that lesson the hard way when his neck lay at the mercy of the guillotine. In any case, even if Kalakia had produced an heir, his paternal instincts would cloud his judgement. There was no room for sentiment in his business. In his mind, to lead The League required a particular breed of person, one who was immune from the seduction of power and who had no attachments which could be used against them; a leader with the wisdom and nerve to hold power strictly for the greater good.

Kalakia was sure that no such person existed in The League. He could have been wrong, of course, but instinct told him otherwise. Men such as Vivar and Vidrik were interested in power only to serve themselves. Sadism, a lust for domination, and greed; even The League was not immune from it. Kalakia recalled the early days. As The League had grown in stature, a scramble for power had broken out among the upper ranks. How ironic, Kalakia had thought at the time, and inevitable. It was human nature. He had promoted Vidrik to fill Felipe's position because the man was a gifted killer. Vidrik was a means to an end, and the end was and always would be the concentration of power under one rightful banner. Placed in the wrong hands, The League would come burning to the ground. He would *never* allow that to happen.

The League needed a prince whom it could groom to take over, someone with experience in the field and able to earn the respect of the men; someone who could emulate Kalakia's rise. Yet even if Frederich proved to be the incorruptible leader The League needed, there was still the question of his reckless nature. Whatever had caused his enigmatic childhood had left something behind. From Kalakia's perspective, it was both an asset and a liability. It seemed Kraas had taught Frederich to hone it in various ways, but impressive as the results were, there was still work to be done. It was early days, but with some patience and effort, The League could mould Frederich into what it needed, and as Francois showed up for the morning briefing, Kalakia had thought of just the man who could begin the process.

"First item," said Francois. "One of our enforcers in Lisbon, Luis Pinto, was arrested yesterday afternoon during a pick-up. There was some trouble, and Pinto broke the man's jaw. A neighbour called the police."

"Where is he now?" replied Kalakia.

"He's in a holding cell."

"Send someone to coordinate the case, and find out who the arresting officer was."

"Antonio Cadija is in Athens right now. I'll get De Bruin to fly in from Amsterdam."

"Good. Next?"

"Kelly Larsen from the IMF wants to meet next week to discuss the tribute arrangements for a handful of Fortune Global 500 companies."

"On behalf of whom?"

"The United States, The United Kingdom, China, Germany and a few others," said Francois, referring to his documents. "They say unemployment is up because the companies don't have money to invest."

"Make her wait until the week after."

"Ok." Francois jotted into his notepad.

"What about Inselheim?" asked Kalakia.

"Matthias Vidrik picked him up this morning in Dahlem. He has him at the interrogation facility and is questioning him right now. It looks like Abel was just using him as a pawn to establish contact and they never actually met."

Kalakia gave a nod of approval. Inselheim had been acting strangely in recent weeks. He had been missing payments and flying out of the country more often than usual. Kalakia also wanted to be sure there was no conspiracy brewing between Frederich and Inselheim. So far the boy had checked out, but Kalakia would leave nothing to chance.

"Have our men search Inselheim's house and office. Do it today," he said.

"I'll make the call right away."

"While you do that, call Scheffler," said Kalakia. "Make sure he handles Frederich's training."

"Elite Squad?" said Francois with raised eyebrows. "Are you sure? Shouldn't we start him in Pulver's unit?"

"He can handle it. Scheffler will know how to maximise his potential."

"Ok. I'll make sure Scheffler receives the necessary instructions."

"Good," said Kalakia.

"Speaking of the boy. His DNA analysis is done," said Francois.

"Yes?" said Kalakia, tilting his head.

"Nothing. It's strange. He has mostly Polish and Prussian German ancestry, but we couldn't find any record of close relatives. He has some distant cousins spread throughout Germany, France, The United Kingdom and America, but it's unlikely they know anything. Intel is digging to find out about his history before Kraas Abel found him in the forest. They know it's top priority."

Kalakia looked out of the window and nodded. He was unsettled by this gap in Frederich's past. His instructions were clear; spare no cost and leave no trail unchecked.

"Last thing. The car will pick you up at midday tomorrow for the meeting with The Council in Budapest," said Francois.

Kalakia nodded.

"Stirner wants to talk about the succession plan," said Francois.

"Of course he does," replied Kalakia.

"I should say, you've been quite preoccupied with the boy recently," said Francois, gazing down at Frederich's file spread out on Kalakia's table. "Surely you're not—"

"Anything else on the agenda?" interjected Kalakia with a hard stare.

"No," replied Francois, smiling politely. "That's everything."

"Thank you, Francois."

Francois nodded and stood up. He organised his papers and packed them into his briefcase then exited the apartment.

"I don't think he knows anything," said Pilz, rubbing his knuckles while walking over to where Matthias Vidrik had been watching him go to work.

Vidrik stared suspiciously at the Berlin-based soldier who often assisted him with interrogations. They were in the middle of playing what Vidrik called the *bad cop, worse cop* routine. Pilz worked the captive over with his fists, and Vidrik took them to hell when necessary. Today their guest was the billionaire Michael Inselheim, and Vidrik was convinced that the head of the Inselheim Group was hiding something.

Vidrik stood up and removed his suit jacket and placed it over the back of his chair. He looked down on the smaller Pilz and gave him a light tap on the back.

"Get the blowtorch."

Vidrik sucked some air through his nose and rolled his shoulders to help enhance the rush of anticipation. He had been looking forward to an intimate moment with Inselheim. As one of the top snipers in The League, and the best in Europe, Vidrik's sharpshooting skills were often needed. Long-range hits provided interesting logistical challenges. Vidrik appreciated the art of the sniper. It required a level of patience which few men had; a days-long wait in some remote, exposed location for a seconds-long window of opportunity to take the shot. Stillness and focus for long periods came to Vidrik like breathing. He was born with it. But long-range still lacked something for him. From 600 feet, his prey was no different to an ant, and stepping on an ant was no fun. He got the most pleasure from seeing the blood, snot and tears of his victim up-close. It was the kind of power he could savour. So when Francois called early in the morning and gave Vidrik the task of investigating a potential conspiracy against The League, he was glad to oblige.

Vidrik looked across and studied Inselheim, chained naked from the ceiling by his arms. He thought Inselheim looked interesting in that position. More *real*.

The world knew Inselheim as the risk-taking businessman with the swagger and sharp suits. But Vidrik knew men like Inselheim better than that. Their entire existence was a show. Beneath his mask, Inselheim was a spoiled brat and a snivelling opportunist. He was calm and controlled until someone pressed the right buttons, after which all his secrets would come pouring out.

Vidrik sauntered over while rolling up his shirt sleeves. He stood in front of Inselheim, who was glazed with sweat and shaking with fear. Pilz returned from the shelves and handed over the blowtorch. Inselheim noticed what was happening and began trembling furiously.

"God, please, no!" he screamed. "I—" Vidrik turned on the blowtorch. Inselheim began speaking frantically and rapidly. "I told you everything! I was late with a payment, and I spoke with Khartoum on the phone. Your men came by a few days later and picked up the money. That was it! I swear! I don't know who killed him!"

Vidrik remained silent. The only sounds were the blowtorch and Inselheim's whimpering.

"You're hiding something," said Vidrik.

"I'm not," cried Inselheim, pouting and shaking his head from side to side.

"You are. We've been tracking you. You're up to something. Tell me what it is."

"I'm not," repeated Inselheim with a sob.

Vidrik took an impatient breath.

"You know, Michael," he said over the sound of the blowtorch. "I'm not the one in control. You are. In my mind, I

131

want to take this blowtorch and work my way up from your knee to your balls. But you have the power to stop me. You're the boss here. Not me."

Inselheim began whimpering and shaking his head more vigorously as Vidrik brought the flame closer to his leg.

"No!" he screamed.

The flame began searing into his leg while he screamed hysterically.

"Don't you want to stop me!?" yelled Vidrik over Inselheim's yells of distress. "Are you not the boss? Are you not the powerful Michael Inselheim?"

"Ahh!" he screamed. "Stop!! Stop!!"

Vidrik moved the blowtorch away, leaving behind a badly charred area on the inside of Inselheim's thigh. His own knees were shaking with excitement. He took the time to steady his breathing.

"Did I hear correctly? Are you the boss?"

"Yes, yes, I'm the boss," cried Inselheim. "I'll tell you everything. Please!"

"Excellent," said Vidrik, keeping the blowtorch turned on. "What is it you need to tell me?"

After an extended, sometimes incomprehensible flurry, Vidrik gathered that Inselheim had never met a young, Estonian boy. He was disappointed at first, and had almost gone back to work with the blowtorch, when the rest of Inselheim's confession came pouring out.

"Do you think he's making it up?" Pilz asked Vidrik, giving Inselheim a sceptical glance as they stood huddled together. "It sounds pretty crazy. A laser that destroys nukes?"

"He's telling the truth," replied Vidrik, squinting and looking at the floor. Vidrik was a seasoned interrogator, and he knew the fine line between truth and hysteria. When he had finalised the next steps in his mind, he looked at Pilz and handed him the blowtorch.

"Take him downstairs and lock him up. I'll call Francois. We need to get a hold of those blueprints Inselheim was talking about."

Kalakia was at his desk, re-reading the Stoic emperor Marcus Aurelius' Meditations, and was currently at "XIII. Remember that all is but opinion and conceit" when his phone rang.

"What is it?"

"We found something," said Francois. "Vidrik got it out of him."

"Tell me."

"What we have so far is a confession and the blueprints from his office, but it seems Inselheim has been working on a project called *Neutralaser*. It's a device which can disintegrate a nuclear warhead. His company ran a successful test in secret in the Kazakh desert."

"He destroyed a warhead with a laser?" said Kalakia, leaning forward.

"As far as we know. Yes."

Kalakia paused to weigh up this new information.

"Where is the device now, and who knows about it?"

"We don't know yet, but we'll get it out of him."

"Where is Inselheim?"

"He's being held at the interrogation facility."

"Good. Send a car to pick me up."

"Ok."

Kalakia began busying his mind as soon as he closed the connection. His instincts had proven correct. *That sneaky imp*. Inselheim was working on something big. Kalakia never imagined that it was anti-nuclear defence. The implications for such technology were enormous. Still, he was not getting ahead of himself. They had to verify the blueprints, and that the device did exist. All things considered, however, if The League did get a hold of such a device, then they could help avoid a geopolitical disaster while tipping the balance of world power even further in their favour. Any nation with anti-nuclear capabilities could hold other countries to ransom. So it was best that The League had caught Inselheim out. Kalakia readied himself for a long night.

Vidrik had one hand on the wheel of his Porsche 911 as he pulled out of the Inselheim Group's data facility in Adlershof. He tugged at his turtleneck collar then lit a cigarette, blowing the smoke upwards before opening the window. With Pilz in the passenger seat they rolled past the four white vans belonging to League Intel, who had quickly shown up to secure the equipment. They reached a long stretch of open road and Vidrik punched the accelerator as they travelled back toward Mitte.

"I need a beer after all that," said Pilz, stretching his neck. "Can we drop by the späti?"

Vidrik nodded and continued driving until they reached Neukölln. He double-parked in front of the convenience store and tossed his cigarette butt out of the window.

"Want anything?" asked Pilz.

Vidrik shook his head. When Pilz jogged into the späti, Vidrik began people watching. He found nothing exciting to look at, just hipsters and tourists. He gave it five years maximum. Berlin was going to hell.

His phone lit up beside him with a new text message:

"*Pilz is no longer needed*", it read.

He tilted his head slowly while staring at the words. No surprises there, he thought. The two of them had struck gold with Inselheim, and a big-mouth nobody like Pilz was too much of a security risk.

A moment later Pilz came back from the späti with his beer already open and got into the passenger seat.

"I changed my mind. Get me a Club-Matè," said Vidrik, figuring he would need the caffeine hit if he were going to dispose of Pilz that evening.

"Ok," said Pilz with a sigh and a reluctant nod.

"Here," said Vidrik, reaching his hand out. "Let me have a sip of your beer."

"Yes, sir," said Pilz, giving Vidrik his bottle before getting out and slamming the door behind him.

Moody bastard.

When Pilz was back inside the späti, Vidrik opened his glove box and got out his small bag of Rohypnol tablets. He took three out and crushed them one by one into the bottle of beer and stirred it around lightly with his thumb covering the opening, careful not to let too much pressure build up. Pilz eventually returned and they exchanged bottles. Vidrik drove off, and Pilz took a large gulp of his beer.

"That's the stuff," said Pilz, burping in the process and looking out at the street briefly. "Crazy, huh?" he continued. "That Inselheim's a wild son of a bitch."

Vidrik said nothing. Pilz would start feeling the effects within a quarter of an hour. They drove on, and Pilz continued to sip on his beer while trying to make small talk before he eventually grew quiet. When he was sufficiently unconscious, Vidrik took the beer out of his lap and tossed it out of the car. He was about to drive back to the facility to dissolve Pilz's body in acid but found himself heading toward Charlottenburg instead. Pilz could wait.

Vidrik decided to ring ahead, dialling the VIP hotline for Madame Sandra's brothel.

"Ja?" said the voice.

"It's Vidrik. Is she there?"

"Hello, Matthias," said Madame Sandra. "Franziska? Yes, wait, let me check."

There was a pause, and Vidrik could hear light whispers in the background.

"I can have her ready for you in forty-five minutes," said Madame Sandra.

"Good. I'll be there soon."

Vidrik dropped the phone on his lap and looked over at Pilz again, whose neck was bent to the side and mouth was slightly ajar. With the wheel balanced on his knee, Vidrik took a few sips of his Club-Matè then put the bottle aside before rubbing on his temple. He was in a grumpy mood. He should have been ecstatic. He had proven himself more than worthy of the promotion. The uncovering of Inselheim's Neutralaser Project was a boon for The League. At the very least, watching Inselheim snivel and come apart should have satisfied him. He should have felt proud about the promotion, and he would have been, had it not come about the way it did. He never liked Felipe. He would have gladly slit the Spaniard's throat himself to claim his position. What agitated Vidrik was how Abel had slithered his way into the organisation on the back of Vivar and Khartoum's lives. He should have finished the kid off instantly. It should have been routine. Instead, Kalakia *rewarded* the boy.

The great man was slipping, Vidrik concluded while pulled up at the traffic lights. He spat onto the road. With Kalakia blindsided, Vidrik decided to take responsibility for the matter. He would keep a close eye on the kid when he came back to Berlin, and if Abel stepped out of line in the slightest, Vidrik would be the one to put his light out. It would not be a painless death for the young Estoni… Vidrik tensed up suddenly, his attention drawn toward an attractive young woman who had just marched out of her building, dragging her luggage behind her on wheels over the cobblestones. She had a tight body, flowing light brown hair and olive skin.

She waited by the footpath not far from Vidrik and watched the oncoming cars. Judging by the bag, she was leaving town. Vidrik recognised her instantly. It was Elias' bitch, the one who started the whole mess. Elias had been foolish to mess with her, but Vidrik had to admit she had a hell of an ass. He watched her coolly for a few seconds. Then he snapped. The traffic light turned green. He bared his teeth and pulled over into a driveway. Without straightening the car, he turned off the engine and reached over the unconscious Pilz toward the glovebox for his pistol before stopping suddenly. "Fuck," he mouthed, his fingers and legs trembling. Kalakia had minced no words when declaring that she was not to be touched.

Vidrik continued watching on while chewing his lip, half of his body on the seat, the other half ready to pounce. A taxi pulled up, and she made for the back of the car as the driver got out to help her. Then she froze. The driver picked up her luggage and tossed it inside the trunk. Still she did not move. After some time she reached into her handbag and took out her wallet. She handed the driver what looked to be money and said something to him. The taxi driver gave her a strange look and shrugged before taking her luggage out of the car again and driving off. Vidrik raised his eyebrows. What was she up to? She remained in her place on the footpath. Vidrik leaned forward and squinted. She was *smiling*. Then she turned back to her building, opened the door and disappeared inside with her luggage. He let his body relax back onto the seat. *Staying, are we?* He continued watching the door before deciding he had seen enough. He took note of the number above the entrance and drove away. Killing her was forbidden, he thought, but Kalakia said nothing about talking. Once the situation had cooled down, he would pay her a visit. She could amuse him while Abel was in Zürich, he decided.

As he drove along, his mood grew flat again. He despised having his hands tied like that. At least in the meantime he had Franziska's glorious tits to cheer him up. He knew what else could lift his spirit. He reached toward the dash and switched on his stereo system. The car immediately filled up with the guitar riff from the song "Die For Metal" by Manowar, which he had been playing on maximum volume earlier in the day. It helped, but he needed something more. He punched the accelerator just as he passed a group of teenagers on the sidewalk. The boys turned their necks abruptly as Vidrik raced off chuckling, enjoying the dopamine rush of not only the g-force but also the thought of skinning alive that scrawny, arrogant little bastard — *and* that whore of his.

16

If only the flight were longer, thought Frederich. Soon after they hit maximum altitude, it would be time to straighten up chairs and prepare for the descent into Zürich. There was a great deal to process in that time. In barely a week, Frederich had twice come within inches of death, had killed two men, made and lost a friend, penetrated the most powerful organisation in the world, and had undergone a strange transformation.

After Ida had stormed off, there was time only for logistics. Frederich did what came naturally and pushed his feelings away, instead busying himself with preparations for the trip. He expected to come back to Berlin, so he set up the auto-payment of his rent with the bank. He shut off the heating and finally got around to labelling his mailbox with '*No Junk Mail*' to avoid having it overstuffed with catalogues and newspapers. He disinfected the shovel and returned it to the basement cleaner than when he had taken it. After scrubbing long and hard over a bloodstain left behind in the trunk by Vivar's body, he decided to cut that piece of the carpet out before returning the Renault to the rental company in Mitte. They had his credit card details.

He then called Johannes on his home phone and let him know that he had made contact with The League. They had reached an agreement, and all parties were now safe. It took all of his persuasive powers to fend off Johannes' suspicion. After much pleading, he somehow convinced Kraas' old friend that the best way to help would be to stay out of it. He promised that he would come to visit as soon as he could. Night came, and he packed his rucksack with the necessities. He managed to get a few hours of sleep before it was time for the early morning flight.

Now that he had stowed his bag and taken his seat, his mind began to drift. Ida ruled his thoughts initially. He wondered where she was and whether she had already fled Berlin. He would understand if she wanted to leave that chapter of her life behind. He felt an ache in his chest, a call from the depths of him which he had no way to answer. It was familiar by now. It appeared the first time during the weeks following Kraas' death. He missed Ida.

He questioned whether she would ever forgive him. It was wishful thinking, he figured, judging by their last encounter. Not even Kraas had been able to forgive what was inside him. Things changed between him and Kraas after he slaughtered the would-be assassin in the forest. They stopped training together, and Kraas began pushing the idea of Frederich moving to Tallinn. Kraas appeared to Frederich to be sad and distracted, guilty almost. He said it was time for Frederich to live a normal life. Frederich grew confused. He *knew* he was not normal. Not even his upbringing had been normal. How did Kraas expect him to live like the rest of the population? Kraas' decision had hurt, but Frederich swallowed it. Nobody could bring themselves to discuss what had happened. That night remained unspoken about, and Frederich did as Kraas told him; he went to Tallinn. He lived a 'normal' life, whatever that was. In any case, a normal life was out of the question now. Frederich was preparing for a career as a killer.

It had evolved quickly. Ida's scream. Suffocating underwater. Putting Khartoum to sleep. The Kalakia meeting. Vivar's failed attempt at revenge. Those events strung together had been a revelation. They showed Frederich who he was, that the first man he killed would not be an isolated incident. Not only did Frederich intend to kill again, he expected to enjoy it. What would Kraas think? It no longer mattered. Kraas was gone. Frederich had to accept that. He would have to make his own decisions now. Khartoum and Vivar.. they deserved to die. The men he would kill in the future? For the right cause, sure, why not. Corruption was a sickness of the Earth. He knew Kraas would agree with him on that point. He had felt that way since he was a boy, as Kraas slowly revealed to him the state of the world around him. He also sensed, in a strange way, that Kraas had been preparing him for this moment his whole life.

The flight attendants passed through the aisle and prepared each passenger for landing. Seats up and seat belts on, they ordered. Frederich shook himself out of his daydream. The time for reflecting was over. He took a deep breath and focussed inside. The void was there. It brought him both calmness and strength — and rage. He realised that his shadow was no longer something to run from. He was now entering a world where, far from having to conceal his savageness, he could channel and unleash it. The discipline to contain it would come in time, and the lessons Kraas had taught him would be indispensable. Regardless of what challenges he faced during his training and beyond, he resolved to let nothing — and no one — get in his way.

It was 2:48 pm at Zürich Airport, 3 minutes until landing, and the man known as Scheffler was at the arrivals gate. While a sea of people shifted around him and chatted excitedly amongst each other with wide-eyes, Scheffler remained steadfast in place like a rock. He watched on as a middle-aged businesswoman marched through the gate with purpose, her leather bag in hand. She was followed by a young, blonde girl with a ponytail who shrieked excitedly at the sight of her waiting friend and sprinted forward, leaving her luggage behind.

Why Scheffler was taking time away from important work to pick up a potential recruit named 'Frederich Abel' was beyond him. He only knew that Kalakia was insisting he pick the boy up from the airport personally, and that he would be the one to overlook the boy's training. It pissed him off to have to drop everything to run an errand. His time was better spent back at the facility. But then again, everything pissed him off these days. Now that he was four weeks into his latest steroid cycle, his trenbolone levels were through the roof. A little bit of extra size never hurt, he figured. Well, not him, anyway. It was those around him who had to look out. Anything could set him off. One of the recruits, the young Pole from Warsaw, was distracted and had not heard Scheffler's instruction. Scheffler did not repeat himself or bother trying to get that idiot's attention. He laid him out on the floor without warning and gave him a concussion to boot. *He listens now*, thought Scheffler, narrowing his gaze.

It was no coincidence that Scheffler's program was hell on Earth. The occasional ass-kicking was good for the boys. It was deep beneath the Alps where Scheffler turned boys into men, inside the abandoned Swiss National Redoubt defence fortress, making his recruits live and train in relative darkness for days on end, going outside only for forced marches through the mountains. Military drills, weapons training, strength training, hand-to-hand combat. He needed his people in top shape and capable of fighting any opponent. Could this Frederich kid handle that? Not likely.

There was no forgetting the attrition phase. Scheffler's favourite. In life and in battle, Scheffler respected only a man's nerve. A real man could take repeated beatings without caving in and could withstand days of psychological torture without breaking. Above all, a man of nerve never gave in to desperation. He maintained his resolve under any pressure. Scheffler prided himself in showing his recruits the limits of their despair. He relished breaking their spirits but also felt a sense of disgust when it happened. Only the finest came out of Elite Squad intact.

Back at the facility, his number two Otto was in charge of inflicting hell, and Scheffler, an elite war machine, was left playing chaperone. He shook his head and looked up impatiently again at the arrivals board, which showed that the flight had landed. He took the photo out of his pocket to study. It had to be some mistake, he thought. This kid belongs on the cover of that JQ men's magazine or whatever it was. Experience told him that it would be a waste of his time. The kid would break within a week. Then again, Scheffler knew Kalakia never messed around. The big man only insisted on something with good reason. So naturally, Scheffler was curious. Still, it was terrible timing for the boy. These days Scheffler had a fuse shorter than the hairs on his waxed chest. He was going to make this Frederich kid sing, and then he was going to break him.

He tensed his bicep and studied it with satisfaction. His t-shirt was stretched to capacity. Progress was good. A flurry of people suddenly poured out through the sliding doors, and among them was a young man who matched the photograph. He had dishevelled light brown hair like a rock star, baby features, and was wearing a black leather jacket with tight black pants. He was carrying a brown rucksack. *Make that Rolling Stone magazine.* Scheffler licked his lips.

"This is going to be fun," he whispered.

PART II

17

THE JEEP CUT THROUGH THE KAZAKH DESERT on the way to the Neutralaser facility, leaving behind a long trail of orange dust. Inselheim gazed vacantly out of the back-seat window, his shoulders slumped. To his right was Kimberley Brunswick, his close friend and Neutralaser head project manager. In the front passenger seat was Vidrik, who had angled the rear-view driver's mirror Inselheim's way. Inselheim occasionally caught his strange, lazy stare pointed directly at him. Behind them were four more Jeeps with a posse of two dozen men, who had been waiting in a convoy when Vidrik and Inselheim's airplane landed at Shymkent International. Brunswick had been in the city hoping to take a well-earned weekend off when she got the unexpected call to meet them at the airport. She had given Vidrik one look, and upon seeing Inselheim's face had silently understood that something was terribly wrong.

The tense journey from Shymkent to the facility took four hours, including twenty off-road minutes before they pulled up at their destination; an inconspicuous, windowless concrete building in the middle of nowhere.

When they came to a stop, Inselheim remained staring at where his leg had been seared. It was treated and bandaged, but the drugs had worn off and it was now throbbing with pain. Vidrik grasped Inselheim by his shirt and forced him out of the car. Inselheim, Brunswick, Vidrik and the other henchmen approached the unmarked grey door. The posse of men stood by silently. They looked military. Their stoic expressions and focussed demeanour showed they had been sent for a reason. Each of them carried a black bag and wore loose-fitting black clothes and combat boots. Brunswick shot Inselheim yet another questioning glance then turned to identify herself through the video monitor. After they were granted entry, they descended the dark, narrow stairs which led straight into the hall. Inselheim remained indifferent while Kalakia's people took time to absorb the bustling scene beneath the desert.

Inselheim had seen the same slack mouths and wide eyes dozens of times with other newcomers. The hall was an astonishing sight; four storeys high and as long as two football fields. There were haphazardly arranged computer terminals, workbenches, testing areas, welding stations, odd-looking robotics equipment and makeshift meeting rooms separated into partitions. A walkway ran through the middle, passing the Neutralaser itself as well as the exit tunnel, and led all the way to the sleeping quarters at the back. The accommodation was organised like a hotel and consisted of a fully equipped gymnasium, cafeteria and large recreation room. A lightly armed security team remained on 24-hour stand-by in case of any unauthorised access or outside threats. Most impressive for the first time visitor was the sheer number of personnel contained in such a remote location. Inselheim had amassed dozens of experts from Germany, Japan, Lithuania, The United States, Russia and more. The various teams were loosely organised into research, design, manufacturing and testing. Each person had been carefully vetted and had signed a non-disclosure agreement. All of them had a history of anti-nuclear activism. Unsurprising to Insel-heim, a significant number of the Japanese team members had relatives who were in Hiroshima or Nagasaki during the Second World War.

With the arrival of Inselheim and his menacing compan-ions, the team gradually stopped what they were doing and took notice. Brunswick approached Inselheim while Vidrik and the rest were busy studying the place.

"Can we talk in private?" she whispered.

Inselheim noticed Vidrik's attention was elsewhere. He nodded and followed Brunswick to her office.

"You want to tell me what the hell is going on, Michael?" she asked, closing the door and leaning against it with her arms crossed.

Inselheim sighed and rubbed his eyes, unsure where to be-gin. When he was away, in Berlin or elsewhere, Brunswick ran the show. Inselheim had known her since university, so he trusted her unconditionally, and she was the most capable person he knew. Still, how was he going to break *this* to her? He was numb, and still reeling from his ordeal. After he was released from lockup, his leg was treated by one of Kalakia's private doctors. He was allowed half a day at home under supervision to sleep and prepare for the flight. With Kalakia's men standing by, Inselheim made the call to Bruns-wick to meet them at the airport but was forbidden to di-vulge anything else. Later they reached Shymkent Airport, where Brunswick was waiting without a clue why. She had waited long enough.

"Those are Kalakia's men. It's over," he said with a flat voice. "They know everything."

"Oh no," said Brunswick, cupping her hand over her mouth. She looked at the floor and hesitated in her speech,

149

letting out a quiet, muffled groan then putting her fingertips to her lips. "How did this happen?" she asked.

"They were tracking me."

"Shit."

"*Ja.* Shit."

"Did they hurt you? I noticed you limping."

Inselheim lowered his gaze to the floor while recalling what Vidrik did to him. Tears glazed his eyes. He nodded.

"Oh, Michael," said Brunswick, walking forward and placing a hand on his shoulder.

Inselheim wiped his eyes and collapsed onto the sofa behind him along the wall. With pouted lips, he looked up at the ceiling to avoid Brunswick's gaze.

"I've never seen you like this," said Brunswick.

"We were so close," said Inselheim. "So damn close."

"What do they have planned?"

"I don't know," said Inselheim, throwing up his hands. "Obviously they're taking over."

"Bastards," said Brunswick with a sharp voice. "No," she added, shaking her head defiantly. "Not going to happen. We've worked too hard for this."

Inselheim sighed.

"It's over, Kimberley. They have us. We give them what they want, or they kill us."

Brunswick gazed into space and ran her tongue side to side over her bottom lip, the way she did when she was thinking hard. Inselheim had already predicted her reaction. First, she would resist the news outright. Then she would carefully measure the situation, including all the facts and possibilities. Finally, she would enforce her will — one way or another.

Inselheim had spent the flight over contemplating the mammoth task of talking Brunswick out of doing anything crazy. He had known Brunswick for over thirty years, and their relationship was as strong as it was complex. He learnt of her true nature the day they met at a mutual friend's dinner party, during their university days in Munich in the mid-80s. Their group was discussing the state of East Germany when Brunswick chimed in. The communist regime would not last into the next century, she declared. Inselheim snickered at the petite brunette with the short fringe, who until then had barely registered on his radar. The deathly stare she shot him vaporised his smugness. After a brief sexual affair, their intellectual discussions overshadowed their desire to go to bed together. Inselheim joined his father at the company soon after meeting Brunswick and was adamant that she should come along. Brunswick understood politics and human nature better than anyone, as well as how to wage war in the boardroom. During Brunswick's rise in the company, Inselheim had never seen her back away from a fight.

"Mass production is going to take time," said Brunswick, turning her attention toward Inselheim. "And there's still hypersonic missile testing. I can reach out to our contacts in the federal government and have them establish a production factory. If we move quic—"

"Kimberley, stop," said Inselheim. "Please. These guys have eyes and ears everywhere. *Everywhere*. They'll find out. And when they do, we're dead."

"Are we?" said Brunswick with a raised eyebrow.

Inselheim noticed her stare sharpen beyond the point of negotiation, and his despair gave way to dread.

"Since when does Michael Inselheim give up so easily?" she asked. "Hmm? Where's Mr. Risk Taker?"

"You don't know what they're capable of," said Inselheim, his lips pressed together. "They broke me."

"So we'll glue you back together. We've been here before. How many hostile governments have we dealt with? How many warlords?"

"This isn't some militia group, Kimberley. Even they know their limits. These people don't have any."

Inselheim turned his ears toward a series of approaching footsteps. The door swung open violently and Vidrik stepped through. The sound of shuffles and men shouting outside came through the door, as well as yells of distress.

"Everyone to the back!" yelled a man outside. "Move!"

"There you are," said Vidrik, closing the door behind him. "Slippery fish. Did I say you could leave?"

Inselheim tensed up and his mind went blank at the sight of his tormentor. Brunswick crossed her arms.

"What's going on out there?" she asked, raising her chin and peering toward the door.

"If you hadn't slithered away, you would know," said Vidrik.

"This is our company. Why do we need permission to speak to each other?" she said.

Vidrik tilted his head and his gaze turned blank. He reached into his jacket pocket and took out a silver pistol, flicked the safety and pointed the gun at Brunswick's head. She flinched and her eyes widened. She slowly uncrossed her arms and lifted her shoulders. Inselheim sat up and gripped onto his knees. He watched on, unable to say a word.

"Yes. It is your company, and you have done an excellent job. For that, you deserve a reward. Come. Come closer. I have a surprise for you."

Brunswick hesitated.

"Come here," said Vidrik with force in his voice.

Brunswick took a slow, cautious step forward.

"Take a look in there," said Vidrik, motioning at the gun with his eyes. "Tell me if it's inside the barrel."

Seconds passed. The tension in the room lingered in stark contrast to the mayhem outside.

"If you're going to shoot me, just do it. I'm not playing your games," said Brunswick.

Vidrik snickered and lowered the gun. He stepped forward and leaned his face close to Brunswick's ear and whispered something Inselheim could not hear. Brunswick's eyes bulged out, and she hardened her face to conceal her reaction. Vidrik then turned and began walking out. When he opened the door, the commotion had already shifted away into the distance.

"This facility is under new ownership," he said. "Come."

Brunswick and Inselheim looked at each other. Brunswick moved first, and Inselheim followed. They walked outside and found the hall had been cleared. The workers were being rushed into the sleeping quarters at the back by the military men, who were now carrying rifles. Six of the militia were standing before a group of six remaining employees who had been lined up beside a partition wall with their hands on their heads. Brunswick and Inselheim exchanged looks of concern.

"Come," said Vidrik, motioning with his head toward the line-up.

"What's going on?" asked Inselheim while looking toward his employees.

He locked eyes with Marius Olson, an aeronautical engineer who had joined recently to help reinforce the team and speed up the final stage of the project. Marius' eyes exuded his terror, his face had turned a deathly pale and was covered in sweat, and his chin was trembling.

"We're downsizing," said Vidrik, before turning toward the armed militia and giving them a nod.

The six men lifted their rifles and aimed at the employees. Before Inselheim or Brunswick could protest, the guns fired. The six employees dropped to the floor. Inselheim went completely stiff. Brunswick screamed hysterically, her voice echoing through the hall. She ran toward the shooters.

"You bastards!" she screamed. "What have you done!?"

She tried to attack one of the shooters with her hands, only to be struck on the shoulder with the stock end of the gun and pushed to the floor. She rose immediately to her feet with a grunt and went over to the dead bodies. She bent down and touched one person then moved to the next, desperately searching for any sign of life.

Vidrik signalled to one of the armed militia. The man put down his rifle and went over to Brunswick. He grasped her by the arms and began dragging her to the other side of the hall.

"Let me go!" she screamed while wrestling with her aggressor. "You damn monsters!"

Brunswick continued to struggle and scream while being forced away. Inselheim could not feel a thing. Brunswick's screams were now coming from the other end of the hall. He gazed at his six dead employees as though in a dream. A hand slapped his face.

"Inselheim, look here," said Vidrik.

Inselheim blinked twice and turned his head.

"That was a message from Kalakia. You do what you're told, or more of your people will die. That includes your smart-talking bitch. You got that?"

Inselheim could not breathe.

"Inselheim."

Another slap to the face. Inselheim nodded.

"Good. Now, everything stays as before. You can have the week off, then we want you in the public eye again. You keep your mouth shut and look normal. Don't do anything to draw attention. Otherwise, you'll have no employees left. You can count on that."

Vidrik paused, allowing the gravity of his words to fully impact Inselheim.

"But look on the bright side. You're still the boss. It's all in your hands. Understood?"

Inselheim blinked and gave a weak nod.

"Say it."

"I understand," he croaked.

"Right, let's go," said Vidrik, nudging Inselheim's shoulder.

Vidrik turned to one of the militia.

"Keep this place locked down until reinforcements arrive," he said, poking the man's chest. "Don't let anyone get out of line."

The man nodded.

Without another word, Vidrik escorted Inselheim up the stairs and back outside where the Jeep was waiting for them. Inselheim offered no resistance. The image of Marius' terrified face was still branded on his mind, and he could barely feel his body. He looked down on himself from a distance, hearing the sound of their feet crunching on the dirt and the breeze blowing. Vidrik led him to the car before it drove away, back through the lifeless desert, leaving Brunswick and the team held hostage by Kalakia's armed killers.

18

No way Scheffler was going to win. Not this time. Not ever. The darkness was no bother to Frederich. In fact, he had learnt to savour it. It invigorated him, like bathing in a warm spa, or based on the smell in the room, like being a pig in shit.

"Knock when you've had enough," Scheffler had said from the doorway with his English accent, illuminated from behind by the hallway light which reflected off his thick head of light brown hair. "You'll be let out, no questions asked. One catch: you pull your head in after that."

Without waiting for a reply, he had shut the metal door and locked it, leaving Frederich in total darkness in the tiny windowless cell carved into the mountain rock. There was no toilet, no bed and no heating. Only black.

During the initial period, Frederich sat by the wall with his legs crossed and his back upright to keep himself alert. His mind eventually settled, and he grew restless. Aches appeared in his shoulders and legs. He shivered occasionally. Within hours his mind's grip loosened and he felt himself floating. Then he could no longer hold it in. He pulled down his pants and squatted in the opposite corner and relieved himself. Then came the nausea. He sat through it all without making a sound and busied himself with fantasies of sticking a knife in Scheffler's throat.

During what he assumed was day two, the various bodily sensations had given way to hunger pains which gnawed mercilessly at him. He could only focus on his breathing and wait as the line between sleep and wakefulness became blurred. He was drifting in the abyss with no grasp of time, anchored only by his loathing for Scheffler. His rage was boundless, but his body had limits. Still, he was alive, and he was holding out. Screw him, he thought again, shivering uncontrollably. No way he was going to win.

"Not a peep in three days," said Scheffler, phone to his face while leaning back on his chair with one leg up on his metal desk.

"Total darkness and no food or water? Are you sure he's still alive?" replied Francois.

"Yep, we've got infrared cameras in the room. He's sitting in some yoga pose. Every once in a while he does some stretching, otherwise he just sits there and dozes in and out."

"How did this all start exactly?"

"Well, I was helping our young friend Piotr Paleski harden up a bit, and that bastard Frederich decided it was too much for his precious eyes."

"Explain what 'harden up' means."

"We were marching at high altitude, and he lost his breath. He was slowing down the unit. He said he wasn't going to make it. So I gave him a helping kick to get down the mountain easier. That was when Abel came up from behind and almost bowled me over. Something's not right with that kid."

"Is all of this necessary?"

"You're joking, right? He's lucky I didn't break his kneecaps. Or at least send him packing."

"That's not an option," said Francois.

"I know, I know, he's Kalakia's golden child," replied Scheffler. "You guys never get this interested in a recruit, do you?"

"What happens next?"

"Same thing that happened to all the ones before him. He breaks, crawls out of his shit infested hole, begs me for forgiveness, and we get on with it."

"Kalakia is not going to like this. If the boy dies in there, it's on you. I hope you understand this."

"Yeah, and if he gets away with what he did, the precedent is set, and we both know what happens after that. Revolt. You want that?"

The line went quiet.

"I'll call you back in an hour," said Francois before the connection closed with a click.

It was hard to know how long he had been inside. It felt like two days, which meant it was probably closer to three or four. He had read all about it. People in total isolation end up with a warped sense of time. Experiments proved that without stimulation, the mind eventually caves. Without a psychological line of defence, a person gets a glimpse at insanity. A front-row seat in extreme cases. Anxiety, terror and hallucinations were not uncommon. He would avoid that if he could. He worked to keep his mind busy by trying to recall every country in the world. He traversed the map in his head, beginning with Europe and travelling eastward toward Central Asia. Uzbekistan, Turkmenistan, Tajikistan. He shot back to Europe. He had forgotten Slovenia. Capital: Ljubljana. And San Marino and The Vatican, both states within a state. Back to Asia. Kyrgyzstan. Mongolia. China. Afghanistan. Pakistan. Eventually he completed all of Asia and The Pacific, The Middle East and the entire American Continent all the way down to Chile and Argentina. Africa, he knew well, including Lesotho, another enclave. He was doing a final sweep of the continents when his mind wandered. He began naming all the planets in the Solar System as well as their moons. Jupiter had too many to remember. Fifty or so, he believed. Pluto had something like five. Hydra and Charon were two of them. He left the Solar System and drifted further into the vastness of the Milky Way.

He woke up with a flinch. How long had he been asleep? He hugged himself and began rocking in place. Was it the cold or the anxiety causing his body to shake? His insides were burning.

"Think!" said a voice from the corner, causing him to jump in his place. He paused and leaned his head to the side.

"Kraas?" he found himself whispering.

"Come, Frederich. I know this isn't all you got. What's your next move?"

He began shaking violently. The burning in his body lifted like a fever. His palms and armpits grew sweaty. Where the hell was that voice coming from?

"Oh, nice try. But where's your *power*? Stop overestimating me. Push! Harder! More! More!"

Frederich shook his head in disbelief, still shivering.

"Kraas?" he called again. "Kraas, is that you?"

He was hallucinating. He had to be. But the voice was *there*. He could hear it. Clearly.

160

"Hey! Hold on. Ugh! Ah, you sneak!"

Finally, he understood. It was his memory in replay. He even knew the precise time. He was fourteen years old, and they had been grappling on the grass outside their home. Kraas had let him win. Or at least it seemed so. Kraas insisted that Frederich had outplayed him. Frederich often looked back on that day. Did Kraas fool him into believing in his own strength? Or did he really outgrow Kraas? It was difficult to know. Either way, it had the desired effect.

"You see? There's always a path forward, Frederich. Always. Never give up."

Frederich felt suddenly warm inside. His eyes glazed over with tears. The mind was a wondrous thing, he thought. It was comforting him with Kraas' voice. The calmer he grew the more the voice faded until he dozed off again.

"Push it! Let's go, let's go!"

Scheffler walked among his recruits while they completed a set of push-ups in the training hall. The men were arranged in rows of ten along the mattresses, all dressed in their black training pants and black t-shirts. Scheffler stopped in front of Piotr Paleski, whose chin and arm were scratched all over from his fall down the mountain. His skinny arms were bulging under the strain. Scheffler loathed his brown puppy eyes whenever they looked at him. He rested his foot on Paleski's back and watched him struggle to lift his body.

"Do you think your girlfriend downstairs is thinking about you?" said Scheffler. "Do you think she misses you?"

Piotr moaned and groaned louder under the increasing weight of Scheffler's foot.

"Come on, let's see those tiny arms work."

Scheffler's number two Otto Litger marched over from the office.

"Phone call," said Otto, brushing over his flattop with both hands.

"Come here," said Scheffler, motioning with two fingers. "Take over."

With Otto now adding the extra weight on Piotr's back, Scheffler marched into the office.

"Scheffler," he said into the telephone handset.

"Word from Kalakia. He believes there are more productive ways to discipline the boy. Let him out and move forward with the training. How you make an example of him after that is up to you."

The connection closed, leaving Scheffler to process Francois' words alone. He put down the handset and gazed into space.

"Fuck!" he yelled, slapping his glass of water off the desk, sending it shattering to the floor. "Fucking bastard!" he screamed and banged his fist on the desk, causing the items on top to shake from the aftershocks.

He exhaled rapidly and scowled. Those damn steroids. *Fine*, he thought. Abel could win the battle of attrition. Scheffler would win the war out in the field. But first, he needed to blow off some steam.

Frederich jerked awake. There was a shuffling sound to his right. His body tensed and the hairs on his head stood up. He choked off his breathing and listened hard for a long time. The room was silent. What was Scheffler up to? He waited and listened. Nothing. Another hallucination? His stomach was in knots. It grumbled again, begging for food. His lips were cracked all over, his mouth felt like paper.

"Raaaw!"

His body convulsed. This time he was sure he had heard it. A mammal of some kind.

"Raaaw," it roared again.

He flipped around and perched himself up with his hands. He underestimated how much his strength had been sapped, growing light-headed and collapsing down onto his shoulders. The shuffling continued. He narrowed his eyes and tried to catch a glimpse of what it could be. He could vaguely make out its enormous outline. His head was spinning. He braced himself.

Scheffler marched into the training hall with his fists cocked. The recruits were in the middle of one-on-one sparring sessions with Otto supervising.

"You! You! And you! Let's go!" yelled Scheffler, pointing at three random recruits.

He planted his legs in the middle then took off his singlet and tossed it aside, revealing his bulging, carefully sculpted muscles. His nostrils were flared and his chest was heaving up and down. He made two swift exhales through his nose.

"Move it!" he yelled with a booming voice.

The other recruits scrambled to the edge of the mattresses. Two of the chosen recruits swapped worried glances. Ralph, the bulky skinhead from London, seemed unsurprised by Scheffler's abrupt entrance. He flared his body and lifted his chin. Otto had his thick arms crossed and looked on from the side.

Scheffler decided on his first victim. He took two quick steps forward and landed a lightning-fast jab in Ralph's face, following it up with a fierce right hook to his chin. Blood sprayed out of his nose and he collapsed to the floor. The life was sucked out of the room. Nobody moved, including Ralph. Served him right for being cocky.

As though sensing the danger they were in, the other two sprang to life. They screamed out in unison and ran toward Scheffler. Scheffler stood firm and allowed the two fighters to rain down a combination of fists to his face and torso. He gritted his teeth and grunted with each punch received, allowing the pain to awaken his endless supply of rage. Finally, he went on the offensive. He gripped one of them by the throat and tossed him aside with one arm. Using a full twist of his torso, he came down on the second fighter with a swift right hook. The recruit fell to the floor, and struggled to lift himself up again. Scheffler stomped on his hip with the sole of his boot, and the recruit let out a deafening scream.

There was now one fighter left standing, but he seemed to have accepted his fate. His hands were cocked but shaking, and fear oozed out of his eyes. He looked over at the other recruits, pleading for their help.

"Eyes here!" yelled Scheffler. "Never let your opponent out of your sight."

He turned his head quickly back toward Scheffler. Scheffler slapped his own chest hard.

"Come on!"

With a final burst, the recruit yelled and marched over to Scheffler and attempted to punch him. At the same time Scheffler reached his arm back and slapped him in the face.

Scheffler's strength was irresistible, and the recruit tumbled over.

The rest looked on dumbfounded at the aftermath. Otto stepped onto the mattresses and looked over the three defeated fighters with a frown.

"Right," he said gently without taking his eyes away. "Everyone get back to the dorm rooms. We march in one hour."

The recruits shuffled away immediately, several of them helping carry the two worst injured by Scheffler's blows. When the room was emptied out only Scheffler and Otto remained.

"Bad news from Berlin?" said Otto.

Scheffler grunted and looked away, shaking his head.

"They're getting soft," he said.

"It's been almost four days. Maybe he's had enough," said Otto, to which Scheffler responded with a dark, wide-eyed grin. Scheffler looked Otto directly in the eyes.

"Enough? We're just getting started," he said, and marched away.

Its breath was stuffy and loud. With slow footsteps it stalked him across the room.

"Come on," he whispered, trembling and alert. "Do it."

It grunted. He knew he would be an easy target, too weak even to stand. He still intended to fight with what little he had left. It moved a step closer. He could almost make it out. The black bear came another step forward, and he scrambled away on all fours to create space, bracing himself against the wall. It came sprinting directly at him. His skin lifted all over and he left his body as it approached. He screamed and leapt at the bear with his fists cocked. He came crashing to the floor and his head smashed against the concrete.

When he came to, there was a loud humming in his ears. His skull was throbbing with pain. He had been knocked out. He tensed his body again. *The bear.* There were shuffles at the door. Not a bear's. Human shuffles. There was a twist of metal on metal. The door opened. Light came rushing into the room and blinded him. He immediately shut his eyes.

"Look at you," said Scheffler from the doorway with a hint of disgust.

Frederich screamed out something incomprehensible, now out of his mind and unable to express himself in any other way.

"Look at you," repeated Scheffler. "You're an animal."

Scheffler stepped forward and grasped Frederich by his wrists and began dragging him out on his back. Frederich wailed and groaned as they crossed the hallway. They reached the stairs, and Scheffler picked Frederich up by his collar and pants and tossed him over his shoulder with no apparent effort. With firm, even footsteps, Scheffler carried Frederich up the stairs. Frederich was still unable to open his eyes or piece a thought together.

"Come on," a voice whispered. "Do it," it said. It took Frederich some seconds to realise it was his own voice.

"Shut your trap," said Scheffler.

"Do it. Do it now. Come on."

Scheffler threw Frederich onto a bed and his footsteps disappeared out of the room. Frederich tossed from side to side, the aching in his head now unbearable. When a hand touched his sweaty face, he yelled and tried slapping it away.

"Shh," said somebody, pressing down gently on Frederich's chest. "Rest, Frederich. Rest."

"Get some water," said the voice to someone behind him.

When Frederich felt metal on his lips he opened his mouth like a child. Water poured in and he began choking. The metal cup moved away then returned to his lips. He steadied the flow with his throat and gradually absorbed the liquid. It had the effect of a healing tonic, injecting some vitality into his body. More water was carefully poured in. He then pushed away with his head to signal that he was done. A hand lifted his head and a pillow was inserted behind.

"What did they do to him?" a voice said.

"Scheffler's gone bananas," said another voice.

Frederich finally registered that he was back in the sleeping quarters with Piotr and the guys. He let go and fell into sleep in a feverish state which followed him into his dreams, along with the black bear, whose powerful energy he could now feel throughout his body.

19

Ida shuffled on her chair to get comfortable then dragged it closer to the table so she could better hear in the noisy environment. She had changed out of her martial arts uniform but was still sweating underneath her clothes. Jitters ran through her as they always did when meeting someone new. Chi sat across from her, leaning back nonchalantly while holding up a cigarette.

"So why Berlin?" asked Chi before taking a drag and blowing outwards, adding to the already smokey air around them.

"What do you mean?" replied Ida.

"You told me before that you visited like fifty cities. Why stay here?"

"Oh. I don't know," replied Ida with a shrug. "One minute I was next to the taxi, ready to go to the airport, and then I changed my mind."

"Just like that?"

"Yes."

"Why?"

"Do I need a reason?"

"Yeah, of course you do! Otherwise I'm going to assume you're crazy. Are you crazy, Ida Garcia?" said Chi with her eyes narrowed. "Are you?"

"It's ok. You can think I'm crazy."

"Ok, then I will. But lucky for you, I only roll with crazy. And if we're going to master the skills of martial arts, we need to bring the crazy out. Right?"

"Yes, right," said Ida, breaking out into a smile and leaning back.

"But no, I get it. Berlin's like that. You go from wanting to leave to spending the next few years here. Then you wake up and you're like: 'What the hell just happened?'"

"Yeah, it's weird," said Ida. "I'm still not sure why I stayed, but I know it was the right decision. I think I really am crazy."

"No, *we're* crazy," said Chi, signalling between them with her finger and nodding insistently. "Speaking of. What did you think of the class? Think you'll keep coming?"

"I loved it. I'll definitely come again," said Ida. The endorphins were still pumping through her, and she liked the way it felt. "And you?"

"If we can end each class with a beer, then I'm in," said Chi, during which she rested her cigarette against the edge of the ashtray and raised her Pilsner. "Cheers."

"Cheers," said Ida, knocking bottles with Chi while making the obligatory eye contact. "This is a cool place," she added and took a sip of her beer.

"Yeah, Gorbachev's Dive is my favourite bar in Berlin."

"I can see why," said Ida, looking around and admiring the lively crowd and cosy feel of the place.

"So what's your plan, now that you're staying?" asked Chi.

"I need to find a job, something part-time."

"Funny you mention that. My friend works at a cafe in Prenzlauer Berg and she told me they're looking for people. Want me to ask?"

"Yes, that would be great," said Ida. "Thank you."

"Consider it done."

Ida took a swig of her beer.

"So... why Berlin?" she asked.

"Why Berlin? That's... Oh, I see what you did there," said Chi, tilting her head and pointing at Ida.

"No, really, California is beautiful. Why did you leave?" said Ida.

"It's not all it's cracked up to be. The grass is always greener, right?"

"Always," said Ida, pouting her lip.

"Plus I needed a break from my crazy family. I mean, I love them, but there's only so many times I can explain why I'm not married."

"Is that what they expect?"

"They expected it five years ago."

Ida looked Chi over again. Her short, scruffy black hair, black lipstick and careless attitude said it all; she had no intention of settling down.

"What about your family?" asked Chi.

"My mama just tells me to be happy. She said it's better to be alone and happy than married and sad."

"I'm beginning to like your mom already."

"I miss her," said Ida, recalling her mother's disappointed reaction when she declared that she was staying in Berlin for the time being.

"I bet you do," said Chi.

"But I'm excited to be in Berlin. And I'll be even happier when I find a job."

"I'll ask my friend tomorrow. Promise. Part-time, right?"

"Yes. Please."

"Not full-time?"

"No, I want to have time to work on a project."

"Oh yeah? What is it?"

"I don't know exactly, I can't decide on anything."

"What's it about?"

"Women. Power. Fashion. That's all I know so far."

"Sounds solid."

"No, it's silly. I don't know where to begin."

"Just decide on something and go with it," Chi said with a shrug before taking a sip of her Pilsner. "Design. Create. Measure. That's what we do at our agency when we have a deadline. If you overthink it, nothing's going to come. Creativity only makes sense in retrospect. Just start, and your unconscious mind takes care of the rest. It all comes together if you trust yourself. When you get stuck, sleep on it, but make a decision and keep moving. The first decision is usually the right one."

Ida thought about which argument to use to tell Chi that it was not that simple. They were different people. Chi was confident, intelligent, witty... *Stop it.* She was underestimating herself again. Did she forget that she had faced up to a killer and survived? That in less than a year, she had uprooted herself from her life and travelled across the world while surviving a horrific trauma? She considered Chi's words again from this new angle. Decide first, worry later. Trust yourself. It made sense, and it was worth a try.

"I need to call it a night soon," said Chi. "Our team has a presentation in Mitte tomorrow morning at 10, which means I have to get to the office early. Yawn."

"Ok," said Ida with newfound energy. She was now overcome by a sudden, undeniable desire to go home and get to work.

They finished their drinks and left Gorbachev's Dive. The two of them stood at the corner in the middle of Neukölln, ready to say goodbye.

"Ok, I'll message you tomorrow when I've asked about the job, and I'll see you Wednesday at class."

"Thanks, Chi. Goodnight," said Ida.

The two of them hugged and went their separate ways. Still tipsy from just one beer, Ida rushed back to her apartment and went straight to her wall of ideas; an extensive collection of sticky notes and magazine cut-outs plastered all over one side of her bedroom. Stilettos. Handbags. Cocktail dresses. Fetish wear. She was ready to decide, but something still felt off. A single yellow post-it note on top of the desk stole her attention. On it was the word 'Unfett,' with a half-formed second 't.' She leaned her head and wondered what it meant. It was her handwriting, but she had forgotten why she wrote it. She found herself thinking about María Félix. What would María do, Ida wondered? She would fight, flirt and create drama. Flick her long eyelashes and draw the attention of every man in the room with her deep brown eyes. None of that was going to help Ida. She was not an actress, and she was no María Félix.

Ida admired María because she represented two things; freedom and control. María used her beauty and sex appeal intelligently. She knew when to flirt and when to play hard to get. It drove men crazy, and it gave her power. Ida then pictured Chi, carelessly swinging her beer around as she talked, brave enough to be herself while rebelling against the wishes of her family. She dressed and behaved in ways Ida could never imagine herself doing. Ida admired Chi, and it had nothing to do with sex-appeal. Sure, Chi got the guys' attention the second she entered the bar, but she barely noticed. She seemed anchored somewhere else. But what was it?

So far Ida knew she wanted to start a business around fashion, and that she wanted it to encapsulate the essence of María Félix. She opened her laptop and ran a search for 'Unfett.' The autocomplete showed what she had tried to write down on the note: '*Unfettered.*' She grinned and remembered the feeling the word gave her when she came across it in an article. The definition of unfettered showed up; *not confined or restricted.* Another word came up in the search results: fetishise; *to make something an object of a sexual fetish.* Was that what Ida wanted her business to be about? Power through sexuality? She scrunched her nose. There had to be another way which appealed to women like her and Chi. She took a scrap piece of paper from her pile and began writing while in a trance: *Unfett. Unfetter. Unfetishise.*

She leaned back on her chair and stared at the words. *Unfetishise.* It would have stripped María Félix of all her power. What would have been left? It was unimaginable. Ida knew no other María Félix. She knew herself, more so after her experience with Elias Khartoum and The League. She let Elias fetishise her, hoping it would win him over. Look where that got her. She shook her head. It was time to decide, and she immediately committed to her first decision; she was moving in a new direction. She brewed herself a coffee and got to work. The next hours passed by in an unconscious flurry, as she sketched design after design. By 8 am not even another coffee could keep her going. She left her desk as it was and crashed into bed without bothering to brush her teeth or get changed, exhausted but with a warm feeling of creative accomplishment.

On Wednesday, after they were done with martial arts class, Ida invited Chi over to her apartment with the promise of showing her something. Chi found a seat in the living room and Ida rushed into her bedroom and came back with an open sketchbook, which she proudly handed over. Chi scanned the page then lifted her head to look at Ida, who was eagerly watching her.

"I didn't know you could draw so well. What is this?" asked Chi.

"I named it the 'Virgin Queen Collection.' Do you know anything about Elizabeth I?"

"Vaguely. She was the Queen of England like way back?"

"Yes, the end of the 16th century. I've been studying her and how her fashion grew with her power. There's a picture of her at the back."

Chi turned to the back of the sketchbook, which had a copy of the Armada Portrait, painted at the height of Elizabeth I's reign after the English defeat of the Spanish Armada. Chi's eyes widened.

"Woah," she said. "Looks like she's wearing her whole wardrobe."

"Not even close," said Ida. "A house couldn't fit her wardrobe. The most interesting thing about her is that she was never married or had children. They called her the 'Virgin Queen.'"

"That makes sense," said Chi, still staring at the portrait. "This lady doesn't mess around."

"She liked to go over the top, and she set the trends for the whole country, even for the men. Fashion was a symbol of her power."

"Ah, I see now," said Chi, flipping through Ida's designs. "You've taken the patterns and shapes and simplified them."

"Yes, every piece takes features from her fashion. I made the sleeves go out a bit around the hands, or the middle of the arm, or used lace where it made sense. I was careful to keep the patterns simple and elegant."

"I'm guessing she never flaunted her boobs?" said Chi, looking up at Ida with a wry smile.

"How could you even say that!" replied Ida sarcastically. "She was a queen."

"Of course. Sorry. What was I thinking?"

Chi flipped back and forth through the designs.

"Pretty impressive," she said. "And what's this?" she added, flipping further through the sketchbook.

"You know Rosie The Riveter, right?"

"Of course. The 'We Can Do It' lady from World War II."

"Yes. I channelled her as well. That one is a cream coloured work overall, styled for everyday wear."

Chi looked back at the page.

"Oh, God, yes," she said. "I love it."

"Turn the page," said Ida with her insides fluttering.

Chi turned the sheet and her eyes lit up like a child.

"No!" she said.

"Yes!" replied Ida with a giggle, unable to contain her excitement. "A white pullover styled after our martial arts uniform. You can wear it with jeans, a skirt, anything."

Chi was laughing openly now.

"Wow! I'm impressed. This is amazing."

Ida's cheeks began blushing.

"Thanks," she said.

"So I see you made some decisions then?"

Ida nodded with a childish grin.

176

"Unfettered. Unfetishised. I get it now. This is great, Ida."

"I couldn't have done it without you. What you said the other night was really helpful."

"Oh, I'm glad," said Chi and placed a hand on Ida's shoulder.

"Orange juice?" asked Ida.

"Sure."

Ida got up and went to the kitchen and fetched two glasses from the overhead cupboard.

"So what's the next move?" asked Chi through the living room door.

"These are just ideas. Designs. I want to know who will actually wear them," replied Ida, returning with two glasses of orange juice and handing one to Chi. "So I'll make samples. Then measure the results."

Chi raised her palm while Ida leaned forward and gave her a high five.

"Do you have time for a fitting by any chance?" asked Ida.

"I finish work early on Friday. If you want we can visit my friend's cafe so they can meet you. After that we can come to yours and do the fitting?"

"Yes, perfect," said Ida.

"Oh, and after that I'm meeting with a couple of the girls at Gorbachev's if you want to come?"

"Sure. Beers are on me. To say thank you."

"Well, isn't that kind of you. I never say no to free beer."

"Excellent," said Ida. "Then prepare to be hungover."

20

The snow was the ultimate purifier, the place where Frederich's consciousness peaked. Focusing was easy in the subzero temperatures. All life-giving energy was swept away, leaving only white vertigo, the harsh burn of ice and the instinct to survive.

Frederich had learnt early to embrace the cold. He adapted his body to extreme conditions with constant, controlled exposure, often shedding the gloves and head cover and allowing his breath to warm him from the core; a Tibetan technique he had mastered over the years. As his platoon worked its way uphill, he drew the crisp air into his belly and forced his legs forward while visualising his inner fire. His body was finally returning to full strength, and it was a relief to be outside in the fresh air, even when it was under the tutelage of Scheffler.

The unit was marching in single file under light snowfall. Two of Scheffler's armed guard flanked the sides with AK-47 rifles, which Frederich noted were perfect for the extreme conditions. Scheffler led the unit, and Otto covered the back. Frederich was behind Piotr and inspected his friend's form for signs of exhaustion. Piotr was on his last strike, and if he slipped up again, Scheffler would send him packing. Frederich was not going to let that happen. It was Piotr who had nursed him back to reasonable strength, and who had risked punishment to sneak in rations of food for Frederich after his time in the hole. Without the extra nutrients, Frederich may not have been able to withstand the training load in the days following his release. After Frederich had stood up for his friend, Piotr had repaid the favour. Now an unspoken alliance had formed between them. Frederich had a hunch that they would need each other, especially since they were the two most within Scheffler's sadistic scope.

Frederich thought about his training with Kraas, which was fundamentally different to Scheffler's approach. Back home, Kraas would push Frederich from sunrise to sunset. The workouts had been gruelling, and Frederich's body had often failed him, resulting in blackouts, cuts and bruises, infections, bouts of vomiting from exhaustion and various muscle injuries. Kraas showed no mercy, and in that regard, he and Scheffler were the same. Where they diverged was in their intention. Kraas looked to test Frederich's potential. Scheffler was looking for a point of failure. Kraas continuously raised the bar while Frederich felt thrust forward to meet it with a kind of warrior energy. He persisted because of Kraas, not despite him. Scheffler took the bar and beat his student with it, simply because he could.

The torture sessions began early under Scheffler, when the recruits were roused at 5 am. During the morning they pushed, lifted, climbed, grappled, punched and kicked themselves to exhaustion before going on to weapons training. In the mid-afternoon they marched out into the cold with their backpacks and supplies. The route was different each time, but always lasted into the night. At the end, random recruits would be selected and ordered to stand on guard duty for the rest of the night.

It was a high-stakes game. If a recruit failed to see out the day, they were permitted to return to the dorms, but they would receive a mark against their name in Scheffler's black book. Three strikes and it was time to go home. Frederich was advised after his time in the hole that he had received two strikes for his outburst, and was lucky not to have been kicked out. For once he agreed with Scheffler. It should have been the end of him. Scheffler had hesitated, then had thrown him in the hole. Stranger still, Scheffler had released him without seeing the white flag. Piotr also had two strikes from two separate occasions, including the one which led to Scheffler kicking him down the mountain. The three strike rule did not apply to those who fell asleep while on guard duty; they were dismissed immediately. As a result, recruits were expelled regularly with no ride back. The exiled were forced to march over the mountains and through the snow to get to the lowlands. Lucky for Scheffler there was a steady flow of new recruits eager to take their place.

They were four hours into the march when Frederich saw the mountain peak ahead. It was well below freezing at the top, and the cold was beginning to burn. Piotr was now hesitating between each step and had his head bowed. Frederich pressed on the pedal and overtook him, elbowing him lightly on the arm as he passed.

"What's wrong tiger, want daddy to carry you?" said Frederich, condescendingly pouting his lips.

Piotr lifted his head and narrowed his eyes.

"Oh," he huffed, struggling to catch his breath. "The way… The way Scheffler carried you out of the hole?" he said as he picked up the pace, bringing him in line with Frederich. Frederich chuckled.

"Low blow," he said.

Piotr also chuckled, his cheeks flushed red, and the two of them marched in unison until they reached the peak, which gave a panoramic view of the Alps. Some of the recruits had paused to take in the sight. Cloud cover and mist weaved their way between the landscape and over the mountains. Laughter and a majestic view, thought Frederich. *Soak it up while it lasts.*

"Waste time enjoying the view and I'll snatch your eyes out!" yelled Scheffler from the front.

"Let's pick it up!" added Otto upon his arrival.

The recruits reluctantly dragged themselves across the peak. As Frederich turned, he saw Scheffler and Otto looking down the mountain and discussing something. He followed their gaze and noticed a body lying on the snow. He moved closer to listen in on the conversation.

"What do you want to do?" asked Otto.

"That's his third strike. Leave him," said Scheffler and walked off. As he looked up, he noticed Frederich staring at him.

"*That's* a sight you can enjoy," said Scheffler, motioning with his head toward the fallen recruit. "It's going to be you soon," he added with wide, predatory eyes, then spat toward Frederich as he passed.

Frederich shifted out of the way and turned around. The fallen recruit was still not moving, and Frederich could not bring himself to leave. *No one gets left behind*; Kraas preached that mantra obsessively. Frederich understood. It meant everything having Kraas around during training. Kraas was a soldier who had committed to facing death along with harsh, inhuman conditions. During the worst of it, in moments of utter exhaustion, despair and terror, a soldier could have no doubt that his team would stick by him. Loyalty to each other was the glue which kept a unit together. Frederich had to remind himself that loyalty meant nothing in Scheffler's twisted world. It was each man for himself.

"Abel!" came Scheffler's voice roaring from a distance.

Frederich gritted his teeth while shaking his head, then turned and caught up with the unit with a sick feeling in his stomach. Piotr was at the back of the line waiting for him.

"What's wrong?" asked Piotr when he noticed Frederich's expression.

"I'm going to break Scheffler's face," said Frederich. "One way or another."

"I hope someone does," said Piotr quietly.

They continued the rest of the march in silence, and the movement helped Frederich shake off his anger. Deep stomach breathing and the cold helped him regain his focus.

They made it back to the facility hours after nightfall. It had been an especially long march, and the recruits all had empty stares. The guards at the front opened the gate leading through the barbed-wire fence, and the platoon stumbled in through the mountain opening on their way to bed.

"You two, guard duty," said Scheffler, pointing at Frederich and Piotr.

"Damn," whispered Piotr.

Frederich's shoulders dropped.

As the platoon disappeared inside, the two previous guards retired from their towers and Frederich and Piotr prepared to take over their positions, which were always filled by the recruits. Frederich assumed this was done for two reasons; to torture the recruits, and to have expendable units as the first line of defence. The armed guard would remain inside throughout the night but would randomly come out to catch anyone who had fallen asleep.

Frederich climbed the wooden ladder and sat on the hard platform in the middle, which had no backrest; the perfect way to stay upright and alert. Above his head hung an antique bell for sounding the alarm. Outside the protected area was a large opening that led to a forest which sloped upwards and merged into an open plain. It would have made sense to cut the trees down to help expose approaching enemies, figured Frederich, but the trees also helped hide the facility from nosy outsiders who might have ignored the numerous military signs intended to keep them out.

His whole body was aching, especially his shins and toes. He took off his shoes and socks and inspected his feet. He pressed against a small blister and decided to leave it alone. He had bigger problems. Too many recruits had already been claimed by the night. He did not want to be the next. Being inside a mountain, the facility only needed guarding from one side, and there had been no incidents since Frederich began, which explained why so many recruits were seduced into sleep and as a result lost their chance to join The League. With the fate of his predecessors firmly in his mind, Frederich put his shoes back on and straightened up to focus on his task.

The night wore on and the temperature dipped. Although his face was burning from the cold, Frederich found himself getting drowsy. His neck would bend gradually to the side, and he would lift his head with a start when he realised what was happening. Sometime after, there was a loud bang and the hut shook all over. *What the..* He leapt to his feet and looked outside.

"Pssst," said Piotr from his hut. "Don't sleep. I heard you snoring."

"What was that noise?" he asked.

"Rock," Piotr said, waving one in his hand. "I have them with me just in case. I'm a sniper with these things."

Frederich grinned and waved then returned to his seat and looked ahead. Lucky. The armed guard could have come at any time. What a way to let Scheffler win.

It was a relatively clear night with the odd cloud in the sky. An almost full moon shone down on them and a carpet of mist hovered over the snow. Nothing stood out. His instinct told another story. He noticed his veins were throbbing and his arms and shoulders were beginning to tense up. He moved closer to the window and hugged the edge. Was there someone out there? He observed the trees and wondered if Piotr could see anything, but it would have been too risky to make a noise or leave his post.

Minutes passed and nothing, except for the light breeze. Then there was a flash from the upper corner of his eye and he shifted his gaze beyond the forest and caught it; a silhouette in the moonlight of someone running over the plain and behind mountain cover. He peered into the other hut. Piotr would have said something had he seen it. Frederich weighed his options. He could alert Scheffler, tell Piotr about it, or leave it. Would Scheffler believe him? What could Piotr do? He left it. Saying he saw a silhouette would come across as thin. Going out there would be too dangerous. He had only one real choice; sit and wait, and remain alert.

With Frederich focussed and primed against a potential threat, the night passed even more slowly. Eventually the adrenaline died down. He did his best to avoid checking the time, and resorted to rapid, shallow breathing and body rocking to keep himself awake, as well as the occasional hard slap to the face. Day finally broke, and he was lightheaded from the fatigue and the cold. Later in the morning, one of Scheffler's armed guard came out with two replacements and told Frederich and Piotr to report to Scheffler's office. Piotr emerged from his guard tower and staggered toward Frederich. His eyes were completely red and his face had lost all colour.

"You look terrible," said Piotr.

Frederich gave him a weak smile.

"You're looking in the mirror," he replied.

When they reached Scheffler's office they knocked on the door and waited.

"Come in," said Scheffler after a long pause.

The two of them went in and stood in the middle. Scheffler was seated at his desk with both his feet up and his hands behind his head. He looked them over.

"Paleski. Get some sleep," he said.

Piotr hesitated.

"Now," added Scheffler with a firm voice.

Piotr looked at Frederich with a frown then reluctantly left the office.

"How are you feeling, Abel?" asked Scheffler when they were alone.

"Great, never been better," said Frederich, his head spinning. He wanted nothing more than to surrender to his mattress and fall into a deep sleep.

"Good. So get to morning drills. You're already late."

Frederich blinked hard multiple times. His brain had no reaction to Scheffler's instruction. Sometime later he was in the hall doing push-ups. Otto's orders echoed in the distance. He watched himself doing rope climbs. He descended

186

to the mattress and made for the back of the line, knocking against someone in the process.

"Watch out, idiot," said the recruit.

Frederich fought to keep his body upright and his eyes open. He kept blinking over and over. More push-ups. He followed the lead of the person in front of him without paying attention to the count. More rope climbs. Then sparring. He moved in slow motion while a barrage of fists landed on his torso. He tried to throw a return fist and was immediately brought to ground. He tapped out and turned his head to the right. Scheffler was standing by the mattresses with a smirk on his face. Frederich had no energy to think. He stood up for the next round. His opponent threw a quick punch and Frederich dodged it reflexively. The next one hit his jaw and rocked his head, bringing him to his knees. He tasted blood. Scheffler chuckled in the distance. *Last strike.* Frederich rose to his feet. His opponent had lowered his guard and was looking at him with a puzzled expression.

"Abel?" he said.

Frederich lifted his fists to prepare for the next round. He leaned too far to the right and tried to straighten up again without success. He was going to collapse. *Last strike.* He had to hold on. A firm hand caught him and straightened him up. It was Scheffler.

"Get some sleep," he said.

Frederich blinked again and Scheffler pushed him impatiently toward the dorms.

"Go. Get out of my face."

Frederich stumbled forward, using all of his focus to find the door. He fell asleep wondering why Scheffler had bailed him out again.

21

Ida studied the interior of Gorbachev's Dive while Chi and the others chatted enthusiastically around her. It was a unique place; candles on every table gave it a warm, orange hue and everything about it looked old and outdated, including the light fittings and furniture, of which nothing matched. The couch they were sitting on was cream coloured with a floral pattern, and the tables and chairs were a combination of light and dark stained wood of different shapes and styles. The young crowd was as unique as the place, and Chi fit right in. She was wearing a tight red pullover jumper with no bra and wide grey corduroy pants. Her short black hair was purposely brushed in all directions.

The way the setting and the people clashed in every way made the man with the black turtleneck leaning against the bar stand out even more. He was thin but had a plump, oval face that hardly fit his body, a broad nose, short brown hair and a lazy but serious gaze. He had a shot glass in one hand and a cigarette in the other. He sculled the drink and placed it on the bar then took a drag, blowing the smoke high into the air. Meanwhile, he looked around at the people with a distasteful look. He obviously did not want to be there. So why *was* he there?

"That place is terrible, there are too many tourists!" yelled Daria a bit too loudly.

Ida leaned over to hear what Chi and the other two girls were discussing but quickly lost interest. They were debating which of Berlin's nightclubs had lost their magic and which ones still had it. Something stole Ida's attention again from the corner of her eye, and she caught the gaze of a guy at the foosball table. He had his elbow resting on his friend's shoulder and one leg crossed over the other. She noticed his broad shoulders and boyish grin then realised she had lingered too long. Before she could look away, he smiled at her. She turned her face and took a sip of her white wine and reluctantly leaned back into the group to find out which club still had the magic.

"No, no, you girls haven't been to Mamma Schaukel. That place is amazing. They have the best house sets," said Chrissi with her high-pitched voice.

"I've been there," said Daria. "It was good until the tourists found it last Summer. I think they list it in some 'Welcome To Berlin' guide."

"What about you, Ida," said Chi. "Where do you prefer?"

Ida thought back to her last visit to a nightclub and shuddered at the memory of Elias approaching her.

"I haven't really partied recently," she said with a frown. "So I can't say."

"How about a drink?" asked Chi, placing a hand on her shoulder.

"Sure," said Ida.

"Come, let's go to the bar. Girls? Drinks?"

"A white for me," said Daria.

"*Weinschorle für mich*, please," said Chrissi with her American accent, proud of the few words in German she could speak.

"You got it," said Chi.

Ida stood up and took her bag from the table and they walked over to the bar.

"Everything ok?" asked Chi while waiting to be served. "You've gone quiet in the last half hour."

"Yes, I'm ok—"

"One second, sorry," said Chi with a raised finger before leaning forward toward the waiting bartender to order their drinks.

"Same as before, right?" asked Chi, turning back once more.

"Uh, yes. Please," replied Ida. "Here," she added, handing over a twenty euro note. "On me."

"You still insist on paying?"

"You got me a job today. It's the least I can do."

"You're damn right I did," said Chi, snatching the note from Ida's hand.

While waiting for Chi, Ida sensed someone beside her. She turned and found the guy from the foosball table at her side. He had his body faced unabashedly toward her and was grinning.

"Hello there," he said.

Ida flinched and stepped back. She looked him over and immediately wondered; was he with *them*? Frederich said they would leave her alone. The guy had a strong presence but delicate features. He seemed too young to be with The League. Then again, so did Frederich. In any case, Ida wanted nothing to do with this guy. What did he want? *Be polite, Ida.*

"Hey," she said with a flat voice.

He was still grinning, but his eyes now showed a hint of concern.

"I've seen you before," he said with a German accent.

191

"Have you?" replied Ida. *What's taking so long, Chi?*

"Yes. A few times. I live in the building across from you."

Ida felt warning bells go off. Her palms grew moist.

"What do you want?" she blurted.

He leaned back and lowered his eyebrows.

"To introduce myself? Is that ok?"

Ida grew claustrophobic from the rising tension and spiralled into a sudden panic. Her fingers and knees began shaking and she had trouble breathing.

Chi turned around and noticed Ida and the guy.

"Are the drinks ready?" Ida asked Chi.

"Yeah," said Chi, staring suspiciously at the guy. "Here, hold this one, I've got the rest. Let's go."

Ida and Chi walked back to the sofa. Ida stole another glance of the guy. He had his arms crossed and was frowning and shaking his head.

"Ida?"

"Hmm?" said Ida without looking at Chi.

"What did that guy say to you?"

"He.." began Ida then stopped. They found their seats again while Ida thought back. What did he actually say? Nothing threatening. Why did she get so worked up? Ida looked at Chi, followed by Daria and then Chrissi. She had no reason to be threatened. She was with friends. Maybe she had overreacted. She turned back and checked the area. He was gone.

"Can you see him?" asked Ida, turning her attention to Chi.

Chi looked around.

"No, I think he's gone," she replied.

Ida scrunched her nose.

"You're being strange," said Chi.

"What happened?" asked Chrissi.

"I don't know. I think Ida brushed some guy off and she's having regrets," said Chi.

"No, it's not like that," said Ida. She had not spoken to Chi about what happened with The League. It was supposed to be behind her. She was supposed to be over it.

"He *was* nice to look at," said Chi.

"Yes. He was, wasn't he?" replied Ida, feeling herself soften.

"Who? What happened?" asked Chrissi again.

"Tell us!" yelled Daria.

"It doesn't matter. He's gone now," said Ida.

"Fine," said Chrissi. "So first of all, cheers. Congratulations, Ida, on the new job."

The four of them raised their drinks.

"Secondly, while you two were at the bar, Daria and I decided that we're all going to Mamma Schaukel to celebrate."

"Not me," said Ida. "I've got work to do."

"Don't lie, you're going to that guy's house," said Chi. "He gave you his address and left. Didn't he?"

Ida leaned her head and stared at Chi.

"Really?" she said.

"I can wish," said Chi with a pout. "You haven't mentioned any guys since I've known you, have you? What's the deal?"

"Yeah, what's the deal?" parroted Daria.

"There's no deal," said Ida, shifting in her seat.

"Uh huh, sure," said Chi. "You can tell me about it later," she whispered into Ida's ear, poking her shoulder and insisting with her eyes.

The conversation then shifted to Chi and Ida's experiences with their martial arts class. Chrissi and Daria entertained the idea of joining them, but admitted that they might feel differently when the alcohol wore off. Chrissi then carefully checked the remaining level of each person's drink.

"Ok, drink up and let's go," said Chrissi. "I want to dance."

"Chi, you're coming, right?" said Chrissi.

"Of course," said Chi with an exaggerated nod.

The girls finished their drinks and took turns going to the bathroom then gathered their things. Chi, Chrissi and Daria went to Hermannplatz to take the underground to Mamma Schaukel, and Ida began walking back to her apartment. It was 3:44 am. She tightened the scarf around her neck and pulled her beanie down. The icy temperatures were on their way, and would be there before Christmas, which Ida realised was only two weeks away. It was going to be her first holidays away from her family. It felt strange just to think about it.

She walked the length of Weserstrasse then turned toward her place. The street she was now on had an industrial park which was secluded on a Saturday morning. She picked up the pace and tried to make it through as quickly as possible. She approached a large empty car park which was barely illuminated by the street lights. It was eerily silent. She looked ahead and saw a figure at the edge of the car park standing against the wall. He had a cigarette and was blowing the smoke upwards into the air. When she approached him, her adrenaline shot up. She walked even faster and tried to ignore him.

"Hello, Ida," he said from the shadows.

Ida tensed up and halted her walk. Was it the guy from Gorbachev's? If so, what was he thinking? It was a creepy move. Wait, did she tell him her name? He lifted himself off the wall and stepped out of the shadow. It *was* the guy from Gorbachev's, but not the one who spoke to her. She recognised the black turtleneck and funny shaped head of the man who had been leaning against the bar. He had been stalking her.

"Who are you?" she asked.

He licked over his bottom lip and slowly moved his gaze over her body.

"You're from The League," she added bluntly.

He smiled at her words, revealing a distorted, unnatural look.

"Am I?" he said.

"Why are you following me?" she asked with more force.

She half cocked her fists and readied herself to fight. He looked relaxed, but there was something beneath the surface. She was unsure what exactly, but she knew enough about The League to guess.

"Don't worry. I'm just a hopeless admirer. An innocent little bird who likes to watch from far away."

"You're very close right now."

"Not as close as I'd like to be."

"Come any closer and I'll make you regret it," said Ida, fully cocking her fists. Her hands were shaking from the anticipation.

"Yes, of course. You think you have your prince to protect you. *Frederich*," he replied, his voice filling with poison as he said Frederich's name. "He's gone away for a while. I don't think he's going to be much help."

"That's not what I meant."

"Ah," he said, lifting his head and flashing his ugly smile again. "You think your karate moves are going to save you."

"How long have you been stalking me, you bastard!?" she yelled, taking a step forward.

His smile turned into a chuckle. He reached into his pocket. Ida's skin lifted with terror and she was about to rush forward and attempt a front snap kick when he pulled out his car keys. He pressed a button and the lights of a sports car on the other end of the car park lit up. He turned and began walking away.

"I hope you like your surprise," he said before turning around. "See you soon," he added with a raspy voice.

Ida's chest was pounding and she could barely breathe. Adrenaline was rushing through her with nowhere to go. He stepped into his car and drove away, leaving Ida with only anger and confusion. *Damn him.* What surprise? She could no longer stand to be still.

She stormed off, taking the long way home to help calm her nerves. When she reached her street she had somewhat regained her composure, but she knew she would not be sleeping that night. She walked down the footpath, hearing only the echo of her steps. As she approached her front door she almost jumped out of her skin. She stepped back and re-coiled in horror at the sight. The guy who had spoken to her at Gorbachev's was sprawled on the step. His dead eyes were open and his throat had been slit. He was covered in blood. Ida began shaking all over. The shock was too much. She screamed, half from terror, half from rage.

"You son of a bitch!" she yelled, turning toward the street, unable to bear the sight any longer.

Hurried footsteps came toward her.

"Hey, are you ok?" said a stranger as he approached. "Oh, shit!" he yelled when he saw the body. He lifted his hand to his mouth and stepped away. With fumbling hands he took out his mobile phone.

"Yes, uh, we need police. Someone's been murdered."

22

Kalakia poured a black coffee and went over to the window while he waited for Stirner to show up for their meeting. The Burj Khalifa in Downtown Dubai was the tallest building in the world, so Kalakia had a perfect view of the city and the surrounding sea and desert. He had visited Dubai a few times after the construction of the ambitious skyscraper, where The League had secured a penthouse high enough to see over the landscape but not too high that it drew unwanted attention. As usual, Kalakia wanted everything within sight while himself remaining out of the public eye.

He might as well have been looking down from a tightrope, considering the diplomatic fine line he had taken in the previous week. The reason behind his latest trip to The Emirates and the circumstances surrounding it had been kept secret, even from the upper echelons of The League. The Neutralaser situation had to be dealt with delicately. Global stability depended on it, and possibly more. Francois had advised Stirner and The Council by phone that a significant development was taking place but told them nothing else. Keeping The Council in the dark was one of Kalakia's biggest gambles, but he trusted that he could keep Stirner on ice until the worst was behind them. The Generals of Africa, Europe and The Americas were told to have their teams on standby, including their interrogators, liquidators, enforcers and espionage teams. Kalakia had feared the worst from the onset, expecting Inselheim's allies to strike hard to protect their valuable investment. As time passed, Kalakia came to realise how much of a lid Inselheim had kept on the project. Securing the facility underneath the Kazakh desert was easier than Kalakia could have imagined. There were no mercenaries or government soldiers protecting the site. Inselheim was alone with his invention. Expecting stiff resistance, Kalakia had taken a second gamble and called Dastan Navolov in Sochi to oversee the Neutralaser takeover. Navolov was the General of Asia, after all, so the facility was on his turf.

Murmurs came from the bottom throughout the week, but they were minimal. As a precaution, Kalakia had Vidrik eliminate Pilz immediately after their interrogation of Inselheim. Pilz was too lowly ranked for such high-level knowledge. Kalakia had thought for a long time then decided not only to let Vidrik live, but to involve him directly in the operation to secure the Neutralaser site alongside Navolov's commandos. Vidrik was smart enough to keep his mouth shut, and too ambitious to let a slip-up ruin his chances of taking over at the helm — a chance Kalakia would never give him.

Kalakia checked the time. Stirner was already fifteen minutes late, which was unlike him. Kalakia dialled Francois.

"Where is he?"

"He's just arrived," replied Francois.

Kalakia closed the connection and continued looking out into the Dubai desert which had sprouted a city at a breathtaking pace.

With his last sip of coffee came a loud beep from the front door. He paced over to the security monitor and saw Stirner in the lobby outside. He pressed the button to grant him access. The door slid open and revealed Stirner, his aged, clean-shaven face glazed with sweat from the heat outside. He was wearing a navy blue suit that had been tailor-made for his round body. He wiped down his head of silver hair and gave Kalakia a nod of greeting.

"Come in, Horst," said Kalakia, motioning with his hand.

Kalakia poured Stirner a glass of water and was about to give it to him when he waved it off.

"No, I'm fine," he said.

Kalakia watched him for a few seconds then gave a shrug and placed the cup back on the table. They were standing beside the collection of black leather sofas in the open living area. Stirner set himself down in a one-seater and Kalakia sat across from him.

"Stressful journey?" asked Kalakia.

"It was fine," said Stirner, waving the question away.

Stirner was not a man for pleasantries or for complaining. Kalakia knew this already. He was not asking. He was probing.

"Good," he said. "So straight to business. Word from The Council?"

"Yes. To be frank, they're concerned," replied Stirner.

"Oh?" replied Kalakia, making an effort to appear surprised.

"Nobody appreciated last month's meeting being cancelled without explanation, or that cryptic phone call from Francois. It left a lot to the imagination. So naturally, they feel like they're being kept in the dark. I must say I echo their concerns."

"Is that so?"

201

"Yes. We've also been receiving troubling news from the Generals. You've been mobilising various teams."

"I have."

"That's why I suggested this meeting. If you can tell me what's going on, I can go back to Budapest and put The Council's mind at ease."

Kalakia was seated with one leg crossed over the other, his fist cupped over his mouth.

"That is not possible at this stage," said Kalakia.

"Can I ask why?" said Stirner, tilting his head and shifting in his seat.

"We are acting to eliminate the threat. That is all I can divulge."

"Can you tell me your reasons for such secrecy?" asked Stirner.

"I have decided that there is too much risk in seeking out a consensus on this issue. The Council's voice is not needed."

"And you decided this alone?"

"Yes."

"Then you're belittling us, Kalakia," said Stirner with a sharp tone.

"I disagree."

"You do remember why you established The Council in the first place? For moments just like this one."

Stirner's face had turned red, and he looked visibly tense.

"This is an exceptional situation."

"So you keep saying."

"Speed, efficiency and a short chain of command is necessary. We must move quickly. You can tell The Council that I will provide a complete summary of events soon."

Stirner pursed his lips and began shaking his head.

"Tread carefully, Horst," said Kalakia with a firm voice. "We must all keep our heads here."

"You're giving me nothing to work with," said Stirner, his voice rising in pitch.

"I'm giving you my personal reassurance. Are you losing faith in me?"

Stirner clenched his fist.

"I trust you," he said, relaxing his hand. "But you know how I feel about these situations. Isolationism never works."

"Yes, and I respect your principles. No one is better suited to represent The Council. The League is a collective effort. But it is also a weapon, and a spear has only one tip, a bullet only one point. I am a wartime leader, The Council is a peacetime collective. Once the threat is dealt with, I will need your voice for dealing with the aftermath. This issue is still in its infancy, and all decisions made will have major repercussions. I will need your help soon enough. Can you keep things together, Horst? Can I rely on you?"

"Of course," said Stirner. "But I can't go back to Budapest empty-handed. I'll lose face."

"I understand."

"Can you give me a timeline?"

"You will know everything in one week."

"One week?

Kalakia nodded.

"Good," said Stirner, studying Kalakia while nodding repeatedly.

"Anything else on your mind?" asked Kalakia.

"No. I'll go back to my hotel now. I fly back this afternoon. The Council is eager to hear from me."

"Of course."

Kalakia and Stirner stood up in unison and Kalakia began leading Stirner to the door.

"Francois will contact you shortly about the upcoming meeting."

"Good," said Stirner. "So I'll see you in Budapest."

Kalakia nodded and pressed the button. The door slid open. The two men shook hands. When the door closed, Kalakia watched Stirner exiting on the monitor. He immediately called Francois.

"Track his journey back to Budapest."

"Stirner?" said Francois.

"Have someone tail him right away. Be very discreet," he said then immediately hung up.

Kalakia and Stirner had known each other for two decades, yet trust remained a fickle thing in Kalakia's world. He wondered for a second whether he was being paranoid. He decided not. As always, he only trusted his instinct. Something was amiss with Stirner. Kalakia was sure of it. Even if it was something innocent, like marital or health problems, he wanted to know. In his experience, it was the greatest threats which at first seemed the most inconsequential, and Stirner's attitude was all the smoke Kalakia needed.

Inselheim was not ready to go back to work. The lack of sleep had him feeling weightless and numb as he walked up the stairs carrying his briefcase and leather gym bag in each hand. It was still not enough to dampen his panic. The mere thought of being confined within the four walls of the elevator had given him palpitations. He needed movement and space. Instead he was back at the office on Vidrik's orders. *Look normal*, Vidrik had repeatedly insisted. Inselheim emerged into the eighth-floor foyer out of breath. His fingers were trembling like he had consumed too much coffee. He checked his tie and stretched his neck out, and tried to relax his shoulders. He then turned the corner and approached the entrance before scanning his ID card to gain access. He pushed the glass door open and marched in with a show of purpose. The security guard gave him a nod as he entered, and he did his best to look like the Inselheim everyone knew. His assistant Martin looked up from his computer and smiled with lifted eyebrows.

"Mr. Inselheim," said Martin. "Welcome back!"

Martin looked genuinely happy to see him. For a second Inselheim envied Martin's naive optimism. When Martin was not at work, he was either shopping for streetwear, getting a new hairstyle or partying at the Berghain nightclub. He would likely never know stress of the kind that Inselheim was being exposed to.

"Thank you, Martin," Inselheim said with a stoic nod.

"How are you feeling?" asked Martin.

"I could use another two weeks break," replied Inselheim. *Or two decades.*

"That bad?"

"Any urgent matters?" asked Inselheim as he came to a stop beside Martin's desk.

"The defence minister has been calling."

"Ok. I'll get back to her shortly. Anything else?"

"I have it all written here," said Martin, turning pages in his diary.

"Can you make a memo and bring it to me?"

"Of course."

"Thank you," said Inselheim, then entered his office.

He shut the door behind him and leaned against it. He closed his eyes, and took one, long deep breath. He reached into his pocket and pulled out the flask he had bought on his return to Berlin, loosened the cap and had a swig of bourbon, followed by another. He welcomed the burning in his throat and the warm feeling in his chest, and savoured it as long as he could. Then the pleasant sensation passed, and he sunk into the familiar position in his chair. The urge came to pick up the phone and check in with Brunswick, to see how things were going. Then he grew sick in the stomach when reality hit. He shut his eyes and rested his forehead on his palm.

The torture was constant. Not even sleep was a sanctuary. When he did manage to doze off, he was always jolted awake, covered in sweat, with a panic attack awaiting him. Now he was afraid to fall asleep without bourbon or sleeping pills. Add to that the flashbacks. Marius' terrified face. Brunswick being dragged away. Those dead, bloody faces, now imprinted in his brain. *Keep it together*. He banged his fist against the desk in frustration and stood up. It was too much. He picked up his gym bag and marched out again.

"I'll be back in an hour," he said as he raced past Martin's desk.

"Wai.."

He rushed out without waiting for Martin's reply. An hour in the gym. It was worth a try. He was ignoring the fact that he had been drinking, and that his leg had not healed enough for exercise. He had no choice. He needed to move. It was that, or lose his mind — a luxury he did not have.

23

Frederich gripped the spoon handle tight and rubbed the wall behind his bed until he had engraved a permanent scratch into the concrete. Beside the newly minted marking were one-hundred and twenty-one others, each representing a day. It was now over four months since training had begun, not counting his time in the hole.

It had taken Frederich weeks to desensitise to the snoring in the dorm room, which had twelve single beds arranged in groups of six against either wall. Twelve young men, driven to exhaustion every day, packed into a windowless cave with little ventilation. A shipment of new bedsheets had been delivered once during those four months, and each recruit was given two sets of black slacks and black t-shirts, one pullover jumper and one insulated military jacket, which were meant to last for the entire training. The result was a nauseating stench and a symphony of snarls and growls which filled the room throughout the night.

Regardless of how tired Frederich was, his internal alarm clock always had him up before 5 am; a stubborn habit he got from Kraas. It was a few minutes before wake-up, and he lay ready in his bed in anticipation of Otto's appearance to turn on the lights and rouse the recruits. Ralph was two beds down from Frederich and was the only one still snoring. The blow Ralph had taken to the nose from Scheffler had caused a break and left a permanent mark on his breathing. If it bothered him, he never showed it. The day after the beating he went straight back to training without a word. Frederich had tapped him on the shoulder and asked how he was doing. The swelling on his jaw and around his eye looked severe. Ralph only shrugged and lifted his t-shirt, revealing scarring on his back from what looked like dozens of lashes. "Scheffler's nothing. You haven't met my old man," was his reply. Ralph was 'AFC', he claimed with his chest puffed out, short for 'Anti-Fascist Crew.'

There was shuffling in the hall, then the light in the next room came on.

"Let's go, men!" yelled Otto.

Frederich's room was next to light up.

"Up, up, up!" he yelled.

Ralph's snoring stopped suddenly. Frederich sat up and looked around. Piotr gazed at Frederich from his bed with swollen eyes and dishevelled hair and signalled good morning with a nod. Frederich gave him a tired smile and nodded back.

The day began like the other one-hundred and twenty-one. They made their beds, got dressed, brushed their teeth and washed up in the communal bathroom down the hall. Then it was time to move, or stumble, in some cases, into the mess hall for a breakfast consisting of porridge, boiled eggs and coffee and tea. Some forty minutes later they were ordered into the training hall, where they ran laps to warm up. Then they began drills. Today Otto was reciting The League's code, which he did ritually every Monday.

"One: Disclosure means death! You do not discuss The League with anyone. Journalists, friends, family, your therapist, not even at confession with your priest!" yelled Otto while pacing among the recruits doing pushups with perfect form.

"Two: No excuses. The League expects one-hundred percent loyalty and dedication, otherwise you are out. Nobody is forcing you to be here."

Otto's boots stomped past Frederich's face as he pressed up and down.

"Three: No prejudice. Race, religion, sexual orientation and skin colour mean nothing here. You will be judged only on your ability to serve."

"Four: No mercy. You kill when told to kill. No human life gets in the way of your duty."

As Otto completed the fourth law, Scheffler appeared from his office and walked up to him. Scheffler nudged his number two's shoulder and spoke something to him. Otto immediately stepped back and Scheffler took his place.

"Right, sparring time! Move it, boys!" yelled out Scheffler.

Nobody argued with the abrupt end to drills. The recruits scrambled and arranged themselves in rows across the mattresses while pairing up with a random recruit. Frederich's first opponent was Piotr, which was no coincidence. Piotr's weight had fluctuated over the four-months. At one stage he looked gaunt and his strength was failing him. Frederich was not managing much better at the time. Once their partnership developed, however, it all turned around. The harsher Scheffler became, the more Frederich and Piotr looked to each other. Throughout the day they exchanged grins, stern looks, playful insults, shoulder bumps and slaps on the back of the neck. Those small gestures acted as injections of energy which helped the two of them persevere through the aches, bruises and muscle strains which they sustained during training. There seemed to be no limit to the power of their alliance.

Piotr was still thin but his body was now muscular and tightly packed. His posture had straightened and his face appeared chiselled and hardened. The same for Frederich. The training had brought him back to his previous shape under Kraas. He felt stronger than ever. His reflexes had quickened, his movements felt almost effortless, and his focus stayed mostly sharp and steady throughout the gruelling activities of the day. Far from breaking Frederich and Piotr, Scheffler had been the catalyst of their transformation into warriors.

"Don't forget to tap out this time," said Piotr, referring to the sparring incident from weeks earlier.

Frederich had not forgotten. He had refused to give in and blacked out after Piotr outmanoeuvred him and put him in a chokehold.

"Cute. Are you still daydreaming about that?" said Frederich.

"Go!" screamed Scheffler.

Piotr shifted into stance with his fists raised and began hovering around Frederich. Frederich stood still and waited. He knew Piotr's fighting style, and was not surprised by the spin kick which came hurtling toward his shoulder. He dodged it with ease. Piotr followed up with a step kick aimed at Frederich's shin and a jab at his face while Frederich stepped back and used his arm to deflect the punch. The follow-up spin kick caught Frederich by surprise, and while he managed to get his arm up, the force sent him tumbling to the mattress. He remained momentarily on his knees and looked up.

"That's new," he said.

Piotr pulsated his eyebrows and shrugged while hopping from leg to leg. Frederich shook his head and rose to his feet. Piotr was getting confident. Cocky almost. It was time to get him off his horse. Frederich faked a right hook and instead jabbed Piotr's nose with his left hand. While Piotr was dazed, Frederich zipped around the side and brought him down. Piotr lifted his legs to hold Frederich back but Frederich shifted in the opposite direction and wrapped his arm around Piotr's neck. Piotr kicked and squirmed, his face flushed red, while Frederich held him firmly down.

"Switch!" yelled Scheffler.

Frederich released his grip and stood up. Piotr moved his jaw around and touched his neck while he caught his breath. Frederich looked down on him and chuckled.

"Saved by the be—"

Piotr pushed his hands down and spun his legs around in one swift move, striking Frederich on the ankles and sending him again to the mattress. He chuckled and jogged over to his next opponent.

"Cheap shot!" yelled Frederich from the floor.

Those on the outside of the sequence shifted to the person on their right so that a snaking motion was created. Frederich's next opponent was Lewis, the young South African with the square shoulders and thick eyebrows with whom he had exchanged a few words here and there. Before either of them could react to the other, Ralph stepped in from the next row and nudged Lewis hard on the shoulder.

"Swap," he demanded.

Lewis looked at Ralph's unflinching eyes and shrugged before obeying and moving off. Frederich raised his chin and studied his surprise opponent. Why was Ralph so keen to switch places? It made no sense. Frederich turned his head and looked beyond the mattresses. Scheffler was staring directly at him. *Of course.* Another of Scheffler's games.

"Fight!" yelled Scheffler.

Frederich turned back to find Ralph running toward him like a bull. He was caught unprepared. Ralph landed a stiff front kick in Frederich's stomach with full momentum and took the wind out of him. Frederich collapsed to the mattresses. Ralph wasted no time. He immediately leapt on top of Frederich and pinned him down. Ralph's fists came hurtling toward Frederich's face as he reflexively put his elbows up. The amount of force was unmistakable. Ralph was not sparring. He wanted to inflict damage. The punches hailed down on Frederich's lowers arms and the occasional one came from the side and connected with his temple.

"Hey, what are you doing? Are you crazy!?" said Piotr, running over and shoving Ralph to the side.

Frederich used the opportunity to roll away and get back on his feet. Piotr was now standing between him and Ralph with his fists cocked by his side. Frederich nudged Piotr's shoulder.

"I've got him," said Frederich. "Thanks, brother."

Brother. The word sounded strange. What made him say that? He had never called anybody that before. Piotr gave him a hard stare, then his face softened and he nodded.

"Anytime," he said.

When Ralph noticed Piotr back away he re-engaged immediately. Frederich finally had some space. Ralph sprinted toward him, and Frederich leapt forward with his knee out, colliding into Ralph's chest. The two of them came to ground. Ralph was dazed and Frederich had the high ground, so the logical next move would have been a choke-hold. Instead, Frederich got to his feet and cut Scheffler a defiant stare. If Frederich fought back against Ralph, he would be playing into Scheffler's hands. Ralph was a pawn. Rather than attack, Frederich relaxed his body and began hopping from side to side with a wide stance. Ralph got up and attacked Frederich with a barrage of kicks and punches, but Frederich remained on the defensive. He ducked, twisted his body and shifted from side to side, not allowing Ralph to connect on any of his attempts. Ralph grew more flushed and sweat formed over his face, but Frederich maintained focus as Ralph's attacks lost both speed and intensity.

"Abel! What are you doing?" screamed Scheffler, forcing his way onto the mattresses. "Fight!"

The rest of the recruits had already noticed what was going on and one by one had stopped sparring. All eyes were on Frederich, Ralph and Scheffler. Scheffler approached Frederich with a red face and his eyes bulging out.

"When I say fight, you bloody well fight!" he screamed, sprinkles of spit flying out of his mouth.

Frederich wiped his face clean then lifted his chin and shook his head.

"I fight my way," he said.

Scheffler's eyes almost popped out of their sockets. He stepped back and sent a left hook streaking toward Frederich's face. Frederich ducked immediately but the fist still connected with the top of his head and almost knocked him off balance. Scheffler's flurry came like lightning. Frederich had never experienced anything like it. The room for error grew less with each punch as he dodged the attacks on borrowed time. Finally, Scheffler connected with a fist to his ribcage. The pain was excruciating. Frederich yelled out and scrambled backwards while clutching at his side. The unhinged Scheffler was worse than he had imagined. He would have to fight harder, or he was going to be badly hurt. He centred himself in the void and got angry. Scheffler came closer and Frederich tensed his entire body, leaping up and giving Scheffler a flying spin kick to the shoulder with all the fury he could muster. Scheffler barely moved.

The next minutes passed like a dream. Frederich went out of his mind, and his reality narrowed into a vortex consisting of only Scheffler's fists and his own. He ducked and dodged Scheffler's onslaught, and used the few split-second windows he had to bash into Scheffler's enormous head and body. A stray punch from Scheffler then found its way through, and he managed to shield it with his arms before he was thrust backwards from the force. He allowed the momentum to carry him and landed on the mattress on all fours, looking up at Scheffler and grunting while baring his teeth. Scheffler hesitated, locking eyes with him and scowling. Frederich's body lit up, and he rose to his feet. He dissociated for a moment, seeing the outline of the forest above him in the moonlight. He shivered from the cold, and the black bear hovered over his tiny body. *Never again*, came a voice in his head. This time would be different, he decided, and shook his head to bring himself back. This time he was going to fight.

Scheffler growled and moved into action, marching straight for him. Frederich punched his own chest and went forward to meet Scheffler. He easily dodged the first attack and landed a counter-fist in Scheffler's ribs. The adrenaline elevated him beyond anything he had ever experienced. His focus was absolute, and as the battle continued, he remained a step ahead. Scheffler might as well have been shadowboxing. Just when it felt like the fight would never end, Scheffler began to tire. He overextended on his next punch and

Frederich seized the opportunity, jabbing his nose and landing a hook punch to the side of his face with a loud pop. Scheffler's head jerked from the impact and he stepped back, leaving blood pouring down his face. He remained firmly on his feet but held his chin and fists lower while showing no sign of swaying or hesitating. Instead, he hardened his stance and came forward again to begin his counter-attack. *He's not human.* Frederich suddenly had the wind knocked out of him. What little was left in the tank dissipated, and he braced himself for the inevitable knockout blow. It was then that Otto stomped through the middle and held his palms out toward each of them.

"No more!" he yelled.

Frederich and Scheffler stood on opposite ends and continued staring each other down while covered in sweat, their chests heaving up and down. Frederich was grasping at his side and Scheffler's fists were still cocked. Two of the armed guard ran forward from behind Scheffler and pointed their rifles at Frederich.

"No, don't shoot!" yelled Otto. "Don't shoot! Stand down!"

The guards lowered their guns slightly and looked at Scheffler. Frederich knew that if Scheffler gave the word, he was dead. He held his breath and waited.

The hall fell silent. All eyes were on Frederich.

"Get out!!" screamed Scheffler in a fit of manic rage.

Otto put a hand on Scheffler's shoulder and spoke something into this ear.

"I don't give a shit!" he yelled, pushing Otto's arm away. "Out! You're done! Finished!" he screamed at Frederich.

Frederich turned stiff. He felt simultaneously relieved and terrified. He pictured the gruelling journey he was about to take over the Alps for which he was in no shape. He had no choice. He turned around and began limping toward the dorm rooms, still clutching his side.

"No, you stay here, or you're out too!" yelled Scheffler.

Frederich turned around and saw Piotr standing behind him. He shook his head.

"Stay," he said. "You didn't go through all this for nothing."

"This is bullshit," said Piotr.

"Hey, back here! Last chance!" yelled Scheffler again from behind.

"I busted Scheffler's face open. I got what I wanted," said Frederich.

Piotr turned to get a glimpse of Scheffler.

"Yes, you did. Nice work," he said with a half-smirk.

"We'll see each other again soon. Thanks for having my back," said Frederich.

"Anytime, brother."

The two of them shook hands, and Frederich turned toward the dorm rooms. In no time he was packed, and with an empty stomach and aching ribs he found himself alone in the snow, deep in the mountains and a gruelling march away from the closest town.

24

The wheels of the black Mercedes hummed and rattled over the cobbled road before braking at the pedestrian crossing. Tourists strolled around Trinity Square in Budapest on what was a crisp, bright morning. Kalakia looked out from the back seat while his convoy was stopped beside the Holy Trinity Statue, which he recalled was built centuries earlier to fend off the plague. It had been lavishly adorned with angels and saints and was eclipsed from behind by the gothic-styled Matthias Church. Kalakia thought about all the kings who had been coronated metres away from him. Then he shook his head at the absurdity of it all.

He could not have cared less for The Castle District. Royalty and grandeur were part of a bygone era. He preferred to stay planted in reality, although he still acknowledged the need for symbolism. It was a core part of the human psyche which pointed toward something more; something sacred yet tangible, and above all, meaningful. The League itself symbolised justice and honour.

The power of symbolism explained why Kalakia tolerated The Council hosting their meetings in a pomp setting, surrounded by the House Of Habsburg. With The League lacking a fixed form, such formalities allowed the leadership to project legitimacy through tradition. To Kalakia, the whole thing was a charade of ageing men living in the past. He believed that power was best demonstrated by action rather than image.

He was feeling more cynical than usual that morning. His strange mood began when Francois told him that Frederich had clashed yet again with Scheffler and had been cast out for good. The news left Kalakia deeply disappointed. He was chasing a pipe dream, he admitted; an incorruptible protégé with abundant potential. He had overestimated Frederich's ability to fall into line, and Scheffler had failed to tame the beast. Harsh reality had won. Now Kalakia would have to pick a name on The Council's list. The amount of hubris within that group was glaring, and it continued to trouble Kalakia. They all had unique talents, but they were also compromised in ways that Kalakia was sure would lead to their downfall. The signs were ominous. The League was heading into dangerous territory.

When the road cleared, they left the Holy Trinity Statue behind and neared the entrance to their destination just before Buda Castle. Kalakia's car was flanked front and back by two SUVs containing his security detail. Their fleet cruised over the cobbles before the front car led them into the underground car park wedged between a museum and a hotel. The security gate lifted and one of the three armed security guards waved as they drove in. Inside there were over a dozen luxury cars already parked, including Stirner's black Bentley Mulsanne. They pulled into three consecutive parking spaces, and Kalakia waited for his men to exit their vehicles and move into position before emerging. Together they marched into the elevator and went up to the fourth floor, where Stirner was waiting in the doorway of the lobby, ready to usher in the new arrivals. When Kalakia reached the door, they shook hands and exchanged nods while some of Kalakia's security detail remained behind to guard the front.

Inside, The Council was already seated around their large, round oak table, and they showed little enthusiasm for the arrival of Kalakia's entourage. Kalakia noted the new, more elaborate chandelier hanging high above the table from the twenty-foot ceiling which matched the 19th-century baroque style of the room. Were the expensive burgundy rugs and gold-plated arched mirrors not enough? The Roman-style columns standing in each corner were also new. Each of them had four lit candles on top.

Kalakia put his cynicism aside and took his seat. There were ten chairs in total at the round table; eight for the members of The Council, one for Kalakia, which was facing the tinted, bullet-proof window, and the last remaining seat for Stirner; the speaker and representative for The Council. Francois and the remaining security detail walked past the congregation and went next door to wait in the library until the meeting was over. Two stewards circled the table to ensure all cups were full of whatever had been wished for. Kalakia accepted a glass of sparkling water and exchanged nods of greeting with the members of The Council. Stirner was the last to take his seat. He waited until the stewards had left the room before majestically reaching his arms out with palms facing the ceiling.

"Welcome, gentlemen," he said. "Let's not waste any time. We have quite a few items on the agenda today. Our last meeting, I'm sure you recall, was more than three months ago, when this Neutralaser *crisis*, shall we call it," he said, turning briefly toward Kalakia, "was first revealed to us. Now, things grew heated, let us openly acknowledge this, but let us also acknowledge that Kalakia's actions were effective. The wisdom of his actions we have already questioned, as it is our duty to do so, but he achieved the required result; the Neutralaser project has been contained, and Inselheim's team has been incarcerated. All fronts seem quiet. The United States, Russia, China and India are still in the dark as far as we know, and their nuclear programs have remained unchanged. It seems, for the time being, that no hostile government will gain access to The Neutralaser."

"Oh come, Stirner," said Richard DeLauer, who Kalakia was not surprised to see interrupting. "Let's not delude ourselves. How long can we hold all those people prisoner? Hmm? And how many sources slipped through our net and are talking to our enemies right now? We all know this is too big to contain."

"Thank you, *Herr* DeLauer," said Stirner with a stiff expression. "Your concerns are shared by all of us. Let's begin with Inselheim. What's his status?"

All eyes turned to Kalakia.

"He is being closely watched," said Kalakia. "We recently learned that the Inselheim Group has been having financial difficulties, mostly due to their over-commitment to the Neutralaser project."

"That's not acceptable. We can't allow his company to draw unnecessary attention to itself at this point in time," said Stirner.

"I recommend we offer him a bailout," said Kalakia.

"Right. Let's do that. And the prisoners?" asked Stirner. "I think we all agree that this cannot continue."

"Our research team has finished creating detailed profiles on each person," said Kalakia. "This will allow us to maintain surveillance and to take swift action if anybody speaks."

"I don't like this," said DeLauer, shaking his head.

"Do you have any better proposals, Richard?" said Stirner impatiently, turning to DeLauer.

DeLauer straightened up and adjusted his glasses.

"Of course. We kill them all," he said. "No loose ends."

The table broke out in murmurs of disapproval.

"Ludicrous!" yelled Boris Parkishkov.

"Are you suggesting a genocide?" asked Phillip Burani.

This time Kalakia held his hands out to calm the table.

"I have considered this idea," said Kalakia. "And it cannot be dismissed. These men and women have dedicated the majority of their recent lives to the project. They are social hermits without family commitments. However, friends and family members have been enquiring. And the news media has been connecting the dots. If we kill them, they will become martyrs, and we turn a difficult situation into a farce. Not to mention we may need their expertise in the future."

"So what do we do?" asked Stirner.

"I have an alternate plan. We will time their release with the destruction of the facility and leave them with a warning. Their six dead colleagues will act as a deterrent. Without solid proof, any leaks will become conspiracy theories. Our disinformation team will take care of the rest. In the meantime, the device and the equipment will be secured at a hidden location."

"Sounds risky," said Stirner.

"In my opinion, it is the best path to take," replied Kalakia.

"When can the relocation be done?" asked Boris Parkishkov with his croaky voice.

"Dastan Navolov can have a team in place in two weeks, but he will need assistance. Do we have any secure locations within Europe?"

"We have the old military bases in southern Romania. They have extensive underground tunnels and nuclear shelters," said Phillip Burani.

"We could transport the shipment through the Danube from the Black Sea," added Stirner.

"In which case we would be moving into Falk Braun's territory," said Kalakia.

"That's right," said Stirner. "Of course we'll get in touch with him."

"Done?" interrupted DeLauer. "Good. Let's talk succession. We've stalled on this issue too long."

"Thank you, Richard. That was the next item on the list," said Stirner.

Kalakia's skin began burning and he cut DeLauer a sharp gaze.

"Perhaps you would like to propose yourself for succession, DeLauer," said Kalakia.

The table reacted to Kalakia's comment with mild chuckles. DeLauer frowned and crossed his arms.

"I have the shortlist," said Kalakia. "And I have carefully studied the names."

"So you're close to a decision then?" asked Stirner.

Kalakia thought about the latest news from Zürich. It was time to be realistic. In his mind, Marco Lessio the Brazilian was the lesser evil. He was exceptionally brutal, even if he had no reason to be, but was still an excellent tactician and a loyal general. The League would grow cruder and more violent under his watch, but would remain an effective force until his hard power strategy began to backfire.

"Yes. I will announce my decision at the end of the month," said Kalakia with great reluctance.

The various members gave quiet nods of approval. The relief on their faces was evident.

"Alright," said Stirner. "Now. Recession. Global investment has shrunk heavily over the last twelve months, and we need to act."

"This is no surprise," said Kalakia.

Kelly Larsen had given him the heads up. Kalakia had acknowledged her and the IMF's concerns but decided that it was too early to act. He had not wanted to embolden world leaders by relieving them so easily of their burden. Some extended economic pressure would do them good and force them to adapt, and it would send a message to the over-ambitious investors and speculators who valued profit above all else.

"We need to act," said Stirner.

"What do you suggest?" asked Kalakia.

"Lower the tribute rate. Five percent should do it. That would ease the situation, give the market some renewed confidence and flexibility."

"It could also signal weakness on our behalf. Loosening the leash emboldens the dog," said Kalakia.

"Why not just expand our portfolio in the affected areas like we always do? We have plenty of emerging markets we can target," came a voice from the side.

"No," said Boris Parkishkov, shaking his head. "We have enough projects. Any more of this and we go down the path of a planned world economy."

"There is another option," said Stirner. "We could funnel the money back through the governments, and they could pass it on via tax-breaks and state and federal projects."

"That could work. We did something similar some years back."

"What do you think?" said Stirner, looking across at Kalakia.

"Do it," said Kalakia. "But run it by Kelly Larsen first. She can help ensure a smooth rollout."

"Kelly Larsen? From the IMF?"

Kalakia nodded.

"She is an idealist, but a capable and useful operator," he said.

"Fine. Is everyone in agreement?" asked Stirner.

The table responded with nods and murmurs. DeLauer was gazing into space with his arms still crossed. He checked the time on his watch and looked out of the window. Kalakia followed his gaze. Beneath was a courtyard which belonged to the museum and across was the hotel. One of the rooms had its window open, and a man was leaning over the edge with the curtain covering his body. He was holding a rifle and looking through the scope. The gun was aimed in Kalakia's direction. Kalakia's eyes lit up and his body lifted and began moving by itself. He reached his arms out in front of both men on either side of him and pushed back with his feet, bringing all three of them crashing to the carpet behind them along with their chairs just as the window smashed into pieces.

"Get down!" screamed Kalakia.

For a second The Council members remained frozen in shock.

"Move!" he yelled again.

Everyone scrambled from their seats, some of them ducking beneath the table, the others trying for the library. The front door opened and the security detail from the lobby came rushing through. Francois was the first to emerge from the library while drawing his pistol from his jacket. The soldier had been reawakened, noticed Kalakia. The rest of the security detail came running behind Francois with their guns drawn. Two of them came to Kalakia's side of the table to join Francois and the rest covered the window.

"The building across!" yelled Kalakia to one of the security detail while pointing frantically to where the shot came from.

"Can't see anyone, sir!" yelled one of the security detail over his back, his pistol pointed outside.

Kalakia rose to his feet, full of adrenaline and his mind sharp and alert, his chest heaving up and down. Francois disappeared through the front door without waiting for instruction.

"You men stay behind and secure The Council," yelled Kalakia while signalling at three of the security detail. "Call Igor Nagy and have him send back up. The rest come with me."

The security detail surrounded Kalakia and they ran into the lobby as one unit.

"Security downstairs says it's clear," said Francois.

Kalakia nodded, and the elevator door opened. He was about to get in then stopped. His mind had been processing the situation from the get-go. Now a voice was telling him not to get in the elevator. The window had shattered from one bullet. It was supposed to be bulletproof. Someone had replaced the pane with regular glass. Someone had positioned Kalakia on the seat which was in direct line of fire. It was an inside job. Kalakia placed a hand on Francois' shoulder as he was about to enter the elevator. Francois froze and turned around. They locked eyes.

"The window," said Kalakia.

Francois considered Kalakia's words. Then he understood.

"Who?" he said with a snarl.

Kalakia had no idea. He only knew that an ambush awaited them downstairs.

"Call Igor back. We need the helicopter."

Francois reached into his pocket and walked away to make the call. One of the security detail came rushing out of the meeting room.

"Stirner's gone," he said.

Kalakia stared at his man with disbelief. *Stirner.*

"Anyone else?" he asked.

"No, the rest are secure. Should we look for him?"

Kalakia thought about what could be waiting at the bottom of the emergency exit. If Igor had also been compromised, the helicopter would not be coming. There would be a shootout, and Kalakia could not afford to lose any men.

"No. Secure the library and wait for my orders."

"Yes, sir."

In less than ten minutes the helicopter arrived and hovered above the courtyard. A rope with a harness was dangled down.

"I'll go first," said Francois, holding his palm out. "To be sure."

Kalakia nodded. The security detail reached out and claimed the rope. Francois clipped himself in and gave the line two firm pulls to indicate that he was ready. Igor had been with The League since the early days in Berlin. Kalakia had always trusted Igor, but he agreed with Francois' precaution. He waited until the rope was dropped again then checked his phone and saw Francois' confirmation that it was safe to go. He clipped himself in. When he was safely inside, the helicopter took off and crossed over the Danube.

"What happened down there?" yelled Igor over the sound of the helicopter blades.

Kalakia heard him but did not respond. He sat stiff in his seat, staring into space with a scowl on his face. His mind was already plotting, asking every question, studying every possibility. Who else was involved with Stirner? The entire Council? Some of them? One thing Kalakia knew with certainty; Stirner's trip to hell was already booked.

25

Frederich got moving straight away. There was no point standing around brooding in the cold. He considered his two options; head south in the direction of Italy, or march north until he reached a town or highway in the lowlands and then hitch a ride back to Zürich. Tracing the routes during the daily marches, he had favoured the southern option. Going north meant he would be funnelled toward the nearby lake, leading to a gruelling mountain climb with a host of unpredictable cliff faces. If he made it over, he could descend to the lowlands and go from there. *If.* He lacked the equipment for that kind of journey. He chose the path of lesser risk and opted to go south.

He crossed through the trees and onto the plain. His ribs ached with every step. He lowered his head and tried to forget about the pain. His stint with The League was over. He was back where he began, and this time he was in the middle of nowhere. What now? What was he supposed to do? He had no desire to return to Berlin a failure. He already knew where that road led. He could travel toward Sicily, he figured. It would at least be warmer there. He could find a spot near the beach. A coffee or a red wine and a dip in the Mediterranean seemed like a good idea. He imagined the blue skies and new opportunities which awaited him, then shook his head. It was too soon for daydreaming. He had not even begun descending the mountain.

The sky was overcast and grey, and snowfall had formed a fresh layer over the ice. He was still hot and sweaty from his fight with Scheffler, and he unzipped his jacket and welcomed the cold as it seeped through. He made it over the plain and then began descending the mountain with careful steps as chunks of snow collapsed under his feet. The wind howled over the surface and raced past him uphill. He zipped up his jacket halfway again and stuck his head in.

While he descended with careful steps he found he had trouble breathing. He stopped and paid attention. His skin was tingling, and not from the cold. He responded immediately to the signals and made for a small patch of trees to use as cover. From his position, he looked up the mountain to check if anyone was following him. He only saw snow falling in slow motion. *What is it, Frederich?* He checked left then right. He was not going to see anything from where he was. He waited a full minute then sprung out of the protection of the trees and went left. As he worked his way across the mountain, he looked down on the ground and saw footmarks in the snow. He counted at least ten fresh sets, all headed uphill. He immediately remembered the silhouette in the night from when he was on guard duty with Piotr. He hesitated briefly then shrugged and turned back down the mountain again. Not his problem. Let Scheffler worry about it, he figured. Then he stopped. The recruits would be leaving for the march at any minute. Scheffler would have two armed guards — maximum. If there was an ambush, it would be a massacre. He felt a strong tug in his chest. *Piotr* was with them. He turned around, pulled the straps of his bag tight over his chest and began jogging up the mountain in the same direction as the footmarks.

When he reached the edge of the plain he crouched close to the ground and looked out. The hairs on his head stood up. Eight men were swarming the trees, dressed in matching white snowsuits and carrying cream coloured rifles. *Professionals.* Two were missing. He turned his attention to the other side of the plain to a collection of large rocks and found two snipers perched over the boulders with their rifles pointed toward the trees, ready to pick off any survivors who slipped through the net. He dropped his bag on the ground and sprinted across the bottom edge of the plain where he would not be seen. He wished he had his pistol, but it was sitting in the drawer back in Berlin. No use thinking about it. He would have to improvise. In any case, the less noise he made the better. He would have surprise on his side when he entered the forest. But first he had to deal with the snipers.

He worked his way around the back and approached the rocks using the slope of the mountain for cover. The snipers were positioned about sixty feet from each other. He looked down and found a rock the size of a melon. He picked it up. It was a high-risk manoeuvre. If the other shooter turned his head, Frederich was dead. He had no choice. With careful steps he approached the shooter nearest to him, careful to avoid treading on any small rocks. The howl of the wind filled the open plain, and the two gunmen remained motionless. Frederich slithered closer, one cautious step at a time. When he was three feet away he lifted the rock over his head. He choked off his breathing and took another step. The shooter cleared his throat while remaining focussed on the trees, the top of his head vulnerable to Frederich's attack.

Bullets rang in the distance. The shooter flinched. Frederich used the distraction to rush forward and bring the rock down on the man's head with a loud thud. He lifted his arms and crashed the rock down again, hearing the skull break from the force. The shooter slumped down onto the boulder and stopped moving. Guns continued to fire in the distance, the cracking noise shattering the stillness of the wild. Frederich turned his head toward the other shooter, who was still focussed on the trees. He picked up the dead sniper's rifle from the ground, aimed at the other shooter's head and fired. The man collapsed and his gun fell out of his hand.

The urgency propelled Frederich forward. He held the rifle against his chest and sprinted across the plain. Upon entering the forest, he aimed the gun ahead, holding it out in front of his chest. Ahead of him were eight shooters with automatic rifles, evenly spread out behind trees and firing in the direction of the facility. Scheffler's guards were using the watchtowers for cover and firing back from the low ground. The recruits were scattered in all directions, some of them scrambling back toward the facility and others heading to either side of the forest to find a tree for cover. Frederich steadied his breathing and aimed at the head of the shooter on the far left. Adrenaline forced its way through his veins, and his arms were on the verge of shaking out of control. He sensed the void and took one, long, deep breath, and fired.

A gush of blood sprayed out of the shooter's head and he fell to the ground. Frederich moved his scope to the next shooter, aimed and fired. He stepped across to get a clear sight through the trees and brought the third and fourth shooters to ground then moved forward a couple of steps and fired again. As the fifth man fell, the others finally took notice. They turned around and spotted Frederich standing behind them. While the sixth shooter took aim, Frederich fired a bullet into his skull. He moved his scope to the seventh man and saw a gun pointed directly at him. The bullets whizzed by while he let go of his rifle and leapt sidewards. He scrambled across the snow on all fours and reclaimed his gun then rolled around and took shelter behind a tree. Some seconds later there was a pause in the hail of bullets. He slowly reached his head out from behind the tree. They were gone. He looked left and saw one of them running through the forest, then right, where the other shooter was sprinting away toward the other side. He lifted his rifle and pointed it left, but was unable to find a direct shot through the trees. He hesitated for a second then gave chase.

He reached the edge of the trees and looked out over the plain while gasping for air. Nothing. Empty. *Where is he?* There was a flicker to his side. A surge of panic willed him to turn around, where he saw the man emerging from behind a tree twenty feet away with his rifle pointed directly at him. He had been out-manoeuvred. He dropped his shoulders and waited for the bullets. There was only a loud thump, and the weapon fell out of the shooter's hands before he collapsed to his knees. He appeared dazed. A rock the size of a golf ball tumbled in front of him onto the snowy ground and rolled forward. Frederich looked to his left and saw Piotr standing thirty feet away on the plain, his arm held out in full extension. Frederich turned back to the shooter, who was conscious but still in a daze. Then he went numb, and it turned silent. Dead silent. When it came, he recognised it but was powerless to do anything. *No, please no.* It came raging out of the void like a shattered dam; pure, unadulterated fury. White turned to black. Green to red. The image of Piotr struggling with someone briefly flashed by. Piotr fell backwards. There was blood. Piotr got back up. Fell backwards again. There was screaming, deranged and unhinged. The terrifying yell of a madman. And finally, black.

When he came to, he felt a heavy weight pressing his body into the snow. Murmurings came from nearby. He tried to get up but lacked the power. The pressure on him was too strong.

"He's conscious," said someone.

He heard a series of approaching footsteps.

"What the…"

"Jesus…"

They were reacting to something. Frederich tried to shuffle his body around so he could see. The pressure on him eased slightly to allow him to rotate. When he turned around he saw Scheffler's face. He had never seen it that way. Was he dreaming? Scheffler looked frightened. Frederich looked down on Scheffler's hands. They were covered in blood. So were his. Lots of it. His knuckles were throbbing with pain. He looked around. The recruits were standing around him with equally dazed looks.

"Why are you all looking at him like that!?" yelled Piotr, facing out at the other recruits.

Piotr bent down and tried to push Scheffler off.

"Get off him!" Piotr screamed.

Scheffler barely budged from Piotr's effort, but he lifted his arms and knee and let Frederich go.

Piotr bent down again and placed his hands beneath Frederich's arms to help him up. Frederich felt weak and lightheaded, and allowed himself to lean on Piotr's body.

"Come on, brother," said Piotr. "Let's get you out of the cold."

Together they walked through the trees in the direction of the facility. Frederich turned around and caught another glance of the stunned faces of Scheffler and the recruits. The shooter lay motionless behind them on the ground. His torso and legs were visible from behind a tree. The snow around him was stained all over with blood.

"Come," whispered Piotr, looking forward with total concentration.

Together they made it through the trees, passing the six dead shooters. The opening was covered with the blood and bodies of dozens of recruits. Among the dead was Otto. The wounded were being carried inside. Cries of agony bellowed from multiple directions. Piotr paid no attention to any of it, keeping his steely eyes forward until they made it inside.

Kimberley Brunswick woke from her nap to quiet chatter in the recreation room. For a second her body remained utterly numb on the couch, and she bathed in the feeling. It was an unexpected moment of bliss, which eventually gave way to reality as it seeped into her awareness like a slow-acting poison. She was a prisoner, a captive of a vicious organisation.

She wiped her eyes and sat up. She had on her old white t-shirt and dark grey sweatpants, and a quick smell test told her that both needed washing. First she would do a quick round and check up on the team, then she would get changed and do the laundry. She put her sneakers on and began walking around the brightly-lit room while observing the pale faces and sleeping bodies sprawled on the floor. Phil and Lena looked up from their card game as Brunswick approached and brushed a hand across Lena's shoulder, then went back to what they were doing. Reiko was scribbling in her journal and paid no attention to Brunswick. Shirvan was on his back, listening to music through his headphones with his arms and legs spread out. When Brunswick's shadow passed over him, he opened his eyes and gave her a tired smile. She smiled back warmly with a nod and continued forward, where Mona was slouched on the sofa with her arms around her knees. Brunswick went over and kneeled in front of her. Mona looked further gone than usual. Brunswick waited patiently, then placed a gentle hand on her leg.

"How are you, Mona?" she said softly.

Mona gave a half-hearted shrug. Her thick red hair was tangled all over from being obsessively played with and her dull brown eyes were focussed on the floor.

"Do you want to come for a walk? Stretch those legs out a bit?" asked Brunswick.

Mona sighed loudly.

"To where?" she said. "The gym or the upstairs rooms? Great choices."

"It doesn't matter. The important thing is to keep moving," replied Brunswick.

"It's pointless. We're stuck here," said Mona. "They're not letting us go."

"You're right," said Brunswick. "Chances are we're stuck here until we die."

Mona glared at Brunswick and tilted her head.

"Right," she said carefully, then nodded. "Exactly."

"Right," said Brunswick. "Or, we can look at it differently. The more active we stay, the more prepared we'll be as soon

236

as the situation changes, and the better chance we'll have of making it out."

Mona gave Brunswick a searching look then her attention shifted toward the front door. Brunswick followed Mona's gaze and noticed that the armed guard was on patrol again. She knew what to ask him, and she also knew what his response would be, but she was still going to try.

"I'll be right back," she said then rubbed Mona's leg before going over to the guard and walking alongside him. "Hello," she said on approach.

"There is nothing new to tell you," he said abruptly.

"That's fine. Then just let us get some fresh air."

The guard shook his head.

"Next week. You already went this week."

"That's too long," said Brunswick. "We're losing our minds in here."

The guard shook his head again and looked the room over thoroughly before heading back to the door.

"Call your people. It's time to negotiate something. It's been four months, dammit!" she said, her voice growing progressively louder and more urgent as the guard got closer to the door. "Plea—"

A shattering explosion sounded in the distance and the floor shook beneath Brunswick's feet. Her body convulsed and she froze with her arms out. The guard sprinted out of the room while everyone looked at each other with grave faces. Brunswick was gripped in place like a toy figurine. Another even louder explosion went off and shook her out of her trance.

She chased after the soldier, running out of the recreation room and going left through the corridor. The front door and only exit from the sleeping quarters had been left wide open. The rattle of gunshots filled the hall outside, and Brunswick crouched low while approaching the front, fighting to control the shaking in her body. Immediately she noticed that the guards were gone from their usual places, and were now in various positions of cover with their rifles pointed forward. An enormous cloud of smoke and dust rose like a plague, out of which dozens of armed men in army fatigues emerged with guns blazing. Brunswick scrambled backwards in terror and collided into Shirvan, who had been standing behind her shoulder. The sheer horror on his face mirrored her state.

"Get everyone gathered together in the corridor!" she yelled.

Shirvan remained distracted by the gunfight outside before he turned to Brunswick.

"What?" he said.

"We need to be ready. This is our chance to escape through the tunnel. I'll gather everyone from upstairs."

Shirvan shifted his attention outside again. Brunswick sensed what he was thinking. Running out into *that* was bordering on insane. Brunswick's gut told her that Inselheim would never risk their lives by going to the government and asking for an incursion to reclaim the facility. Whoever was attacking, their tactics were reckless and ominous. Brunswick was certain that staying put would pose the highest risk.

Shirvan searched her face.

"You have to trust me!" she yelled.

"Ok," he said with a nod, still appearing doubtful.

"We'll meet at the edge of the corridor over there," said Brunswick, pointing back toward the recreation room.

"Yes. Ok," said Shirvan and slowly moved away from the door while catching another glimpse of the chaos outside.

Brunswick sprinted upstairs, running into members of the team cautiously descending one step at a time.

"Go down to the corridor!" she yelled. "Be ready to move out!"

Brunswick sprinted by the rooms while the clatter of gunshots continued outside.

"Down to the lobby! Gather in the corridor!" she screamed at the shocked faces standing in the doorways.

"What the hell's going on?" someone yelled.

"Just be ready to move out!" Brunswick yelled back. "Leave everything behind."

Brunswick completed a sweep of the entire floor and banged her fist against any doors she found closed. Then she went downstairs to join the rest of the team, where dozens of wide-eyed faces in the corridor awaited her and everyone was huddled close together. Brunswick looked over them, trying to determine if anyone was missing.

"Is everyone here?" she said to Shirvan.

"I believe so," he yelled back.

The gunfire had not ceased for a second. Brunswick carefully approached the front door again. The plume of smoke had settled, and several of the guards lay bloodied on the floor. Members of the invading army were now halfway through the hall and quickly approaching, covered by a deafening amount of gunfire. She studied the path to the tunnel door, which lay just behind the Neutralaser a hundred feet away. She began trembling again when she thought about going out there. Her teeth chattered uncontrollably. She was now sharply aware of the risk she was about to put her team in, not to mention herself. She closed her eyes and tightened her jaw, gripped by terror and doubt. Time was quickly running out to decide. She steeled herself and sprinted back to the corridor.

"Ok, let's move!" she yelled. "Make a line behind me."

The team began shuffling around to queue up behind her, a number of them moaning from fear. Brunswick was drenched in sweat, and she brushed away parts of her hair which were covering her eyes. Jittery hands rested on her shoulders. She turned around and found Mona, her jaw slack and eyes bulging. Brunswick nodded and tried to smile, and Mona tightened her face and nodded back.

"Let's go!" yelled Shirvan impatiently from behind.

Brunswick shuffled forward with the team behind her. There were two loud bangs, and smoke began to seep over the guards' positions outside. Mona's body pushed up against Brunswick from behind.

"God protect us," whispered Brunswick and took off.

They sprinted off with Brunswick in the lead, and she snaked her way around the desks and boxes to maintain cover from the gunfire. There was a loud, sharp thump to her left. A bullet had found its way through. She grew weightless, and for a second lost contact with her body. Then she found herself behind the partition wall next to the tunnel door. They had been allowed through there once a fortnight to get some fresh air at the tunnel exit. This time Brunswick was determined that their freedom would be permanent. She moved to the touchpad without looking back and began entering the pin code. She stumbled through the eight numbers way too quickly, unable to control the adrenaline in her body. The screen showed 'ERROR' in red. She tried again. Her hand twitched when she was midway through as someone screamed behind her. She spun around and saw a body on the floor. There was blood. Bullets were now crashing into the desks, chairs and boxes behind them and the guards had been pushed right back to the sleeping quarters. Another of her team fell to the floor, then another. The rest made it behind the partition wall and huddled around Brunswick so that she lost sight of those who had been shot. She tried to catch another look.

"Open it!" screamed Shirvan. "I'll go," he said and forced his way back through the crowd.

Brunswick's urge to join him was overwhelming. She was responsible for the lives of her team. She turned back to the touchpad and rapidly entered the code without a thought. The door began lifting and everyone moved forward. Brunswick felt a tiny flicker of relief and turned around to have it sucked out of her. Shirvan was sprinting back in her direction, with the invaders now metres behind him.

"Back!" screamed Shirvan, and wrapped his arm around her as he passed and forced her into the tunnel.

"We can't leave them!" screamed Brunswick.

"Push the button! Close it!" screamed Shirvan, refusing to let Brunswick out of his grip.

Brunswick struggled and screamed but Shirvan held tight. One of the invading soldiers turned in the direction of the tunnel and saw the moving door.

"No!" yelled Brunswick.

She watched on helplessly as the door slid shut, and the terrifying sound of bullet fire tapered off.

26

The private jet cut through the clouds over the Czech Republic on the way back to Berlin with Kalakia gazing out of the window. His eardrums were pounding and his fingers were still trembling. His thoughts were in vile places. He was picturing Stirner being tortured and bled dry like an animal, that traitor's body dissolved in hydrofluoric acid and unceremoniously disposed of. Before that, Kalakia decided, Stirner's home would be burnt to the ground and his closest family members murdered in unspeakable ways by The League's most sadistic killers. His assets would be sold off, his legacy erased from the face of the Earth.

Francois placed a light hand on Kalakia's shoulder. Kalakia flinched and looked up.

"Hmm?" he said, blinking twice.

"I just spoke to Igor."

He turned his body around and signalled with his eyes to the chair across from him. Francois sat down.

"Tell me."

"Igor's men stormed the car park. You were right. A death squad was waiting for us. They were taken care of."

"Stirner?"

"No sign yet."

"What about The Council?"

"Igor has them at a secret location. They're playing dumb."

Kalakia ground his teeth while tapping his finger on the little table beside his seat.

"There's more," said Francois.

Kalakia stopped tapping and looked at Francois.

"They weren't only going after you. There have been over two dozen confirmed attacks on our soldiers and facilities in the last six hours. New York, Rio, Moscow, London, Zürich, Doha, Tokyo, Cape Town. We're still gathering information, but already dozens of our people have been injured or killed. Whoever did this, they're extremely well informed. They knew what spots to hit and when. Also, we've received calls from U.S., British, Chinese and Russian intelligence. They insist their governments knew nothing of the attacks."

Kalakia clenched his fist until his knuckles turned white. There was no doubt now that it was an inside job. When he spoke again, his voice sounded coarse and unfamiliar.

"Transport The Council to Berlin. I want them interrogated, but not touched. Not yet. Speak to our contacts at Interpol and have them monitor the airports in case Stirner shows up. I want him alive."

"Should we declare a state of emergency?"

"You should have done that as soon as you got on the plane. Do it now and do it first. The men need to be prepared for further attacks."

Francois' phone began vibrating in his hand. He checked the screen.

"It's Dastan Navolov," he said.

Kalakia sat at attention. Francois lifted the phone to his ear.

"Yes."

244

Francois listened carefully, then his eyes lit up.

"Attacked? When?" he said.

For a time Francois listened, shifting often in his seat. Kalakia remained upright and waiting.

"Hold on," said Francois then lowered the phone.

"Someone hit the Neutralaser facility. They bombed the entrance and stormed the hall. One of our people made a call from inside during the firefight, and now Dastan says he can't reach him."

Frederich sat on the cold concrete with his back against the wall, rubbing on his knuckles in a dazed state. His hands were red all over and still throbbing. Groans of agony came from inside the rooms, which had been turned into makeshift hospital beds. Scheffler had already accounted for the dead and the injured were being brought inside. Ralph walked by carrying two enormous plastic jugs of water for the wounded on each shoulder. He and Frederich exchanged silent nods before Ralph disappeared inside. A shadow descended on Frederich. He looked up and saw Piotr's tired, frowning face gazing at him.

"I wasn't going to ask, but we need help moving the bodies."

Frederich placed both hands on the floor and pushed himself up.

"Let's go," he said.

They walked toward the middle of the training hall where Scheffler was coordinating the recruits, who were now armed and being instructed to cover the front alongside the surviving guards.

"Don't stray!" yelled Scheffler. "I don't want to lose any more men."

Scheffler's face was pale and he appeared exhausted, but he was as steadfast as ever.

"Scheffler! Helicopters heading this way!" yelled someone from the entrance.

Frederich's skin flared up in anticipation. Scheffler's eyes bulged open and he ran to the front with Frederich and Piotr trailing him. The sound of helicopters chopping through the air grew louder. Outside, the armed guard and recruits were standing or crouched in various positions with their rifles pointed in the air. The trees began blowing around when the three helicopters approached. Scheffler had his hands on his hips as he carefully watched the choppers descend while the force of the blades stretched his hair and clothing to one side. Then he began waving off the shooters.

"Don't shoot! They're with us! Don't shoot!"

The armed guard and recruits slowly lowered their guns. Frederich shielded his eyes and watched the black military helicopters descend onto the opening, where traces of blood could still be seen beneath the snow. The attack helicopter landed first followed by two transport helicopters just behind it. Six armed men in military uniform and six civilians got out of the transport helicopters. Three men and three women were carrying medical bags. The door of the attack helicopter opened and two more armed soldiers hopped out. They turned around and helped two other soldiers bring out their prisoner. The captive had his hands bound behind his back and was dressed in the same white military uniform as the attackers. He was forced onto the snow, and had his head bowed. *Son of a bitch*, thought Frederich. It was the one who got away. The last shooter.

They had found him.

At close to sunset Kalakia's jet descended on The League's private runway in the Brandenburg countryside. No risks were taken. The surrounding area had been searched for possible threats and awaiting them on the tarmac were six carloads of armed soldiers. After the jet landed and came to a halt, Kalakia and Francois made straight for the second vehicle and the fleet drove off.

Back in Berlin, they approached the penthouse at Zoologischer Garten with extreme caution. Soldiers from Hamburg, Frankfurt, Munich and Cologne had arrived to help protect Kalakia and reinforce the city. Many had been arranged into armed carloads of four which were parked in random locations in the surrounding area. A unit of twenty soldiers was on stand-by in the car park, ready for battle in case of an incursion. Scouts in civilian clothing patrolled the streets on foot, instructed to keep an eye out while remaining inconspicuous. Snipers were also in place on the rooftop by the time Kalakia arrived. The fleet pulled into the car park, and Kalakia made it to the elevator under armed cover. Soon he was inside with Francois by his side, where they made connection with Navolov's commandos.

"The team is approaching the Neutralaser facility," said Francois while turning his mobile phone to loudspeaker mode and laying it on the coffee table.

The sound of helicopter blades came bursting through. Kalakia and Francois waited and listened.

"There's a fire ahead," said a distorted voice.

"What fire?" said Francois, turning his ears toward the speaker.

"We've arrived at the coordinates, and there's black smoke coming from a hole in the ground. Looks like they blew it wide open and torched the whole thing."

Kalakia and Francois exchanged sharp glances. Kalakia leaned forward.

"Any sign of life?" he asked.

"Nothing. Just the fire. We didn't see anyone on approach."

"Split up. Check the entire area," said Kalakia. "Do not stop until you find something."

"Roger that," said the voice.

The connection closed with a click.

"They had to have come by air," said Francois. "If they were trying to move the device by road, we would have found them by now."

"The device is already destroyed beneath those flames," said Kalakia bitterly.

"That makes no sense. Why would they do that?" replied Francois. "Stirner knows we still have the blueprints."

As Francois spoke the word 'blueprints,' he and Kalakia immediately locked eyes. Francois lowered his head and dialled League Intel.

"The Neutralaser blueprints," he said into the speaker. "Has anybody had access to them recently?" There was a pause. "Yes, I need to know if anyone has requested access in the last months." Another pause. "Good. Call me back."

Francois hung up and lowered the phone onto his lap.

"They're checking."

Kalakia went over to the window and his thoughts drifted. The prototype had been destroyed, and Inselheim's Neutralaser team was either dead or captured. If Stirner had access to the blueprints or had taken the Neutralaser team alive, The League would lose monopoly over the technology. There would be a global crisis. The age of mutually assured destruction would be over. Panic would break out among the superpowers. War would follow.

Francois' phone rang and he quickly answered and raised it to his ear.

"Yes."

Francois listened for a short time then hung up.

"Nobody accessed the blueprints."

"You seem sure of that," said Kalakia.

"We have multiple checkpoints in place. It's air-tight."

Kalakia had complete faith in Francois and the intelligence team, but that knot in his stomach continued to bother him.

"Do we still not have a fix on the attackers?" asked Kalakia.

"About that. Scheffler's training facility was also hit. They were ambushed from the trees."

"What?" said Kalakia. "Scheffler?"

"He's alive. Otto Litger was killed in the crossfire, along with twenty-one others. Dozens are injured. Some critically. A backup team is assisting and medics are looking after the wounded."

Kalakia considered the terrain around the training facility.

"How did the attackers escape?"

"Well, here's the good news. The boy. Frederich. He saw the enemy approaching and attacked them from behind. He killed two snipers then picked off six other shooters. He was almost killed but another recruit managed to intervene. He.."

Francois stalled in his speech.

"He saved them," said Kalakia impatiently.

249

"Well, yes, from what I understood his intervention helped avoid a massacre. Scheffler and the others were sitting ducks. It's just… the way he killed the ninth shooter sounded rather strange."

"Strange? How?"

"According to Scheffler, he mutilated the man. Beat him repeatedly with his fists and the butt of a gun. Nobody could contain him. He beat the shooter to a pulp before Scheffler and the rest could come and pull him off. Scheffler said he was completely deranged, like an animal, that he's never seen anything like it."

"I can only imagine what he means," said Kalakia. "Let us not forget about Khartoum and Vivar. We learned early what we were dealing with. We cannot act surprised when he becomes unhinged."

"Maybe you're right," said Francois.

"Is he still posing problems?"

"No. According to Scheffler, it was a temporary episode. He's back to normal now."

"Good," said Kalakia. "Let us focus on the fact that he slaughtered nine of our enemies. I want the bodies identified."

"Ok," said Francois. "I have more good news. The last surviving shooter was spotted by our helicopters while fleeing over the mountain. They have him at Scheffler's facility."

Kalakia felt a rare shot of relief pass through him. His shoulders relaxed. *Finally.*

"Fly him here for interrogation," said Kalakia.

"Of course," said Francois.

"Have Frederich brought also. I would like to speak with our vicious young brute."

27

Standing beneath the bright, moonlit sky, Frederich drew comfort from the glow while holding his rifle against his chest with both hands. Finally, some space to clear his head. They had been ordered over and again not to pass the fence. For their own safety, Scheffler insisted. Frederich had no intention of listening. As soon as he took over guard duty, he crossed the opening and entered the forest while ignoring Ralph's shouts of protest. He had already been ousted. He was no longer under Scheffler's command, so nobody could tell him what to do.

The cold felt good against his skin. With the situation inside somewhat under control, he began to think about that trip to Sicily. The open road. Solitude. Maybe not a good idea after what he had experienced, but he was craving it nonetheless. There were no flashbacks this time. He felt nothing. Too much had happened in a short time. Nobody had spoken a word to him about it. Those final, frenzied minutes were blacked out from his memory, and Scheffler had already disposed of the body. Meanwhile, the look on each person's face told him all he needed to know. The truth was out. They had seen Frederich the lunatic. Their responses had been typical; shock followed by a cautious distance. Except for Piotr. He had not flinched.

There was a loud thud against a tree behind him. *Speak of the devil.* He half turned his head toward the approaching footsteps.

"You're a lousy aim," he said.

"If I were aiming, you would have a sore head by now," Piotr replied.

A hand rubbed Frederich's back from behind as Piotr came to his side.

"How is it in there?" asked Frederich.

"As good as it can be. No one else has died. Thank God."

Frederich nodded.

"That's a damn relief," he said. "I heard a helicopter before?"

"They flew Lewis out. He's not doing good."

Frederich gave a sombre nod and looked back at the sky, and they remained for a moment in silence.

"Scheffler's looking for you," said Piotr, breaking the quiet.

"Is he? What does he want?"

"No idea."

"Doesn't matter. It's probably best if I leave soon," said Frederich.

"Why?" said Piotr, pulling his head back in surprise.

"Scheffler already wanted me out. Plus everyone knows now."

"Knows what?"

Frederich went quiet and looked at the ground.

"Knows what?" repeated Piotr.

"Don't play stupid."

"I don't know what you're talking about."

"Come on!" yelled Frederich with an unexpected burst of emotion. "Enough! I know. You know. Everyone knows."

Piotr narrowed his eyes and trapped Frederich with his stare, then stepped forward and grasped him hard by his shoulders.

"Listen here, you bastard! You're a hero, remember that," he said with a scowl.

Frederich bowed his head and let his shoulders drop.

"What are you doing here, Piotr? The rest of the guys had the brains to stay away. Why are you still talking to me?"

"Because you're my friend, and you got me this far," said Piotr, letting go of Frederich's shoulders.

"You saw what I did. How can you still want anything to do with me?"

"Yes, I saw. And I don't judge you."

"Why not?"

"Because I've seen it before. We all have the beast inside. All of us."

"What do you mean you've seen it before?"

Piotr straightened his long neck and leaned back.

"Back in my hometown, in Poland, there were two serial killers in the area. Nobody knew at the time because the police were still connecting the dots. The killers were going around with a hammer and screwdriver and butchering anyone they saw. Children, women, homeless people, anyone who couldn't fight back. One day, Juva, this kid from our town, he was playing with his friend in the woods and they both got killed. A man from our village was driving by and saw the killers through the trees. He stopped and went closer without them seeing him. He recognised them. It was Luka and Robert. They lived in our town. They were standing over the bodies and laughing. Instead of telling the police, the man went and told Marja, Juva's older brother. When Marja saw the bodies, he lost it. Really lost it. It was the devil's work. You couldn't even recognise the boys' faces. Marja went after Luka and Robert. He stabbed and beat them both the same way they did to Juva. Most people agreed that he did the right thing. But that look everyone gave you before, that's how everyone in our town looked at Marja. That's the look people give when they don't understand. They can't see how someone can go there. Everyone was shocked. But not me."

"Why not?" asked Frederich, engrossed by Piotr's story.

"Because I was with Marja when he did it. We were childhood friends. He told me to stay home, but I went with him to look for Luka and Robert. I held the gun so they wouldn't escape. Marja loved his little brother more than anything. Seeing the young boy die like that, it broke him. It was never supposed to happen. Not like that. It was a horrible thing. Once Marja went over the edge, he was never coming back. I saw the devil in his eyes. He had no choice. Nobody chooses to cross over. And I know you didn't choose it either." Piotr studied Frederich's face. "You've done it before, haven't you?" he said.

Frederich looked up and locked eyes with Piotr, unable to breathe, unable to say a word.

"Whatever made you like this, it wasn't your fault. I'm telling you, nobody chooses the devil. The devil chooses them. So stop blaming yourself. That bastard pointed a gun at *you*. *He* took you there. Every choice I've seen you make tells me you're a good person, and I'm sorry you have to carry this. Just like I was sorry for Marja. But you have to accept that it is there."

Accept? What did Piotr know about it? It was one thing to witness it. Having it inside you was something else entirely.

254

"You tried to stop me," said Frederich. "Why did you help Marja kill those guys?"

Piotr gave an ugly, lopsided smile.

"Because the devil was in me too. The hate came like fire. I *wanted* Marja to kill them. Not hurt them, or scare them, or take them to the police, but destroy them. After, I was ashamed. Like you. I felt like a monster. I didn't want to feel that kind of hate again."

"Does what happened have anything to do with why you joined The League?"

Piotr nodded.

"The police came looking for us, and Marja gave himself up. I ran away. The League was my only chance to avoid being locked up."

"Do you regret what you did?"

"No," said Piotr with a cold voice. "We did what was necessary. I just regret that we had to do it."

Frederich said nothing. He could only nod his acknowledgement of Piotr's torment. Piotr looked away over the plain.

"I can't get rid of it, can I?" said Frederich.

Piotr shook his head.

"I don't think so."

"So what do I do?"

Piotr turned to face Frederich.

"You go back and see what Scheffler wants, and you keep being yourself."

Frederich nodded and placed a hand on Piotr's shoulder.

"Thanks," he said, then leaned in and gave his friend a firm hug. He then pushed off and marched away through the trees toward the facility to look for Scheffler.

Frederich reentered the facility and found the training hall empty. A light was on in the mess hall with murmurs coming from inside. Scheffler appeared in the hallway in the distance. When Frederich noticed him, Scheffler turned around and walked back inside. Frederich followed.

He found Scheffler in his office, leaning against the front of his desk with his legs spread and his arms crossed.

"Door," said Scheffler.

Frederich shut the door behind him and leaned on the other end of the desk next to Scheffler.

"That Kalakia, I swear," said Scheffler, shaking his head and biting his lip. "He knew. He had you pinned from the start."

Frederich waited. *Where's he going with this?*

"You know," continued Scheffler. "I went through some bad shit when I served. But I was never helpless. We did our homework and we took care of business. Planning. Precision. Preparation. Twenty-four seven. We were always a step ahead. I don't know what's happened to me. I've lost the edge. There was no way anyone would get the slip on me if it were a few years ago."

"You served with the British military?" asked Frederich.

"SAS," replied Scheffler. "Who dares wins, ey? Those bastards today got us at the perfect time, when we were the most exposed. They'd have cleaned us up if you hadn't shown up."

"If I wasn't already outside, I would have been killed with everyone else."

"That's right. But destiny doesn't give two shits about what-ifs. You were a magician out there. Who trained you, Abel?"

"My father, Kraas Abel. He was Spetsnaz."

"Ah," said Scheffler, lifting his head to the ceiling. "Now it begins to make sense."

"Was your father military?" asked Frederich.

"No, my old man was a boxer. Dirk 'The Cobra' Scheffler. You probably never heard of him?"

Frederich shook his head.

"He had a name back in England. My grandfather left Germany before the war and settled in London. That's where he met my grandmother. You can imagine what growing up in London after the war was like with a German name. My old man got picked on a lot, so he had to learn how to fight. He started spending time in the boxing ring. Later on he blew up nationally. Won some fights. Then his drinking got in the way."

"I guess he taught you some tricks? I've never fought any-one as quick as you."

"Yeah, I got my start from him. Everyone knew me as Dirk The Cobra's kid. That's why I went into the military. To carve out my own legacy."

"I can understand that," said Frederich, feeling a strange buzz when he realised he was having a civilised conversation with Scheffler. "I think that's why I joined The League. I didn't realise how much my father influenced me until he died."

"Sorry to hear."

"Thanks. I'm sorry about Otto. He was an honest man."

"He was. And much more. Rest in peace. Took me having to carry his dead body to finally see it."

Scheffler exhaled and shook his head.

"I was just so angry all the time. You ever had that feeling like you've just woken up from a long, dark dream?" he asked.

"Yes, I know that feeling well," said Frederich with a reluctant smile.

Scheffler's face fell flat and he turned his body toward Frederich.

"Right. About what happened out there. That was some intense business. You usually get like that? Or was it the situation that tipped you over? Wouldn't blame you if it was."

"It's happened before."

"I see. Well, anyway, I'm glad you were out there, Abel."

Frederich looked on, unsure how to respond. He never expected to hear that from Scheffler.

"Ok," said Scheffler, lifting himself off the desk. "Last thing. You're wanted back in Berlin."

"By who?" asked Frederich.

"Who do you think? The helicopter is coming back at 06:00 to pick you and the prisoner up."

"What's going to happen here?"

"The training program is on hold for the time being. Something big's brewing. They hit us hard. Even went after the big man."

"They hit Kalakia?"

"He's lucky to be alive."

Frederich's lips slowly parted. *They went after Kalakia.*

"Go get some rest, Abel," said Scheffler, slapping Frederich on the shoulder. "We've all had a rough day."

Frederich nodded and left the room in a daze. It looked like the trip to Sicily would have to wait.

28

When Frederich stepped onto the countryside runway, the tension was thick in the air, infecting what should have been a peaceful day. The tarmac was surrounded by lush green and tall, thick trees, but it might as well have been a picture hanging on a wall. League soldiers were spread around along the fence, dressed in all black with their hands close to their jacket seams. All eyes were on the prisoner, who was now in plain clothing and both handcuffed and blindfolded. When the prisoner neared the waiting SUV, one of the soldiers took hold of him and punched him hard in the stomach then pushed him roughly into the back seat, causing his head to bang on the edge of the car roof in the process. The men scowled, grinned and nodded with approval. One of them spat on the ground, his fists clenched.

The back door of a second black SUV was held open by a League soldier, who had his menacing gaze on Frederich. Frederich noted the man's skull-bare undercut and flawless posture. Ex-military, he assumed. While he approached the car, the ex-soldier gave him a friendly nod. He paused for a second before getting in. Had he imagined that? Inside the car were three other men including the driver, all staring forward. None of them acknowledged him. Yes, he had imagined it, he decided.

They travelled from Brandenburg to Berlin in silence, crossing farms, small towns and bright yellow rapeseed fields. At close to sunset they reached the city from the south and the two cars split off, with Frederich's driver turning westward and the other car continuing north, Frederich assumed, to the torture chamber at Potsdamer Platz.

They approached Zoologischer Garten and drove into the underground car park of the Grand Luxus hotel, descending the ramp in circles until they reached the bottom level. There they were met with more League soldiers dressed in black, some at the ramp entrance, others guarding the elevator. Frederich then realised that there were a handful more soldiers along the street outside, dressed in civilian clothing with casual t-shirts and jeans.

Their SUV pulled up and Frederich and his companions went to the elevator. Inside there was only one button, and they went up to what felt like the top floor. They reached the lobby, where again there were more men standing guard, all of them as tense-looking as the others. It was now clear that The League was in a state of war.

The metal door slid open, and the ex-military soldier directed Frederich to go inside, where there was another room with another metal door. It too slid open, revealing Kalakia standing in the doorway with his thick frame and predatory eyes.

Vidrik and his captive locked eyes. It was a brief moment to get acquainted. Vidrik was measuring the man's fear while drawing him into his sphere of dominance, where pain would be the only form of communication. Did the despicable worm tied to the table understand that? Vidrik looked deeper and concluded that no, the worm did not understand. Not yet. The worm blinked once and licked his lip while trying to look disinterested. Vidrik knew that game. The worm would be interested soon enough.

When going through his tool chest, Vidrik had looked past the blowtorch and the cutter. He had something special in mind. The League's absolute dominance was being put to the test by the worm and his friends. Under such exceptional circumstances, the worm had to be made an example of. The soldiers were aching for revenge. Kalakia, in his typical fashion, was taking his time planning a response. Meanwhile the big story making the rounds was all about the amazing Abel, who had killed nine enemies with unprecedented efficiency and mutilated the last one just to send out a message.

The soldiers were getting over-excited. Understandable, figured Vidrik, considering how weak and indecisive the leadership had been in recent times. He was going to put their minds at ease with a message of his own; their protector at the gate was *him*, not Frederich Fucking Abel.

He looked down at the worm, strapped naked on his back. The worm was a handsome young man, with his tanned face covered in freckles. The questions could wait. Vidrik turned the scalpel in circles by its handle and inspected the tip. The handsaw was waiting ready on the table beside him. A dozen high-ranking soldiers stood around the table and looked on. Among them was Falk Braun, the General of Europe, whom Vidrik had specially invited to witness the spectacle. At the back with his arms crossed was Francois. He had not been invited. He was going to run home and spill the details to daddy. A problem for later. It was time to go to work.

261

"Now," said Vidrik, giving careful, equal attention to each person in the audience before turning back to the worm, who seemed more engaged once the scalpel neared his body. "Let's peel back the skin and see what we can find out."

"Come in, Frederich," said Kalakia without offering a greeting.

Frederich entered the apartment, feeling Kalakia's eyes on him from behind. He took note of the sheer size and unusual layout of the place. He had no interest in the artefacts and paintings. He approached the window and looked out over Berlin, able to see far into the distance, where most buildings were no more than five stories high.

"Nice view," he said.

"I assume you saw far more magnificent sights during your training?"

Frederich spotted Kalakia in the reflection, standing upright with his head raised and his hands clasped together behind his back.

"For brief moments," said Frederich. "But we weren't there to enjoy the landscape."

"No, you were not. That was the first time you had been to The Alps?" asked Kalakia.

"Yes," replied Frederich. "I was about to say I'd never left Estonia until recently, but you already knew that, right? You know everything about me."

"Well, who would know if Kraas took you for a family trip through Europe by car?" said Kalakia.

Frederich turned around and narrowed his eyes. A smirk appeared on Kalakia's face and disappeared just as quickly.

"Were you harmed in the firefight?" asked Kalakia with a change of tone.

"No, I'm fine," said Frederich.

"Good," said Kalakia and signalled toward the sofas.

Frederich moved away from the window and found a seat. There were two glasses of water on the coffee table, as well as a bottle of whiskey and two empty whiskey glasses.

"Outstanding," said Kalakia when he sat down. "You single-handedly saved the lives of dozens of your peers. Scheffler is integral to our organisation. Because of you, he is still with us."

"I did what I had to," said Frederich.

"Did you? Who told you to risk your life? From what I was told, Scheffler cast you out like an animal."

"I didn't do it for him."

"Then for who? For me? The League?"

"That's part of it. I also went back because of my friend, Piotr Paleski."

"A fellow recruit?"

Frederich nodded.

"So you acted out of loyalty and friendship?"

"I guess so."

"Yes, well, you have made quite the impression on our men. Your story is spreading. In a time of crisis like we have now, your heroics have raised their morale."

"I heard you also had some trouble?" said Frederich, uncomfortable with the praise being doled out.

"I did."

"Who's behind this?"

"The answer to that question will not be a straightforward one. The enemy achieved total surprise, which is no easy

263

feat. This can only mean that a shadow organisation has formed in secret. Untraceable and without form."

"Just like The League."

"I did suspect this time would come. Our enemies have been adapting and evolving. When power is not permitted to concentrate, it loses form and spreads. Now our strategy is being used against us."

"Who's the mole? This couldn't have happened without inside help."

Kalakia sighed and looked away briefly.

"Let us return to you. Tell me about your quarrel with Scheffler."

"What's there to tell?"

"A significant amount, I suspect. You dared stand up to him not once, but twice. We already know how you feel about death. But why risk everything because of a squabble? This I do not understand."

"It wasn't just the snow giving Scheffler vertigo up there. He was getting carried away, and it was only going to get worse if nobody stood up to him. I didn't want to risk my place with The League. I want this more than anything. But.."

Kalakia lifted his eyebrows.

"But?"

Frederich shrugged.

"I don't know. I was angry. Sometimes I do stupid things without knowing why."

"No," said Kalakia, shaking his head. "That will not do. You act foolishly at times, yes. But I suspect something else was at play. Tell me."

Frederich paused and searched himself. He was aching to see Kraas again, a feeling he had not had since leaving for Zürich.

"Because it's what Kraas would want me to do," he found himself saying. "I couldn't back away. I had to face Scheffler no matter what."

Kalakia nodded repeatedly.

"You are your father's son."

Frederich nodded, feeling suddenly vulnerable under Kalakia's gaze.

"Did your father ever tell you why he joined the Spetsnaz?" said Kalakia.

"Yes," said Frederich. "He said it was his duty to fight. He hated the conflict between the Soviet Union and the West. He felt that both ideologies were flawed, but he said nothing would ever change if he stood on the sidelines."

"I understand this notion," said Kalakia. "Ultimately, his attempts were futile. The collapse of the Soviet Union must have broken his spirit. Which is likely why he retired to the woods, no?"

"I guess so," said Frederich. "I never really thought about it that way."

"And now? The mantle goes to you."

"Hmm? No way," said Frederich, shaking his head.

"Why not?"

"Because. Kraas was… He was…"

"He was what? A hero?"

"Well, yeah," said Frederich.

"A decorated soldier?"

"Right. I'm nothing like that."

Frederich looked down and began picking at this thumbnail.

"No, you are much more," said Kalakia.

Frederich stopped his fiddling and looked up. What was Kalakia talking about?

"Look at what you have achieved in this short time. You carry Kraas' bravery with you. You stand for the greater good, as he did. Only you are not bound by flawed ideology. As you said, Scheffler became consumed up there without checks and balances. He is an honourable man, but a man nonetheless. It was *you* who brought him back. It was you who stood up to injustice. You can fool yourself, if you please, but not me."

"I don't know," said Frederich. "I think the ambush had more of an effect on him than I did."

"Have you any lingering ill-will toward him?"

"We had a chance to speak and clear things up. I prefer that to fighting him."

"He is an exceptional warrior. His methods are brutal, but he does so out of loyalty to us. He wishes to see only the best graduate his program and enter our ranks. Only the strongest can win his respect. You have done the latter. I hope you two can find a way to work together."

Frederich tilted his head.

"Together?"

"You have captured the imagination of the soldiers, and we find ourselves in the eye of a storm. Changes are being made before we face our new enemy. Which is why we are fast-tracking you. We will need your skills for this next phase. Are you ready to serve?"

Frederich felt suddenly weightless. Only a day before he was planning a long holiday down south. Now The League Of Reckoning wanted him after all? He cleared his throat.

"What do you need me to—"

Kalakia's phone rang. He answered immediately.

"Tell me," he said, then listened for a long time without speaking. As the call progressed, a scowl slowly appeared on his face. "Fine. Thank you, Francois," he said before closing the connection.

The mood in the room had shifted. Kalakia's mind was now elsewhere. Frederich waited silently.

"We will have company soon," said Kalakia before collecting himself and standing up. "Make yourself comfortable. Have a drink if you like. I will return shortly."

Kalakia then went inside and shut the door while Frederich wondered what had just happened.

"Has Vidrik arrived?" asked Francois.

"Not yet," Kalakia replied into the phone.

"Ok. Falk Braun wants you to know he's pleased with what he saw."

"Is he?"

"Vidrik is trying to send a message."

"There are better ways to do so than by skinning a man alive."

"This sickening act is his way of undermining you. You already know my opinion of him."

Kalakia had a few ideas on how to clip Vidrik's wings. Felipe Vivar had created similar problems in the past.

"I will handle Vidrik. Anything new?"

"Yes. Stirner showed up. He's in France. We have CCTV footage of him being picked up at the airport in Nice."

Kalakia flinched at the news.

"By whom?"

"We checked the plates. It's in the name of an off-shore company. The team is digging."

Kalakia clenched his jaw.

"I understand this upsets you," said Francois after a short pause.

"Just find him," said Kalakia with a low voice.

"We will."

"What about this captured shooter? What did we find out?"

"We know he's Israeli ex-military. His team was made up of disgruntled ex-soldiers. American. Russian. British. Iranian. All of them mercenaries. We also have the name of their contact; Christian Haargersen. He lives in Copenhagen. Haargersen fed them intelligence for the attack on the training facility."

"We need to move on this now."

"Who do you want to send?"

It was a good question. Who could Kalakia trust? There was no way of telling how much the enemy knew. Anyone The League sent could be compromised. It would have to be someone outside the ranks who had the nerve to get the job done. Someone capable and invisible. Kalakia leaned back into his chair. He knew just the right person.

There was a buzz at the door before Kalakia emerged from inside. Frederich had been at the window again looking out at the city landscape and turned to see who it was. The door slid open and a tall, unpleasant looking man with a thick head of brown hair walked through. He was wearing a black turtleneck with black slacks.

"Frederich," said Kalakia while standing beside the man. "Meet Matthias Vidrik. Felipe Vivar's successor."

Vidrik stood stiff and stared at Frederich with wide eyes. He then grunted and went over to the coffee table and poured himself a whiskey.

"I take it the little bird already told you everything," he said.

"What was Falk Braun doing there?" asked Kalakia.

"He was enjoying the show. What else?"

Vidrik took a sip of his whiskey and sauntered around the sofas, making a turn around Frederich.

"So this is the hero. How old are you, boy? Sixteen?"

Frederich found no use in acknowledging or interacting with the man. He clasped his hands behind his back and turned toward the window. From the corner of his eye he saw the reflection of a scowling Vidrik, his stare growing even more demented. Before Vidrik could react, there were fast approaching footsteps. Frederich watched calmly in the mirror as Kalakia grasped Vidrik by the throat. The glass fell out of Vidrik's hand and shattered on the floor.

"Vidrik," said Kalakia with a sharp voice. "You are distracted. Eyes here."

Vidrik rasped and squealed and lifted his hands to try to counteract Kalakia's grip.

"Hands down!" yelled Kalakia with a booming voice.

Vidrik held his arms out to his side then slowly lowered them.

"First," said Kalakia. "Know that your despicable stunt at the facility will be dealt with in good time. For now, we have graver concerns, and I have no patience for your games."

Vidrik blinked multiple times, and Kalakia released his grip, allowing Vidrik to collect himself and catch his breath while grasping at his neck.

"Yes, yes, yes," said Vidrik, forcing out a cough. "War. When I'm back from Copenhagen—"

"No," interjected Kalakia, shaking his head. "You stay here and wait for my orders."

"What?" said Vidrik, his face contorting. "I have the situation under control. Who else is going to figur—"

"You have done more than enough," interjected Kalakia again.

"But.."

"Go home and wait for orders."

Kalakia went over to the door and looked impatiently at the visibly stunned Vidrik. Vidrik stayed in his position momentarily then slowly joined Kalakia at the front. He gazed longingly at Kalakia, urging him to change his mind. The door opened. Kalakia ushered him through. Vidrik then shifted his gaze toward Frederich, and his face stiffened, his eyes sharpened.

"Goodbye, Vidrik," said Kalakia.

Vidrik stood in his place outside, his attention completely fixed on Frederich. The door slid shut.

"Right," said Kalakia, rolling his shoulders and appearing relaxed again. "Let us discuss your first assignment."

29

His name was Christian Haargersen. He lived waterside on Havnegade Promenade, where his rent was three months overdue. Recently he had resigned from his diplomat job a mere seven months before his ten-year anniversary. The six-page report provided by League Intel had a headshot clipped to the corner along with a regular photo, which showed Haargersen and a young female companion sitting close together at a football game, the woman wearing an F.C. Copenhagen team shirt with a thick jacket over it and Haargersen dressed in a grey suit and trench coat.

The forty-six-year-old Haargersen was a chubby man with leathery, sun-stained skin, a thick head of blonde hair and a natural squint. In the photo he was leaning back with his arm stretched protectively over his companion's seat and looking smugly at the camera while the surrounding spectators were focussed on the game. The woman was sitting up with perfect posture and staring into the camera with a childish grin. It was clear from the photo that Haargersen had no interest in football. He had come because of her. *Ladies man.* Never married. Worked for the Danish government until his recent resignation. Now he was still living waterside, but his circumstances had changed considerably.

Frederich sat between the trees along the water's edge in Freetown Christiania; the vehicle-free, graffiti-covered Anarchist commune in the centre of Copenhagen. Meanwhile, Haargersen was slouched in an old outdoor chair on the other bank. The ex-diplomat had been biting his nails and staring into the water for a good hour. Frederich had to double and then triple check the photo to be sure it was him. Compared to the confident ladies man in the picture, Haargersen now looked aged and depressed in his bargain basement shorts and t-shirt.

Haargersen's shanty had been crudely built out of wood and iron sheets. In the yard along the water there was a tyre-swing hanging from a tree and a wild collection of plants and bushes which merged into the surrounding forest. Haargersen's place was modest compared to the other dwellings in the commune, although many of them looked to have been built using recycled and old material. Haargersen had gone off the grid without leaving the city, yet Frederich still tipped his hat to League Intel for managing to track Haargersen down so quickly. He remembered too well how they identified him in Neukölln after only a two-minute exchange in front of the kebab store.

He saw two options. He could break into the shanty at night and wake Haargersen up for his interrogation, or he could shadow Haargersen's movements outside of Christiania and hope that Haargersen met with someone of significance. He had already ruled out the second option. Haargersen was perfectly positioned where he was. Outside the commune there would be too many variables to deal with, and Frederich could not afford to lose his target.

He also had other reasons to close out the mission quickly. He looked down at his jittery fingers and tried to breathe through the panic. Instead, it spread throughout his body. His palms and armpits grew sweatier. He closed his eyes and found himself back in the Alps among the dead bodies on the reddened snow. The groans of the wounded gnawed at him, and there was nothing he could do to stop hearing them. The horrified stares of Scheffler and the recruits were unflinching. *Why is this happening now?* His legs then began shaking, and he knew he would need something to put him at ease.

He took out the cannabis cigarette he had purchased on Pusher Street in the main town. 'Silver Haze,' the dealer had called it while insisting it would allow him to stay clear-headed during the effects. He lit it up and took a long, deep drag and held it inside for a few seconds before exhaling. After a short delay, his skin began tingling, and a calming energy descended on him like a warm blanket. The trees suddenly came alive, and the shimmers along the water started glowing. It was a foolish move, he admitted, but also a calculated one. He would have far more trouble focussing as long as the flashbacks were still playing out.

The drugs had the desired effect. As his body melted, so did the paranoia and visions. The weather was mild and sunny, the breeze slight and cool, and Haargersen was still biting his nails. Frederich lifted his head and took joy in his surroundings, feeling at one with the nature around him and bathing in a welcome feeling of calm. And for the first time in a long time, Ida crossed his mind.

Just as the sun was preparing to set, Haargersen shook himself out of his daydream and forced Frederich to come alive. He rushed inside his shanty then reemerged after a few minutes and marched toward the footpath with clear purpose. Frederich scrambled to pick up his rucksack, which had been overloaded with equipment for the mission. *I told them I don't need all this crap*, he thought as he moved out with the extra weight on his back and legs.

He shadowed Haargersen in a lightheaded state from inside the trees as the ex-diplomat crossed the bridge to the main side of Christiania. Haargersen passed him on the footpath, going in the direction of the main town, and a hundred-foot gap opened between them before Frederich began trailing Haargersen. While Frederich followed the path, propelled by Haargersen's rapid march, his attention was drawn toward the trees. He slowed down, expecting to see something deep inside the forest. During that brief time Haargersen passed out of sight. It had to be a side-effect of the drugs, thought Frederich, even though he was sure he was sensing something real. *It's the weed. Go.* He broke into a light jog until he caught up with Haargersen and resumed trailing his target.

Before Haargersen reached town he turned off into an obscure space between the trees covered in overgrown grass. Frederich used a tree trunk as cover and watched as Haargersen moved toward a small, lone brick structure half-submerged in the ground. Haargersen ignored the entrance steps which descended to the door and went around the back, where the grass was even longer. He treaded through the thick weeds and then ducked out of sight. It was too risky to go any closer. Frederich stayed where he was and waited. Less than a minute later Haargersen emerged carrying a large black sports bag on his shoulder. He pushed through the wild grass and passed Frederich again, going back the way he came. A dark, heavy-set man with dreadlocks and a hyper-coloured yellow singlet was also walking along the path. The man stopped and turned his head when

Haargersen passed him and stared for a long time. Frederich concurred with the man's suspicions. It looked like Haargersen was done hiding out and was going on the run.

While Frederich waited for the dreadlocked man to resume walking the other way, he remembered to check his phone. He cocked his head as he read the three-hour old encrypted text message on the screen sent by League Intel: *"Vidrik missing. Seen boarding commercial flight to Copenhagen. Proceed with caution."*

Vidrik chewed on his lower lip while weighing the situation. Where the hell did Abel go? He was right there next to the tree before that hippie with the filthy hair moved in the way.

Meanwhile Haargersen was getting away. Vidrik reluctantly turned and pushed through the trees, travelling along the river until he was back in position behind his sniper rifle. He looked out and saw Haargersen crossing the bridge. Which way Haargersen turned would decide Vidrik's next move. Vidrik tightened his grip around his weapon and braced himself to take the shot. Haargersen turned right, and after disappearing behind the trees for some seconds, appeared again and went straight down into his hut. A minute passed with no movement. Then another. Vidrik maintained his finger on the trigger.

Frederich managed to force the back door of Haargersen's shanty open and rush inside just as Haargersen approached from a distance. He was thoroughly drenched and his veins were pulsating all over, his heart pounding like a jackhammer. He sucked in another breath of air and tried to centre himself. The lightheadedness rose up like a sand cloud and he felt himself on the verge of passing out. He quickly reached his arm out and found support against the wall. A long sprint through the trees and underwater dive through the river mixed with drugs and a heavy load was a lousy cocktail. He had even re-aggravated the bruising on his ribs from Scheffler's punch. Considering the situation, however, he had no other choice.

There was a thump at the front door. He reached in and took out his pistol. Quick, loud steps filled the hall before Haargersen appeared in the bedroom.

"Don't move," said Frederich with his back to the wall beside the bed, his pistol pointed at Haargersen. "Not another step."

Haargersen flinched and turned quickly. He looked at the dripping wet Frederich and almost jumped when he noticed the pistol, his eyes opening wide and his lips parting.

"Wh… Who are you?" he asked.

"I'm not going to hurt you," said Frederich. "I have orders to let you go as soon as you tell me about your friends."

"What? Which friends?"

Frederich waited. When no answer was forthcoming, Haargersen's shoulders dropped.

"You're with The League Of Reckoning, right?" he said with a low, flat voice.

"Right."

Haargersen hesitated, appearing to be thinking hard. Frederich was not going to offer him time to think up a lie.

"Talk. Quickly," said Frederich.

"You'll let me go if I tell you what I know?"

"Yes."

"No, you won't. You'll kill me anyway."

"We want the people who hired you. By now they already know you've been compromised. I'm guessing that's why you're hiding out here. You knew they would be looking for you. This is your one chance to make it out alive. Don't waste it."

There was a long pause.

"What do you want to know?" Haargersen said, keeping a nervous eye on Frederich's pistol.

"Start from the beginning."

"The beginning. Ok. Can I sit down first?"

"No. Start talking."

Haargersen breathed deeply and turned his attention to the floor. He dropped the bag from his shoulder.

"They contacted me a month ago. They said The League is pushing the world toward economic collapse. They wanted to put together a counter-organisation to fight back. They said they had the intel to hit you where it hurt the most. My job was to organise the attack on your training facility. To kill Vince Scheffler and inflict maximum casualties."

"And you just said yes to all this?"

"I wasn't contacted by coincidence. My feelings about The League are no secret. Plus their offer was through the roof. You have to understand—"

"Who contacted you?"

"I don't know who she is. She said her name was 'Tina.' We spoke a few times on the phone. Then we had a meeting here in Copenhagen. The money was in my account the next day. She gave me a phone to communicate via encrypted chat. The whole thing was being planned with a short turnaround. To avoid your people finding out."

"That's not enough. I need something solid. Something we can use."

"She said she was a recruiter for them. She's British, serious brown eyes, fit body, shaved brown hair. Olive skin."

"Still not enough," said Frederich and stretched his pistol arm out.

"Shit. Ok, ok," replied Haargersen, lifting his arms above his head. "I have photos of her. I had a private investigator tail her. As an insurance policy in case she tried to screw me. He followed her to Sochi. She met with some people in a cafe. The photos are in here. You can have them." He kicked his bag in Frederich's direction. "The phone is in there too. It's got everything on it. All the intel documents, chat history. Maybe that can help you as well?"

"Better."

"Don't kill me," said Haargersen. His lips were trembling and his body was slowly collapsing, like he was sensing his end. His eyes watered up. "Please," he sobbed.

"I won't kill you if you keep cooperating. I want to see what's in the bag. Take it and put it on the table and unzip it," said Frederich, motioning toward the antique table by the window.

Haargersen sniffled. He lowered his arms and took the bag over to the table and unzipped it, then turned around and faced Frederich. Frederich nodded, stood up and went over. As he walked in front of the open window, he turned around and bent his neck down to search the bag. Two bullets were fired from a distance, less than a second apart. A sharp pain pierced Frederich's back as he and Haargersen collapsed to the floor.

278

Vidrik's skin gushed and tingled. He blinked over and over, unable to contain his joy. What a stroke of luck! How did Abel get in there? He froze for a long time, trying to make sense of what had just happened. Then he shrugged, and went about disassembling and packing his rifle into the bag. Who gave a damn. Abel was a corpse. That was all that mattered.

With his bag all packed and tossed over his shoulder, Vidrik walked back through the trees. The car was parked across the road. By the time the police were called and the crime scene investigated, Vidrik would be long gone. He had a long drive ahead of him before he got to France.

When he reached the path again, he made sure it was clear before cutting through and traversing the edge of Christiania under tree cover. He emerged at the exit and calmly walked out and found his car parked by the side of the road. Once the bag was in the trunk he got in and drove off. With one hand on the wheel, he fought to take off his leather glove with his teeth but had to stop when his phone began vibrating. He peered suspiciously beside him. Private number. Stirner? He answered without saying anything.

"Thanks, Vidrik," said the voice on the other end. "Man, what a complicated situation. Haargersen was getting away and I had you creeping in the bushes. I had to make sure he was taken care of while getting you off my case. You solved both those problems."

Vidrik's mind went blank. Before he knew it, his hands were shaking and his body was numb. *Abel. Alive? How?*

"You.." he began, unable to find the words.

"Don't feel too bad, it wasn't all me. Kalakia must have had a feeling you would do something stupid, so he had you

279

tracked. I smelt you in the trees and saw where you had that rifle set up."

Vidrik was having trouble breathing. He had taken his foot off the accelerator and the person behind him was honking their horn as his car slowed down.

"I swear, swimming underwater with a ceramic vest is hard work. Where's your lateral vision, Vidrik? I crossed the river from right behind you."

"You... When I find you..."

"Yeah, yeah. Worry about that after Kalakia's done with you."

The call ended abruptly. Vidrik's car drifted slowly toward the side of the road before he pushed the brakes. The shaking took on a life of its own. His mind drifted to another place. All he could do was scream, yell at the top of his lungs and slam his fists on the steering wheel over and over again while descending into pure madness.

Frederich tossed the phone onto his lap and leaned back while chuckling to himself, then grimaced in pain from where the bullet had struck his back. Lucky it missed the spine, he thought. The ponytailed man stared at him for a second through the rear-view mirror then turned his eyes back to the road. He was justified in wondering why Frederich was wet all over, and Frederich was fine with the silent scrutiny. It was the public's eye he was relieved to have escaped. Nearly every person on the street had gawked at him after he had jumped over the fence and onto the footpath, one bag on his back and Haargersen's next to him on the ground. Luckily The League's car was in position to pick him up.

280

Frederich ran a hand through his hair to find it was beginning to dry off, then turned his face toward Haargersen's bag beside him. He reached over and unzipped it. There was a bundle of photos inside held together by a rubber band. There was also an IBM laptop, the smartphone Haargersen had mentioned, a light grey cashmere sweater and Haargersen's rainy day fund; a thick stash of 50 euro notes. Frederich took the photos out, pulled off the rubber band and began flicking through. The first couple of pictures were of the woman supposedly called 'Tina' getting into the driver's seat of a white sedan. Two things were immediately clear; Tina was a serious individual, and she was incredibly fit. The first photo showed the outline of her body while she crossed the road, wearing black stilettos, tight grey business pants and a cashmere sweater. The second photo showed a shot of her face as she opened the car door. Frederich gave extra attention to her squinted brown eyes and tightly pressed together lips and at once felt a strange urge to meet this woman.

The second set of photos were likely taken in Sochi, judging by the Russian writing on the window in the background. The sign at the top read 'Rose's Cafe.' In focus was Tina, shaking hands with a male associate at the front of the cafe among passers-by. Frederich studied the man carefully and decided he was at least sixty-five years old. The man was also a relic of the 70s. He had a round belly, a full head of greying hair and a thick moustache. If that was not enough, then his short-sleeve vintage brown shirt and cream corduroys confirmed it.

Whoever the man worked for, he was high status. He looked overly confident and entirely at ease in public. Tina, to her credit, seemed unfazed by him. She kept her body straight and had her chin up in all of the photos. In the series of shots they shook hands, exchanged some words and then went into the cafe. After carefully rechecking each picture, Frederich took snaps of the photos with his phone and sent them to League Intel via encrypted message. He had a hunch that the man in the picture would be of immediate interest to The League. He then bound the photos back together with the rubber band and tossed them into the bag before letting his head fall back. He closed his eyes and tried to relax for the long drive back to Berlin.

30

Multiple helicopters buzzed through the gloomy morning sky over the Swiss Alps and landed on the mountainside. Each wave brought with it another of the Four Generals, accompanied by dozens of his most trusted warriors. The Generals disembarked with their guards and treaded uphill from the landing zone toward The League's mountain fortress. Kalakia met them all at the entrance, surrounded by his own guard. At his side was Francois, as well as Vince Scheffler, who was a last-minute inclusion for the meeting and only had to travel a short distance from the training facility to attend. Kalakia greeted each of his Generals with firm handshakes and invited them inside. The last to arrive was the grinning Dastan Navolov. The General flattened his bushy moustache with his thumb and index finger and sped up his walk on approach, placing a hand on Kalakia's shoulder as he came near.

"Apologies," said Navolov. "I had some urgent matters to take care of in Sochi."

"Come, Dastan," said Kalakia, noticing the gun resting in a holster under Navolov's brown shirt. "The rest are waiting inside."

Before turning around, Kalakia looked at his man for confirmation that the outside was secure and received the nod he was looking for.

"All clear, sir. Sniper team is in position, and the scouts say the perimeter is secure."

Kalakia nodded and turned around. Followed by their personnel, Kalakia and Navolov walked side by side through the tunnel, passing the series of former weapons storage rooms, and entered the dimly lit cave where the meeting was to take place. Three of the Four Generals were already seated on a row of chairs in the middle. At a right angle to them the remaining members of The Council sat stiffly with hands on their laps and frowns on their faces. Along the edges of the cave, the rest of the soldiers stood by in audience.

Kalakia took position at dead centre, standing upright with his arms at his side, his shoulders back and relaxed, and his chin raised. He looked over his Four Generals one by one and silently reflected on their careers. Nanda Diop, the small-statured Zambian and General of Africa, was a tactical genius who united most of the tribal militia and criminal groups on the continent and made them loyal to The League. Falk Braun, the General of Europe, went from scraping a living as a street fighter to becoming a critical member of Kalakia's journey toward world domination. Dastan Navolov, General of Asia and ex-mob soldier, who murdered his boss and convinced hundreds of members of his organisation to defect to The League. Johnny Fez, ex-cartel boss and General of The Americas, had consolidated his power on the back of his victory in the brutal, years-long war between the cartels.

"Gentlemen," said Kalakia, his penetrating, resonant voice echoing through the cave. "I will not waste time. Today, we find ourselves facing into the abyss. The League is under attack like never before. Our underbelly has been struck. The enemy has made its opening salvo, and Horst Stirner, a member of our own Council, has defected."

At the mention of Stirner, Dastan Navolov spat on the floor and mumbled a series of curse words in Russian. Kalakia paid no attention to him. He began pacing slowly as he spoke.

"Our first cause for concern is the shape which our enemy has taken. They have emulated our shadow form, combining precise intelligence with an extensive web of mercenary soldiers. This model, as we all know, can only thrive when grounded in truth and honour. Without strong principles, no entity can withstand the test of time. This is where we differ from these soulless cowards. *Nothing* can break us if we stand firm in our mission. Like a wave crashing onto a rock, our enemy will crumble."

"We're collecting limbs from those sons of bitches," said Dastan Navolov.

Kalakia stopped pacing and clasped his hands behind his back. Navolov's men kept their eyes on Kalakia and said nothing.

"Yes," said Kalakia, turning to Navolov. "However, we cannot prevail without a united leadership. Corruption is a cancer which must be cut out, and Stirner will remember this soon enough."

Navolov and the other Generals nodded in agreement. Kalakia paced slowly toward Navolov.

"And like cancer, corruption can spread into the most important organs of the host body."

Kalakia came nearer to Navolov and his skin began crawling.

"It can spread into our ranks," he continued, adding a growl to his voice. A fire moved into his chest and spread out. Navolov looked around nervously then back at Kalakia.

"Into the hearts of those we trust!" yelled Kalakia, now a few feet away from Navolov.

Kalakia could almost see his reflection in Navolov's terrified eyes. Navolov began lifting out of his chair as Kalakia drew the hunting knife from his jacket pocket.

"You swine!" bellowed Kalakia, clenching the knife with an iron grip.

Kalakia moved swiftly while Navolov reached for his holster and thrust the knife into Navolov's throat, twisting it and forcing it inside until it emerged from the back of Navolov's neck. Navolov gargled and croaked. His eyeballs protruded out of their sockets. Kalakia scowled and looked directly into them. The other Generals jumped to their feet in alarm and cries of protest rang out everywhere. Francois, Scheffler and another guard scrambled forward and pointed pistols at each of the Generals' heads before they could act.

"Don't fucking move!" yelled Scheffler.

Warm blood poured out of Navolov's throat and ran down Kalakia's arm. Kalakia forced the knife out and let Navolov's bloodied, dead body fall to the floor with a thump. Some of The Generals' soldiers stood stiff in shock, while others had drawn their guns and were scrambling forward in a collective state of disbelief. It was the decisive moment. Kalakia flung his knife to the floor and held his arms out with palms facing forward.

"Whoever wishes to avenge their General, do it now!" he yelled. "Those who have lost faith in me fire the first bullet! Show me your honour!"

Kalakia's entire body was shaking in a fit of rage. Those who had drawn their guns hesitated.

"Do it!" bellowed Kalakia with all his might.

The cave went quiet. The moment froze. Kalakia waited with every inch of his body and prepared himself for the impact of a bullet fired by a rogue soldier. Dozens of them stood armed and on edge, scowling, their eyes fearful and fierce. The shot could come from anywhere. The tension lingered for what felt like an eternity, until the clang of a pistol falling to the floor finally broke it. The first soldier took a step back. After a slight pause, another gun fell. More soldiers followed suit. Kalakia looked at each of them one by one, challenging them with his stare. Soon every gun was either holstered or laying on the floor. Kalakia sensed that the worst was over. He took a deep stomach breath and came back to himself.

"Kill them," he said coldly over his shoulder.

Three bullets were fired into the remaining Generals' skulls. Splatters of blood sprayed onto the floor followed by the three collapsed bodies. Kalakia turned to The Council. Boris Parkishkov had his nose lifted defiantly in the air but could not stop his lips from quivering. Richard DeLauer was leaned forward on the edge of his chair and staring at Kalakia with all the spite he could conjure. The rest were quietly trembling.

"Today, we replace The Council with new leadership," said Kalakia. "One better suited for war, and one that has not been violated by greed."

Terrified wails rang out among The Council.

"We had nothing to do with this!" shrieked DeLauer. "How many times do we have to say it?"

"Like our Generals, you are a single unit. You share equal responsibility for the successes and failings of your peers," said Kalakia. "And also the same fate."

Kalakia clasped his hands together behind his back and nodded. His guard came forward with rifles and pointed them down at each of The Council members.

"We told you! We had nothing to d—"

The gunfire combined to cause a deafening blast. The heads of the eight old men were pulled back by the impact before their dead bodies slouched down into the chairs. Boris Parkishkov had been hit to the side of his face and was still moving, struggling to draw air with blood pouring down his chest. The shooter responsible for him stepped forward and fired another bullet.

Kalakia lowered his head to allow a full minute of silence to take over the cave. The echoes of the final bullet slowly died out, and nobody moved or spoke while Kalakia honoured the men he had sacrificed for the good of The League. He had considered all the options; expulsion, imprisonment, even a trial to determine guilt. Most of the leadership had been with him from the beginning and had given everything for The League. The mere thought of annihilating his Council had given Kalakia palpitations. Then the pictures of Navolov meeting the enemy in Sochi reached him, and he was shaken out of his indecisiveness. Deep down he had known the correct line of action to take, and the strength to carry out the plan finally came to him.

He straightened up and turned to his soldiers to give his concluding address.

"Soldiers. Our leadership has failed you. *I* have failed you," he said. "Yet we are at war, and we must adapt quickly if we are to prevail. Today, we began by striking out the old

288

so that we may enter a phase of necessary renewal. Today, we declare new leadership, so that we may return order, strength and purpose to The League. And once we have vanquished our new enemy.."

Kalakia paused and observed the faces of his men more closely. They were hanging on his every word, their faces filled with doubt and fear.

"… I will stand down and make way for a new era."

Loud murmurs broke out among the soldiers.

"The League will never falter!" yelled Kalakia, reclaiming their attention. "We are lions, and we are not afraid of death! When the war is over, the new head will usher in an even greater era of peace and justice. The League will continue to do what so-called moral men cannot. We are the last line of defence between prosperity and chaos."

Kalakia paused, allowing the weight of his words to impact the men.

"The new head will begin by electing a new Council," he continued. "For now, we do not require men of wisdom. We require warriors. We require kings. We look now to new Generals who will lead by their fine example. I expect they are prepared to do their duty. In the Americas, Marco Lessio will take his place as General."

The faces of the crowd turned back and Marco Lessio stepped through, wearing black slacks and a black singlet. He brushed over his short black hair and crossed his tattoo-covered arms, and nodded at Kalakia.

"Asia we entrust to Tamju Lau. May you bring order and honour back to your region of the world."

Lau was already standing at the front in a black suit. His greying hair and moustache were neatly trimmed. He rested his hand on his chest and bowed his head. Kalakia felt safe in his selection of Lau. He was the opposite of Navolov; humble, level-headed, and only used violence when it was tactically sound.

"Daps Limbaba. I know you will lead Africa well with your ferocious strength and proud family heritage."

"Until my death!" yelled Limbaba with his husky, booming voice.

"Your father would be proud," added Kalakia with a nod. Limbaba closed his eyes and bowed his head.

"Vincent Scheffler, you will take the reins in Europe."

Scheffler's face lit up with surprise and Kalakia pulled him in with a sharp stare. After some seconds, Scheffler's shock faded and his face softened, and he bowed his head in acceptance.

Kalakia studied his riskiest choice. He hoped that Scheffler's recent transformation after the attacks was permanent and would allow Scheffler to put aside the brute and lead with wisdom and reason. Scheffler was otherwise a worthy selection. He was military elite, a loyal soldier of The League and most importantly, he held the respect and fear of hundreds of veterans who had graduated his tutelage.

"Gentlemen, I commend you," said Kalakia.

The soldiers began taking turns congratulating the newly promoted Generals. Kalakia looked down at his clothing, stained red with Dastan Navolov's blood. There would be more spilt in the coming weeks and months. Much more, he predicted. Meanwhile, the necessary sacrifices had been made, and The League could emerge from its rebirth with a readiness for the war ahead.

"Long live Kalakia!" screamed Marco Lessio, raising his fist into the air.

"Long live Kalakia!" repeated the rest of the soldiers while copying Marco Lessio's gesture.

Cheers and war cries broke out as the tension created by the killings erupted in a violent display of camaraderie. The men's new-found sense of purpose roused Kalakia's affection for them, and he could not help but be swept up by their passion. A warm tingle washed over his body, but he maintained focus as he studied the scene around him. The purge was over, and the war was about to begin.

31

Inselheim unlocked his front door and stepped into the foyer of his Dahlem home. He dropped his briefcase on the floor and stood in the dark, observing the silhouettes of the furniture in the living room. Another day gone, blurred out by meetings, phone calls and trying not to think about whether Brunswick and the team had been harmed. Inselheim was planning on collapsing onto his bed without brushing his teeth or changing out of his shirt and trousers. Holding him back was the knowledge that after two or three hours he would wake up breathless and covered in sweat. His thoughts would be stampeding and the panic amped up to the maximum.

Not worth it, he thought. He went into the living room and switched on a lamp, then headed to the bar. He picked up the expensive crystal bottle and poured himself half a glass of bourbon. He paused for a second then topped up the glass until it was almost full. He then shifted over to the window to check the street. The three cars with Kalakia's men inside were parked in the shadows. All of them black with a dark tint. They had been there since before yesterday. It must have had something to do with those attacks Inselheim saw on the news. The media had come to the usual conclusion. The global mafia war had boiled over again, but world leaders were confident they could de-escalate the situation. Arrests had already been made in multiple cases, the news media reported. Naturally Inselheim was not buying it. The League was up to something. His anxiety jumped to an eight when he saw the news. After he noticed the reinforcements guarding his office building and home, he went into full-blown panic mode.

The turmoil was inside him. Outside the street looked calm. He took a sip of bourbon and rubbed his sore eyes. His reflection in the window looked back at him. It had dark patches beneath its eyes, a ghostly pale complexion and looked ten years older than him. He looked away in disgust and was about to go into the kitchen to get a snack when his phone rang. His shoulders tensed up instantly. Vidrik. Only he called that late. Inselheim reluctantly answered.

"Yes," he said with a flat voice.

"Michael!" screamed Brunswick through the phone speaker.

Inselheim jumped up and almost lost grip of the phone.

"Kimberley!" he yelled. "How did you… Are you ok?"

"Yes, I'm ok. It's so good to hear your voice."

"How did you get access to a phone? Where are you?"

"We're in the emergency facility. We escaped through the tunnel."

"You escaped? Oh, that's excellent," said Inselheim, nodding repeatedly. "Is everyone safe?"

Brunswick fell quiet while he paced around the room. His pulse began racing.

"Kimberley?"

"We're safe," she said quietly. "But we're three short. Aiko, Lena and Jonas were shot while we were getting out."

Inselheim stopped moving. He tightened his hand into a fist. A strange sensation came over him.

"Who killed them?" he said with a hoarse voice.

"Someone attacked the facility. It was mayhem. Michael, it was my fault. I made the decision to try for the tunnel. They died because of me. Michael... I'm sorry." Brunswick's voice grew teary. "It was my fault."

Inselheim's body began trembling and his face grew hot.

"No, Kimberley," he said with a low voice, picturing himself shoving a grenade inside Vidrik's throat. "*They* did this. They did all of it."

The line went quiet. Whatever ordeal Brunswick had been through, it was big. Inselheim could sense it in her voice. She never broke down. She was the one who stood firm during challenging situations. Her silence was a call for help. For the first time since Vidrik had tortured him, Inselheim found a pocket of clarity.

"Hang tight," he said. "Help's coming, ok?"

Brunswick sniffled.

"Ok," she said.

A loud rattle broke out outside and snatched Inselheim's attention. He lowered the phone and scrambled to the window. A sharp pain cut through his chest, and he gasped. A dozen men in balaclavas were on the street firing on Kalakia's soldiers with assault rifles. The windows and windshields of the cars smashed into pieces, revealing the bloodied bodies inside. In the middle of the road were three black vans. The door of the third van opened, and more masked men came running out. The clattering of gunfire continued, before a frightening explosion made Inselheim flinch. He groaned when he saw masked men running through a plume of smoke at the front gate, which forced him toward the bedroom. He reached the door just as there was a crash at the front. He turned his head and saw the masked men

295

come sprinting inside. One of them spotted him, and he instinctively ran inside the room. There was nowhere to hide. *Shit*. Panic shot through him. He could barely react before one of the men ran in and tackled him to the floor. The phone fell from his hand.

"Michael? Michael! What's going on?" came Brunswick's distorted voice.

Two men picked him up and began carrying him out. He bobbed up and down while being taken to the street, accompanied by the men's loud breathing. When they got inside the van, the rest of the shooters jumped in and the door slammed shut. The van took off with a loud screech. Inselheim tried to focus on the men surrounding him until someone slipped a mesh bag over his head. His arms were forced behind him and his hands bound tightly together with a cable tie, which cut into his wrists. His legs were then tied together and he was shoved up against the side of the van with his face pressed up against the metal, where he remained while they sped away.

Home at last.

The sun was shining outside as Frederich studied the streets of Berlin from the back seat with reawakened fascination. The city felt both strange and familiar after so much time away. There would be little chance to get comfortable, considering the situation, still he looked forward to at least one night in his bed. The last stopover had been tense. Now with his first mission in the books, he was beginning to loosen up.

He had not forgotten how lucky he was to be alive. Vidrik had outmanoeuvred him, and would have effortlessly picked him off had it not been for League Intel's intervention. Frederich spent the hours-long drive analysing his decision making, and his stupidity. He had killed Haargersen and obtained precious information while under exceptional pressure. The price paid was allowing Vidrik to live. He also could not help phoning Vidrik just to brag. It was a cocky move, and as much satisfaction as it gave him, he knew Vidrik would not let the humiliation go so easily. He would no doubt come back for revenge. Frederich would just have to be better prepared next time.

They drove by Kalakia's penthouse at the Grand Luxus Hotel. Kalakia would be away for the week, Frederich had been told. It seemed like a typical evening at Zoologischer Garten. Tourists were dressed up and heading to dinner, and grinning teenagers loitered around. Spread among them was the random soldier dressed in civilian clothing while trying to blend in. As long as things stayed that way until the morning, Frederich planned on getting a decent night's rest before preparing for his next mission.

The ponytailed man drove them west down Kantstrasse and pulled into Frederich's street. Haargersen's bag was already in the passenger seat, ready to be delivered to League Intel. Frederich took his rucksack by the strap and braced himself to get out as they approached his apartment block. The ponytailed man pulled over to the side of the road and turned his body toward the back seat. He then shocked Frederich by smiling and reaching out his hand. Frederich hesitated before shaking it.

"See you tomorrow morning, Abel," said the ponytailed man.

"Uh, sure thing," said Frederich. "What's your name by the way?" he added, sensing the opening.

"Erik," said the ponytailed man.

"With a K?"

"Yes."

"Erik. Ok. Call me Frederich."

"Ok. Frederich."

There was a lull while Erik looked out politely at the street. When he dropped the strong silent act he seemed to be a friendly and straightforward person. Frederich noticed for the first time a small scar above his eye and that his hairs were beginning to grey.

"So what do you think about this whole situation?" asked Frederich.

Erik pouted his lip and shrugged.

"Kalakia is our leader. We take care of the street, he handles the chessboard."

Erik had a slight American accent fused with the intonations of his mother tongue.

"You trust him, don't you?"

"He's faced many enemies, and he always wins. The attack in Budapest, he saw the bullet coming. Nothing misses his eye. There's no one like him."

"No, there isn't," said Frederich.

"Or you," added Erik. "We heard what you did up there. The men are comparing you to a young Kalakia."

Erik paused, then smirked.

"Only a bit more crazy," he added.

Frederich's face burnt up and he looked away.

"Thanks for the lift, Erik," he said. "See you tomorrow."

He shook Erik's hand again and got out of the car, taking care not to aggravate his back. He was busy unzipping his rucksack to get his house key out when he froze. He looked

298

ahead toward the front door to his building. He knew those legs.

"Hi, Frederich," said Ida.

He looked up, and blinked once. Then twice. Was she really there? Wait, *what* was she doing there?

"Hey," he said, his voice barely audible.

Ida had her hands in her pockets. She looked tense.

"I need to talk to you," she said. "The League broke their promise."

32

"Wait here," said Kalakia before opening the back door of the SUV and stepping out.

He stood in place and sucked in the fresh country air while he studied the surroundings. Little had changed in the last thirty-five years, he noticed. The cows were still lazily grazing, and the nearby forest was as dense and green as he remembered it. He closed his eyes and tilted his head. It had been a long time since he had heard the sound of birds chirping.

In front of him stood his childhood home, to which time had not been as forgiving. The roof tiles had long been replaced, and the front porch now extended around the back. Otherwise the house remained untouched. The paint had mostly been stripped by the sun, and sections of wood had broken off from the walls and porch. The garden was gone, and in its place were wild weeds and grass.

The old car in the driveway looked even worse. It was rusted and filthy all over, and was standing on bricks and flanked on all sides by weeds.

It seemed like no one was around. He walked over the path which he had crossed thousands of times as a child and approached the front entrance. He pulled the handle, and was not surprised to find the door unlocked. He stepped inside, and the floorboards creaked beneath his feet. The air was musty and heavy. He looked into the living room. The old bookshelf was still there, filled from floor to ceiling. All the other furniture was different from what he remembered but nonetheless appeared years old. His eyes tracked up the stairs then to his right, to a pair of photo frames standing on the hallway table. He stepped forward and took hold of the first frame, which showed an old black and white portrait of his father, his stoic expression and tweed jacket a sign of the times. Looking at his dead father's face, Kalakia felt nothing until he turned to the next photo. The emotions from that day came flooding back with surprising intensity. He felt heavy with sorrow and simultaneously fired up with rage. The event captured in the picture had changed his life forever. Standing dead straight in the middle was his father in his tweed suit, his hands by his side. Kalakia was to his father's left, frowning at the camera with his chin lowered. At his father's right hand was Kraas. He was in his military uniform, his posture impeccable. Twenty years of age, Kraas was leaving that day to begin his service with the Soviet Armed Forces. Kalakia had been beside himself when he found out. He had screamed, kicked, cried and wailed in protest. He did not want his older brother to leave. To him, it was the worst kind of betrayal. He was fifteen years of age.

He looked up and turned his attention outside. Someone was at the back of the house. The back door then opened, and a person came stomping inside accompanied by clanging sounds. He went toward the racket and halted when he reached the kitchen, having found her standing there in a brown dress. Unlike the house and the car, she had aged gracefully. She stared intently at him, carrying with both hands a metal pot filled with milk. Her wrinkled skin was glowing, along with her grey hair which she had tied into a tight bun. Kalakia was immediately drawn to her gentle grey eyes.

"Hello, mother," he said.

The pot left her hands.

Made in the USA
Coppell, TX
06 November 2021